SHE AWOKE TO FIND
THE BARREL OF HER LOVER'S .25
NUZZLING AT HER LIPS

After pulling the trigger, the lover turned
to leave. He was almost out the bedroom
door when he saw the fur coat on the floor.
He thought about how she had been wearing nothing underneath. Nothing except
the ring. That was one nice piece of glass.
Except it wasn't glass, was it?

The lover returned to the bed. Looking
past what was left of her face, he focused
on the stone on her finger.

He'd take the ring. The cops would expect
that. Just another housewife who disturbed a burglar. And got her head blown
off for her efforts.

Other Mysteries by
Marc Berrenson
from Avon Books

SPECIAL CIRCUMSTANCES

L.A. Snitch

MARC BERRENSON

AVON BOOKS ◆ NEW YORK

L.A. SNITCH is an original publication of Avon Books. This work has never before appeared in book form. This work is a novel. Any similarity to actual persons or events is purely coincidental.

AVON BOOKS
A division of
The Hearst Corporation
1350 Avenue of the Americas
New York, New York 10019

Copyright © 1991 by Marc Berrenson
Published by arrangement with the author
Library of Congress Catalog Card Number: 91-91780
ISBN: 0-380-76324-9

First Avon Books Printing: August 1991

AVON TRADEMARK REG. U.S. PAT. OFF. AND IN OTHER COUNTRIES, MARCA REGISTRADA, HECHO EN U.S.A.

Printed in the U.S.A.

RA 10 9 8 7 6 5 4 3 2 1

To my wife Karen
for listening to
all of my stories

Many thanks to Carol Mark and Stan Berkowitz for reading the manuscript. And to Dan Klamkin for letting me pick his brain on the book business.

CHAPTER 1 ━━━━━━━━

It was payoff time for Vincent Romero. He had taken care of the woman's husband and sweated out the last couple of months waiting for the check. Now she had the money, and he was going to be a whole lot richer.

She lived in the hills off Laurel Canyon on the Valley side. A big place with a view that was like from an airplane. Vincent took the back route, along Mulholland. He passed the place where he had arranged the husband's little accident. You could hardly tell where the poor slob had gone over the edge, just a few pieces of metal and glass where the flaming car had finally come to rest. He could barely distinguish the burned-out patch from the other charred spots on the hillside where kids had set fire to garbage so they could watch flames leaping into the nighttime sky, blazing in the deserted darkness.

Vincent snaked his way along Mulholland toward Laurel Canyon. He had one finger of his right hand on the wheel, making believe he was in one of those television commercials that showed how great his gunmetal gray BMW CSi handled. For a moment, he was young, successful, and handsome, in complete control, just like the guy driving the car in the commercials. He had taken charge of his life and was making all the right choices.

Let those other assholes grunt away their lives for a few bucks, a thirty-year pin and a farewell dinner in the banquet room of the Sportsman's Lodge. Not him. He was too smart for that. What did they say about survival of the fittest? Well, there were the beasts of prey, and there were those there to be eaten. Vincent Romero had no doubt to which group he belonged.

Right now, he was getting pissed off because he had to slow down behind a Plymouth station wagon filled with kids.

Vincent thought about the woman. Since he had taken care of her old man, he'd spoken to her only a couple of times. She'd come on to him from the very beginning, like they all did, but he had put her off. He didn't want to queer the deal just to slip it to her. He'd told her there was time for that later, after the money was in. And he'd meant it, at least the part about the money. Vincent thought the woman was okay, nothing great. Probably worth fucking, though.

Vincent was glad she was nothing special, otherwise he might have fucked her anyway, and that might have caused problems. She'd have thought they were going to ride off into the sunset, just because he'd fucked her. That was the problem with all women. They all assumed that because they spread their legs for you that they had you for life. Like parting with a little pussy was such a big deal.

Vincent floored the accelerator, crossed over the double yellows, and passed the Plymouth. When he got to Laurel he made a left, heading down into the Valley. Another quick right and he was on the street that led up to the woman's place.

When he made the turn, he was reminded in an instant of his days as a rookie on patrol. The places off Laurel up in the hills were always getting ripped off. Lots of rich folks who were gone all day made for easy pickings. Not like your Ozzie and Harriet neighborhoods where Mom was always home baking a pie and watching the street for suspicious characters. The people who lived in these hills didn't want anything to do with their neighbors. They were too busy making money to buy more things to make them feel important.

Vincent liked that. It fit right into his plan: just another burglary in the hills, where things got a little out of hand. Well, maybe more than a little. He mulled the idea over a few times, liking it even more.

The woman was there, standing on the front porch at the end of the driveway in a full-length fur coat. Jesus, how stupid can you get? Just like when she called him at the station to tell him she had the money. Incredible. He just about shit when he found out who it was.

He pulled the car alongside the garage, behind some overgrown star jasmine that hung from a trellis attached to the side of the house. The scent of the jasmine was still strong and reminded him of a woman he'd once had. When he walked around the back of the car toward the front door, she was still standing there, fondling that coat, waiting for him.

"Let's go inside," he said, looking over his shoulder quickly, then placing his hand on the small of her back and guiding her inside. Vincent could feel the smooth silk lining on the inside of the fur coat slide along the contours of her back. He let his hand drop lower, gently pressing with thumb and fingers the soft curve of the woman's ass. It made him think about what he was going to do. He was surprised to feel himself getting hard.

"Don't be such a worry, honey," she said, once inside the door. She had a drink in her hand, and Vincent thought that by the glazed look of her eyes it wasn't her first of the afternoon.

"You've been a bad boy," she said in a drunken sort of baby talk. She came right up against his chest, causing her coat to fall open, and Vincent saw that she was wearing nothing underneath. She looked down at herself then up at him, smiling. Then she reached up and rested her hands on either side of his neck. He could hear the sound of the ice tinkling in the glass near his ear. He could feel the tips of her breasts against his shirt as she moved them in small half circles against his chest. She was softly kissing him around the mouth, starting, stopping, then starting again, as if she were warming up for the one long kiss.

He didn't want to rush things. He wanted to stay cool, make sure he was in control. But the woman was darting her tongue inside his mouth, making soft moaning sounds while she moved her nipples back and forth against his chest. He felt himself getting harder, and he knew that she knew it.

"You've got the money?" He tried to pull away but she held him to her.

"You haven't said a thing about my new coat," she whispered, close enough that he could smell the scotch. "Do you like it?" She was still kissing him, now around his ears and on his neck.

"Yeah, it's great."

She pushed him away, playfully, as if she thought playing the little bitch was going to get his mind off the money and onto her. She headed for the stairs, crooking her finger, motioning for him to follow.

He followed her up the staircase and into the bedroom. She was giggling like a schoolgirl, looking back at him. When she reached the bedroom she walked straight to the bureau and removed an envelope from one of the drawers.

"Happy celebration day, baby," she said, holding the envelope in her hand. The scotch was making her unsteady. She reached out with one hand to grab the dresser.

Vincent took the envelope and looked inside at the thick packet of hundreds. Just putting his fingertips on the crisp bills made him feel good. Better than that, triumphant. The conqueror savoring the spoils of battle. It made the woman look even better to him.

"I spent a little already," she said, modeling the fur coat like she was on some sort of game show.

"You look great in it," said Vincent, still thinking about the hundreds.

"And that's not all," she said. She held up the back of her left hand, within inches of his face.

"I bought it today," she said. "That fucking cheapskate . . . All the years we were married, he never bought me nothin' like this."

Vincent was looking at the rock on her finger, a huge diamond solitaire that made the knuckle on her finger look small. He had never seen one that big, except in the dime store when he was a kid.

"And the asshole *had* the money!" she shouted. "He drove around in his fucking little Porsche so that he could impress those teenybopper secretaries of his. Get 'em to jump in the sack with the fat old fart. Fucking their goddamn brains out."

Vincent said: "Nice rock, baby."

"Damn right it's nice," she said, holding the ring up to the light, mesmerized by its brilliance.

She looked away from the ring at Vincent, then casually shrugged the coat off her shoulders. It fell in a heap of fur to the ground. Vincent was surprised that she could do that in one motion, considering what she'd had to drink. She was just standing there now, looking at him. She looked better than he wanted her to.

"I think we should *consummate* our relationship, don't you, baby?" She giggled using the word.

Vincent didn't answer. Just stared at her. Her legs were spread and she was fingering her vagina with both hands. Her arms pressed against the sides of her breasts, elevating them and pushing them forward. Vincent liked that.

He stepped closer, and with his fingers traced small light circles around her nipples, watching them stiffen. He continued doing that, while she played with herself, her head thrown back, gazing at the ceiling and moaning with pleasure.

Vincent got to his knees. He grabbed her hands in his and placed them on the back of his head. He put a hand on each side of her ass, and with the tip of his tongue he followed the opening of her vagina, up and down slowly. He could taste her slightly sour smell as her lips began to part. He moved his tongue faster, feeling her hands pressing him against her, hearing her short high squeals of delight.

When he pulled away, he knew she was ready. Vincent carried her to the bed. He slipped off his shoes, then his pants and shirt. She had propped her head against the pillow and was watching him through glazed eyes. He liked looking at her as she watched him undress.

He grasped his stiff cock in one hand, gently caressing it for her to see. He held it near the base, trying to show her as much of it as he could, wanting her to see how big he was. He'd always done it that way, letting them admire his size before he showed them who was boss.

"I like that word, *consummate*," he said, moving toward her on the bed. She just kept moaning, "Oh, baby, oh, baby . . ." He straddled her chest, his hand still in a fist around his dick. She balanced her hands on his hips, taking his cock in her mouth and moving him slowly back and forth. Then they changed positions. She came first while on top of him. Then they both came with him between her legs thrusting hard, using the headboard for leverage. Then once again, because she had wanted it.

When she awoke after her nice little nap, Vincent already had the barrel of the .25 nuzzling at her lips, just like he had done with his dick earlier. He was playing with her. He liked the look on her face as she was waking up, the cool steel of the barrel moving back and forth. She caressed it with her tongue, just before she opened her eyes and saw him standing over her, ready to blow her brains out. Vincent smiled when he saw that look. Like she wasn't sure whether this was just a part of her dream or not. Not horrified, just confused. Trying to get her bearings, maybe even close her eyes and get back to the dream.

He had picked the .25 because it was a clean throwaway. He couldn't use his service revolver, and the rest of his guns might get traced back to him. Also, he thought the .25 was big enough to do the job without making too much of a mess.

After he pulled the trigger he knew that he'd at least been right about it doing the job.

Vincent was almost out the bedroom door when he saw the fur coat on the floor. It made him stop for a moment, thinking about how easily she had shrugged the coat off and how she had been wearing nothing underneath. Nothing except that ring. Jesus. That was one nice piece of glass. Except it wasn't glass, was it? No, the fucker was real.

He turned and came back to the bed, not looking at what was left of her head splattered on the sheets and the wall behind. He focused on the ring, just sitting there, right on her finger. Vincent lifted her hand off the bed and noticed a drop of blood across the face of the diamond. He rubbed it off on the bedspread.

It was quiet in the house, except for the ticking of the clock on the nightstand. He could hear the muted sounds of traffic on the freeway, like the hum of some distant transformer, barely audible.

He knew he should leave things like they were. He told himself that. Everything he had learned up to now told him to leave the ring right where it was. Then he started thinking. He didn't like the idea of passing up such an easy score. His mind raced, trying to rationalize what he had already decided to do: he'd take the ring, like it was a robbery or something. Sure. The cops would expect that. After all, it would explain the shooting: just another housewife who disturbed a burglar in the course of a burglary and got her head blown off for her trouble.

But the more he thought, the more it didn't sound right. There she was, naked on the bed. They'd run all kinds of tests, find out she'd just fucked some guy. Now, how do you explain that?

But he wanted that ring.

Vincent went to the bathroom and grabbed a towel and the woman's shower cap off a hook on the door. He draped the towel over part of the woman's body, then dropped the shower cap on the floor near the nightstand.

There. That looked better. Just taking a shower when she discovered the bad guy in the bedroom. He sees her, panics, and throws her on the bed. Yeah, that sounds good. The bad guy decides he may as well fuck her since she's there for the taking. Vincent knew lots of guys, straight burglars, who got into that kind of stuff when it was available. Maybe they scuffle while he's slipping it to her, and he blows her brains out to keep her from yelling for help.

Yeah, that sounded right.

He pulled the ring from the woman's finger and stuck it in his pocket. In the back of his mind he was thinking that even if the cops bought the shower story, taking the ring was a gamble. Something that could be traced back to him. Something that could put him in the bedroom with the woman whose brains were hanging from the headboard.

But he'd figure a way around that. He'd have to. It was too good to pass up, a rock that size.

He smiled to himself as he turned onto Laurel Canyon and headed back toward the Valley. Yeah, he thought, feeling himself get hard again, a rock that size was just too good to pass up. Even after being ripped off by the fence, it would make a nice little unexpected bonus—his reward, he thought, for being such a great fuck.

CHAPTER 2 ━━━━━━━━━

It was raining outside, must be.

But it couldn't. Too hot . . . Like an oven yesterday.

Still, that hissing sound.

Not rain, much too hard and constant for rain.

He opened his eyes, stared at the cottage cheese ceiling, blinked twice, and started over.

Not rain.

A hose, somewhere outside. That's it. Manuel, the gardener, was spraying down the concrete near the pool.

He rolled over slowly, not certain how his head would react, and looked at the clock. Six-thirty, as always. For as long as he could remember he'd been waking up at six-thirty. Initially he considered himself lucky, not having to worry about getting a late start on the day. Over the last year or so, at least since it had happened, he put his inability to sleep longer more in the category of a curse than anything else.

Ben Green rolled onto his stomach and tried to find a cool spot on the pillow to rest his cheek. There was none. The sound of the water outside, hissing against the already hot concrete, set the tone for the day. He gave up trying to find a cool spot on the pillow and got out of bed, swinging his legs over the side first so he could take a moment to clear his head. He walked over to the window of his one-bedroom apartment, poked a finger between the blinds, and looked down at the Mexican gardener. There were dark liquid splotches on the white concrete pool deck, like a map of the lake region of northern Michigan, where the heat of the concrete had already begun evaporating the water. Ben thought about the day before, and the one before that. One-hundred-plus temperatures, enough to make driving in a car without air-conditioning not only unpleasant but downright dangerous. His air conditioner had decided to take a vacation about three hours into this latest heat spell. Not that it didn't work entirely. There was still air being blown from the vents. It was just that the supposedly *conditioned* air was coming out about five degrees hotter than the temperature outside.

The gardener looked up and waved to him, then yanked on the length of hose that was snaked across the planter and over the pool deck. A half dozen chaise lounges were stacked atop each other in the corner beneath two large palms. Ben continued to peer from the window, watching the gardener unstack the metal and plastic pool lounges one at a time, hosing each one with a quick spritz, then set them side by side along the shady side of the kidney-shaped swimming pool.

Ben headed for the kitchen, flicking on the television along the way. He could hear the sound of voices coming from the portable as he searched through the refrigerator for coffee. He should force himself to get used to instant, he thought, his arm and shoulder inside the refrigerator, reaching into the back where he thought he had last seen the can of ground coffee. He extended his arm as far as possible, turning his head away from the opening in order to reach an extra few inches. He felt something cold and round and metallic underneath the large plastic bag of peaches that his neighbor, Bryan, had given him, and behind the half gallon of Donald Duck orange juice. He tugged on the can, feeling the bag of peaches fall onto the glass shelf. As he pulled the coffee can free of the bag, the peaches began rolling toward him and over the edge of the shelf and onto the floor. Ben cursed himself and quickly tossed the peaches back into the refrigerator, then closed the door.

On the television he could hear Bryant Gumbel's soft, articulate announcer's voice. Perfect, pleasant. Not a word or syllable mispronounced. Soothing and proper, and, Ben thought, not the voice of a black man. Bryant Gumbel . . . Now there was a guy that had it all together. From that silky voice and controlled demeanor, to those marvelous clothes, always perfectly matched. He had to be the most appealing, most pleasant, most nonthreatening black man on television.

Having set the coffee maker into motion and taking pleasure in the rhythmic gurgling sound it was making, Ben ambled back into the bedroom. Bryant and Willard Scott were seated in canvas-backed director's chairs. Bryant's suit fit perfectly, not showing too much shirt cuff, and displaying just the right amount of sock peeking out between the cuff of his suit pants and his soft, shiny Italian leather loafers. Willard, on the other hand, was wearing a short-sleeved white shirt with a string tie he claimed had been sent to him by a ninety-nine-year-old viewer from New Mexico. His pants, chino-type trousers cuffed on the bottom, looked wrinkled and slept in. He had one leg crossed over the other, displaying a pair of argyle socks and about four inches of hairy leg.

Ben shucked off his underpants, letting them fall to the carpet, and made for the shower. The hot beads of water against his neck and shoulders were welcome. He stood beneath the spray for a few minutes, trying to piece together the day's expected events: a Monday, but nothing special. His usual first-of-the-week review of cases, setting aside the ones that still had work that needed to be done. After that, the new cases, if there were any, would be on his desk and he'd have to set each one up in its own file with his chronological checklist stapled to the inside of the manila file folder. Then there'd be time for a few phone calls, a chance to tie together any loose ends so that he could cut down on the time he'd have to spend in the car driving around town to interview witnesses.

This is what had become of his weekly routine over the last six months. What had followed Julie's death, and his own emotional breakdown. After the hospital and the convalescent home—he found that he could no longer face the familiar. He was only aware now that almost two years had passed. His home in the canyon, his law practice, the long morning bicycle rides, even Claire . . . Each had become all too painful reminders. Like fun-house mirrors in which his own guilt and despair were reflected.

And after a time, his old friend Francis Powell had said that there was a place for him as a special agent in the Internal Affairs Division of L.A.P.D. if he was ready to reenter the world, if he wanted it.

Ben stepped from the shower and quickly dried himself, rubbing the towel first over his head, then the rest of his body. He glanced at his face in the small mirror over the sink, and saw that his hair was tousled and spiked like the kids were now wearing it. He ran a smoothing hand over his hair, then bent closer to the mirror and inspected his eyes. First both eyes together, wide open, getting a general impression. Then just the left, and finally the right. Then he stepped back and squinted, watching the small bags of skin under each eye contract so that they appeared to disappear. He looked ridiculous. He couldn't go around squinting, holding up the bags under his eyes. So he relaxed the muscles in his face and looked normal and the bags reappeared and, he thought, looked worse than before.

He decided he'd take a break from this morning inspection, this daily monitoring of his own aging—his death watch, as he had come to think of it. He walked back into the bedroom, the towel wrapped around his waist. The "Today" show had switched to the local networks for the news. He stood in front of the television, feeling the carpet slightly sticky between his wet toes. He sat on the edge of the bed, facing the television but not listening. It was happening again. Ben's thoughts raced away from him, as if fueled by their own power, no longer under his control. He began falling, tumbling back over the years to the time when Julie was alive. He saw himself standing outside his Malibu Canyon home listening to the young, scrubbed Highway Patrol officer telling him that they'd found Julie, that he'd have to make an identification of what was left of the body. Then another scene, himself standing in front of a stainless steel coroner's gurney looking down at a young woman, his daughter, naked, her skin and nails covered with oily dirt, a coroner's thermometer protruding from her side as if she were a rump roast ready for the oven. And he remembered the little man, the coroner's deputy, running around apologizing for the thermometer, saying he wasn't supposed to see that.

There was a picture of a black city councilman on the television, Ben couldn't remember the guy's name. The councilman, looking uncomfortable, was standing in front of a bank of microphones and television cameras. On either side of the councilman was a black youth dressed in what Ben, and every policeman, D.A., and criminal defense attorney in the city of Los Angeles recognized as the gang uniform of the day: baseball cap; black-on-black sunglasses; white T-shirt under a dark, shiny, silk-like windbreaker; jeans; a few gold chains; and brand-new, perfectly white, high-top leather athletic shoes with laces hanging untied at the side. The councilman and the two gang members had their hands joined in a sort of three-way handshake for the benefit of the cameras and still photographers whose cameras whirred, flashed, and popped as the three blacks stood grinning into the bright lights. The voice-over by the newscaster explained that the city councilman had created a task force for the purpose of bringing together various warring gang factions in the city in an effort to "curb the violence" between rival gangs that had "plagued the city in recent weeks." Ben recognized the words as those he'd heard many times before. He also recognized one of the gang members as La-Charnelle Washington, a high-ranking member of the Rolling 60s Crips. LaCharnelle wore the Crip colors, a blue calico bandana over his close-cropped Afro and underneath a blue corduroy baseball cap. The bandana was tied in a knot at the back of his head. The other gang member, the one Ben didn't recognize, was similarly attired except for the red cap and jacket of the Bloods, the Crips' rival gang.

Ben snickered at the thought of either of the two gangs getting together for any purpose that didn't involve drugs, or thievery, or violence, and more often than not, all three. The political types were always trying something like this, more, Ben thought, for the free publicity than the heartfelt expectation that any gang-banging member of the Crips or Bloods was salvageable as a human being.

Ben slipped into a fresh pair of underwear, then resumed his seat on the edge of the bed and started pulling on his socks. The local news still had center stage and they were showing a clip of some guy who had recently struck it big on the Big Spin. They were handing the guy an oversized check with lots of zeros on it while the band played and people in the studio audience cheered. The guy getting the check, the winner, smiled but looked uncomfortable, almost embarrassed. Then the picture switched back to the studio and the news-caster wished everybody a nice day before sending it back to Bryant and Jane in New York.

Ben finished dressing, deciding to leave his usual synthetic camel's hair sports coat on its hanger inside the closet. It was just too hot, and he knew the tie would be the first thing to go even before he got to the office.

On the TV, Bryant was interviewing Antonio La-Russo, the head of the U.S. Attorney's Office in New York. Ben recognized LaRusso's face from all the times he'd seen him on the evening news, holding press conferences about the organized crime figures or inside stock traders that his office was indicting. LaRusso, Ben thought, was a master at self-promotion, never missing an opportunity to go before the cameras to portray himself as the tough Italian crime-fighter of New York. There had been rumors about LaRusso's aspirations for the senate, but the clever trial lawyer deftly sidestepped Bryant's questions about that, saying that he had no definite plans other than to continue fighting crime in high places and to protect the good people of the state of New York. The picture then switched to a videotaped clip of the arrest of a group of middle-aged men, some older, outside a small restaurant in New Jersey. The men, all organized crime figures according to the newscaster, were coming out of the restaurant, one after the other, some still wearing the white paper-napkin bibs with the restaurant's logo around their necks. Each of the men was being guided by a young clean-cut FBI officer dressed in a suit. The men being arrested each held their arms or open newspapers over their faces, in an effort to hide from the cameras. Ben watched as the group of arrestees, along with their captors, were bundled off into the open doors of a waiting van and, presumably, taken away for booking.

Ben flicked off the television. Those G-men really have a tough life, he thought, then chuckled. The feds had the best of everything. While the local cops banged around in the muck trying to catch burglars, auto thieves, heroin dealers, and the like (and then tried to convince a court that most of these slime-buckets were truly dangerous people who deserved more than a slap on the wrist and a ninety-day sentence that was reduced to forty-five with good time and work time and early release credits due to jail overcrowding), the feds, in their permanent-press suits and their all-American haircuts, planned elaborate stings of businessmen and stockbrokers and old men sitting in Italian restaurants sipping on red wine and shoveling down linguine with clams. And it was no wonder that most federal indictments never made it to trial. The feds didn't mess around with any of that bullshit plea-bargain stuff. At least not like the local courts. Any defense lawyer who practiced in federal court knew that federal judges, with those lifetime appointments in their back pockets, tolerated no bullshit. They didn't have to worry about such pedestrian problems as being reelected. If you were indicted in federal court, it was a safe bet that you were going to get convicted, unless you were very lucky and very rich. And once convicted, if you wanted to still play tough guy, you were looking at a lot of hard time. Most decided that it just wasn't worth it. Instead, a guy could, like Nixon's boys, cut a deal for a few years in one of those federal country clubs they called detention facilities, all the time feeding the G-men a steady stream of information about some other mob guy, who, when caught, would do the same.

Before leaving, Ben gulped a few cups of coffee, turned off the coffee maker in the kitchen, and checked the small square of cork nailed to the wall that he used as a bulletin board. A piece of notepaper pinned to the cork had the name ''Dr. Mellnor'' written in his penciled scrawl, along with tomorrow's date and the time of his appointment. He paused for a moment, registering the name and the reason it was there. He felt himself drifting back again, his mind flashing pictures he'd seen dozens of times before: the day it happened; afterward; over and over again, burning itself into his psyche. He no longer willed it to stop; he'd learned that that didn't work. The more he tried not to think about it, erase the pictures from his mind, the more vivid the images became. He knew that this gruesome slide show of the mind, allowed to run its course, would only get worse, that there was no happy ending. That if he stayed where he was, motionless, helpless, trapped by his memories, he'd begin to crumble. It had happened before. It angered him that he was not over it. He'd reconciled himself to always having the memories with him like a hand inside his stomach flexing its fingers open and shut. Still, it maddened him that after so much time he'd still not gotten over the paralyzing grief, the feeling of total despair as the hand grasped at his vital organs and yanked and pulled, rendering him helpless.

Ben willed himself away from the reminder on the bulletin board, from his memories. He ran out the door and down to his car, hopping down the steps three at a time and landing with a thud on the paved walkway. He made himself smile at the gardener, who smiled back and waved, saying: *"Buenos días,* Señor Green." The gardener said something more in Spanish that Ben didn't understand.

Once inside his car, Ben backed out of the carport, not looking for cross traffic, intent only on heading for the office. He shoved a tape into the slot and turned up the volume, then rolled down the windows, hoping that the music and the noise of the Monday-morning traffic crush would distract him. Anita Baker's soulful, plaintive voice—like the numbing high of a hype's fix—began to take the edge off his anxiety. He let his mind drift with the music, trying not to think of anything, especially that afternoon eighteen months ago when his life came to an end.

CHAPTER 3 ━━━━━━━━━━━

All she had said was, The boss wants to see you right away. By the boss, Ben Green knew that his secretary meant Francis P. Powell, the chief of police, whose office was three flights above his.

Did he say what it was about? he had asked. She just shook her head back and forth, pencil clenched between her teeth, not even looking up, not missing a beat on her typewriter.

Ben and Francis Powell had gone through the police academy together. In the early years, as rookie cops, they'd spent time sharing the same patrol car. Ben considered Francis both his friend and his boss, but more his friend.

Since their first week in the academy, Francis Powell had taken Ben under his wing, an older brother kind of thing. It was Francis Powell who had come to visit Ben in the convalescent home after his breakdown. It was Powell who spent long afternoons walking with him, shoring him up, discussing Ben's feelings about Julie's death, his guilt, his perception of what his life had become. Like a film editor, Powell relived scene after scene with Ben, subtly directing the conversation one way or the other, until Ben fell upon a path that would help lead him out of his emotional confusion. It was Powell who, after a sufficient time had passed, suggested that Ben come to work for him in Internal Affairs, as an investigator-at-large, as he had termed it.

The joke between them was that the "P" in Francis' name stood for "Politico." Powell could cajole and backslap with the best of them. From the time they first shared a squad car, Francis Powell had had his sights set at the top.

Now, as Ben stepped off the elevator on the top floor of Parker Center, he was curious what his old friend wanted. Powell had pretty much left Ben alone since he had started with Internal Affairs, popping by every so often only to say hello. Ben knew his boss was more concerned than he let on. He also knew that Francis Powell would want him to feel that he had as much space as he needed, that nobody was looking over his shoulder to make sure that he didn't flip out. Powell was scrupulously careful not to draw any more attention than was necessary to Ben's situation. That was why this command performance intrigued Ben.

There had been rumors, both in the department and in the local papers, that Francis was considering running for mayor in the next election. Ben discounted the talk as merely rumor; yet because he was familiar with Francis Powell's penchant for power, he didn't discount it altogether.

Ben signed the log at the security desk outside the entrance, then pushed through the two large wooden doors into the waiting room of the chief's office.

"He's expecting you," said the secretary. "I'll tell him you're here." She walked off through a doorway.

Ben started thinking about the rumors. If Francis Powell was actually serious about running for mayor, he'd need help in the form of large donations, which was not the kind of help that Ben could give.

After Ben left the department to start his own law practice, the two onetime close friends didn't see much of each other. It was Ben's breakdown, ironically, that brought them back together. Ben had been surprised to find Francis Powell waiting patiently in the lobby of the convalescent home that January day over a year and a half ago, bundled against the cold, forcing an optimistic smile and pressing back the tears. Until that day, other than the occasional phone call, and seeing Powell in the newspapers or on the six o'clock news, Ben had kept his old academy buddy in the back of his mind. Their paths rarely crossed, with Ben busy representing the criminals that Powell and his men had put in jail. By the time Ben's criminal practice began to take off, Francis Powell was already ascending the ladder into the upper echelons of the L.A.P.D.

"He can see you now," said the secretary, coming back into the waiting room.

Francis Powell's office occupied a corner of the top floor of Parker Center. It was the kind of office you'd expect that the chief law enforcement officer for the city of Los Angeles would have. One wall was completely covered with photos and governmental proclamations. The pictures were of various dignitaries and celebrities with whom Powell had rubbed elbows over the years. It was like a *Who's Who* of Southern California.

On the wall behind Powell's desk were three photographs of Francis in full uniform. In one of the photos, Francis was shaking hands with Ed Meese in front of a large carved wooden symbol of the attorney general's office which hung on the wall behind the two men. In the photograph just to the right of the one with Meese, Ronald Reagan was handing some sort of medal in a black leather wallet to Powell. Both men were smiling and shaking hands at the same time. The third was a picture of Powell being sworn in, the day he became chief of police.

One entire wall of the office was a window from which you could look down on downtown Los Angeles, City Hall, the Criminal Court Building, and the Federal Building. A large desk spanned almost the entire width of the office, and behind the desk, almost lost amidst the papers, files, newspapers, trophies, and awards, sat the chief of police, Francis P. Powell.

"Benny," he said, smiling and standing behind his desk, reaching a hand across the desk toward Ben.

Ben shook his hand, then plopped into one of the two large cushioned chairs opposite the desk. They looked at each other for a moment, silently taking stock.

"Everything okay down in the pits, Benny?"

"Couldn't be better. I'm busy, which is good." Ben averted his eyes from his friend, not wanting to catch the look of concern that he knew would be there. Francis Powell was a hard case for Ben. From the beginning, he'd had trouble faking it with Powell.

"That's good to hear," said Powell, staring at Ben, allowing himself the split second necessary to evaluate the truthfulness of Ben's response. "You know our deal, Ben. Things start climbing up on you, you just let me know, and the two of us will work it out together, right?"

"Jesus, Francis. I'm not that bad off." Ben tried to laugh. "Hell, it's been at least a couple of days since I had thoughts about climbing into some tower with a high-power rifle and shooting someone." Powell remained expressionless. Ben shifted uncomfortably in his chair. "Okay, okay, I shouldn't have made that crack," he said. "I owe you a lot, Francis. You went out on a limb for me with the department, setting me up here and all, and . . ."

"Bullshit about the department," roared Powell. "I *am* the fucking police department! If I say I want a special investigator to handle touchy cases, to work with the D.A.'s office on sensitive prosecutions, then that's exactly what happens." He paused momentarily, catching his breath. "The fucking department should be tickled pink to get an ex-cop, ex-prosecutor defense attorney with your experience. We tend to see things too one-sided over here. That's why we lose some of the cases that we shouldn't. Hell, Benny, you're gonna be our fucking secret weapon!"

"Okay, okay, you've convinced me," said Ben. "So what's so important that I gotta drop everything and rush up here? You gonna run for president or something?"

Powell smiled, playing with a plastic pen on his desk.

"Who knows," he said, looking up at Ben. "You wanna be 'my V.P.?"

"No chance, buddy. But I might be interested in one of those ambassadorships. You know, like in the South Pacific or one of those places. I can see it now. The Honorable Benjamin Green, ambassador to Tahiti. Half-naked island girls at my beck and call . . . I think I could get used to that real quick."

"Don't rush out and buy your grass skirt." Powell laughed. "Not just yet."

Then his smile disappeared. "Listen, Benny," he continued. "You've heard the rumors about me and the mayor?"

"It's hard not to."

"Yeah, I'll bet. Well, the bottom line is that they're true. I've been giving serious thought to challenging Hernandez in the next election."

Ben saw a what-do-you-think-of-that look on Powell's face. He didn't answer the look immediately. He wanted to make sure what was really on his friend's mind before he ventured an opinion.

"Hernandez is strong in the Latin community," said Ben, figuring that saying the obvious was nonjudgmental, safe.

"That's true," snapped Powell. "But I've done a lot for minorities in the department, you know that. We've got a lot of black and Mexican faces out front where everyone can see them."

"You don't have to convince me, Francis."

"Thanks, Benny. It's just that I think Hernandez is vulnerable right now. What with that business about his hiring his relatives for city jobs, and that crack he made at that N.O.W. conference about his respecting his wife for knowing that her place was in the home."

"Yeah," said Ben, laughing. "That was pretty stupid."

"And there's plenty more," said Powell. "I tell ya, Benny, the man can be beat."

"And you figure you're the guy to do it?"

"I do, Benny. I do. I've received some very discreet inquiries, from some big-money people. They're interested in me challenging Hernandez the next time around. These are serious people, Benny. With serious money. Enough to mount a full-blown campaign."

"Are you already committed?"

"Not yet. I told them I was interested, though. They expect an answer soon. If it's not me, Benny, it'll be somebody else."

"Big money doesn't like Hernandez, huh?"

"Hernandez has pissed off too many people. He may be the candidate of the people, like he likes to have everybody believe, but that's not gonna get him reelected. He's going to need lots of cash. And those *people* of his are not long on cash. Hell, most of them don't even vote!

"Anyway, I know I gotta be careful. I figure I already got the black vote, they've always distrusted that Mexican. As long as there's not a black running against me, I'll get most of them. As far as the white vote goes, I'm not real worried. I mean, who better to run a law-and-order campaign than me? Hell, I've been the guy fighting to keep the black and Mexican gangs out of their nice little bedroom communities. They gotta vote for me."

"So you got it all figured out, huh?" said Ben. "What do you need me for?"

Ben watched the smile on his friend's face match his own.

"You know me too well, Benny." He started playing with his pen again, looking out the window. Outside, there was the usual glare of sun on haze, like some giant cigarette was being puffed on and the smoke blown in an even stream, covering the windows of the city's buildings.

"We got a problem," said Powell, returning his attention to Ben. He stood behind his desk, shuffling through a stack of files until he found the one he wanted.

"Take a look at this," he said, handing one of the files to Ben. Ben looked through the paperwork: a photograph of an officer in uniform whom he didn't recognize; a copy of the same officer's personnel file; three or four confidential reports on the officer's promotability signed by various lieutenants; and a sealed manila envelope with the word *Confidential* stamped in red ink on the front.

"Can I open this?" Ben asked, holding up the envelope. Powell nodded.

Ben pulled out a series of loose pages, standard crime report forms, along with a confidential memorandum from a detective in Vice, and a photograph of a man and woman, both wearing dark glasses, standing between two cars in a parking lot.

"What's all this?" asked Ben, sifting through the papers.

"The cop's name is Vincent Romero," said Powell. "He works West Valley Division, a sergeant. Moonlights as a security guard over at the Boulevard Mall. Decent record. Been with the department close to fifteen years, no major marks against him."

Ben was holding the departmental photograph of the uniformed officer taken shortly after his graduation from the academy. The guy looked great in uniform. This Vincent Romero looked like one of those silent-screen movie idols. Clean-cut, jet-black hair plastered back underneath his cap, white smile with perfect teeth. A good-looking guy.

"We got a report from one of the detectives in Vice," said Powell. "You should have it there."

Ben held up the confidential report.

"Yeah, that's the one. Go ahead, read it."

The detective's report dealt with a case that Vice was handling involving an arrest for lewd exhibition by a twenty-year-old male suspect named Arnold Lever in the men's room of the Biltmore Hotel, downtown. According to the vice detective, the suspect exposed himself to an undercover vice officer while standing in front of one of the urinals, saying, "I'll suck yours for free," and masturbating himself at the same time.

The detective's report went on to say that Lever's case was pending trial in municipal court. Further, that recently, the detective had been approached by one Murray Lever, the suspect's father, regarding information that the elder Lever had about another case. According to the detective, Murray Lever wanted to trade his information in return for favorable treatment for his son.

"What kind of information?" asked Ben.

"I had the detective talk to Murray Lever, off the record," answered Powell. "You know about these do-me-a-favor routines. Everybody figures they can get the cops to cut them a little slack by trading information.

"Well, anyway," Powell went on, "this Lever, the father, that is, works in the Jewelry Mart. He's got a little shop, mostly secondhand stuff. He's clean, we checked him out. Anyway, it turns out that some guy comes into his shop one day and tries to pawn a very large diamond without a setting. Lever tells him he doesn't have that much cash laying around, but that he can arrange the sale, and tells the guy to come back the next day. Meanwhile, he starts thinking about the guy with the diamond. There's something about the guy and the deal that doesn't smell kosher."

Powell continued: "Lever can't do the deal himself anyway, so he figures he'll call up the cop that arrested his kid and tell him about the loose diamond, act like he's doing his civic duty. You know, like it has nothing to do with him wanting us to do his kid a favor.

"As it turns out, the guy with the diamond never comes back. The vice cops that took Murray Lever's report tell him that they'll look into the matter, and promptly proceed to round-file the whole thing.

"Nothing more happens for a couple of weeks. Lever's kid cops a plea to trespass and gets community service and probation, and the whole thing is pretty much closed. That is, until the detective gets to talking to his wife's brother, who's some kind of claims adjustor for an insurance company. They're sitting around the pool one Sunday when the brother-in-law starts talking about this claim he's got where the wife's the beneficary. He says that the husband got killed in a car crash near Mulholland Drive, but not before the husband had hired a private investigator to follow the wife because he thought she was messing around while he was at the office.

"To make a long story even longer," said Powell, "the private dick gets pictures of the wife talking to some guy in a parking lot. Those are the ones you got there in the file."

Ben looked at the parking lot photo again.

"Well, the brother-in-law shows the pictures to our detective, and it turns out he recognizes the guy in the picture as a cop, of all things! It seems that this cop in the pictures and the wife of the dead guy had been getting it on right under the old man's nose, just like the husband suspected."

"What was the name of that movie?" asked Ben, his eyes turning to the ceiling as if the information he wanted hung there ready to be plucked. "You know, the one where the wife and the boyfriend take out this insurance policy on the husband, then knock him off?"

"There's been lots of them," said Powell. "Remember that one with Fred MacMurray as the boyfriend?"

"Double Indemnity," answered Ben. "That's the one."

"Right. An old scam, but the brother-in-law's boss figured it was worth looking into before they parted with their half million."

"Half million?"

"Yeah. The wife had taken out a policy on the husband a few months before he died."

"And he bought it in a car crash, you said?"

"Went over the cliff, just west of Laurel Canyon."

"An accident?"

"Who knows. It's pretty convenient though, you gotta admit."

Ben didn't answer right away. He was looking at the parking lot picture. Finally he asked, "So what's the connection?"

"Look at the guy standing next to the broad in the parking lot . . . Look familiar?"

It was hard to see facial features, the picture having been taken with some sort of telephoto lens so that faces were more grainy than normal.

"I'll save you the trouble of ruining your eyes," said Powell. "The woman in the picture is the dead guy's wife. The guy she's with is Vincent Romero."

"Sergeant Romero."

"Exactly. It seems our Sergeant Romero had been seen with the wife on several occasions prior to the husband's death."

"Could be totally legit," said Ben.

Francis Powell leaned back in his chair, put his hands behind his head, and smiled, like a father listening to his child explain why he couldn't go to school on the day of the big test because he suddenly didn't feel so good.

"Okay, okay," muttered Ben. "So it does sound fishy."

"Wait," said Powell. "You haven't heard the best part. It seems our favorite housewife used part of the insurance payoff to buy herself a little trinket, an eight-carat diamond solitaire."

"Lever," said Ben.

"Now you're catching up, Benny. The wife paid for the ring with a check, according to the detective. The detective and a friend who worked L.A.P.D. Bunko-Forgery, got ahold of the bank records. The insurance company, because they thought something wasn't quite right about the whole thing, traced the check back to the jeweler who sold the ring. They got a complete description of the ring: size, price, the whole enchilada.''

''So?''

''So a couple of days after she gets the money—the same day that she buys the ring—she has her head blown off in the upstairs bedroom of their house. And you know what the cops *don't* find when they start scraping her off the wall?''

''The ring.''

''That's right.''

''What about the shooter?''

''What about him? Sure, the logical thing is that it was some sort of rip-off. That the woman was shot by the thief, and he took off with the ring, right? That's what the homicide guys figured.''

''And our boy, Romero?''

''Ah, that's where the story gets really interesting. You see, when the sergeant in Vice finds out about the wife getting killed, knowing what he does from his brother-in-law, he mentions it to the homicide detective who's handling the wife's case. Just for the hell of it, he also tells him about the loose diamond that Lever almost bought right about the same time as the wife was murdered.''

''Romero . . .''

''You got it,'' said Powell, his eyes lighting up. ''Lever I.D.s Romero as the one who tried to pawn the diamond within days after the wife was killed.''

''Jesus!''

''Just a fluke, Benny. A total fucking fluke.''

''So now what?''

Francis Powell picked up his pen and began cleaning his nails with the metal clip.

''There's no way we can prove that both diamonds are the same, not without the actual stone, which may or may not still be in Romero's possession. Even then, diamonds, to the casual observer, look alike. It would take an expert who had seen the diamond the wife bought, along with a detailed gemological report of that diamond, to give an opinion whether it's the same one Romero tried to pawn. And even then we'd be stretching.''

"We could call Romero in and . . .''

"And he'd just clam up. We'd be dealing with his lawyer and we'd never get further than where we are right now. No. We can't let him know that we're onto him, not just yet. I've had them pull the burglary reports for the last year from the Boulevard Mall where Romero works. Interestingly enough, there's been a noticeable upswing in the amount of burglaries and insurance payoffs at the mall since Romero took the job. It looks like our sergeant has got his hand into a lot of different pots.''

"Keep him under surveillance,'' said Ben. "Hope that he makes a mistake.''

"He will,'' said Powell. He reached over and grabbed the photo of Romero from off the top of his desk.

"A cocky bastard like this,'' he said, tapping his finger on the photograph, "is bound to make a mistake. And when he does, we'll be there, waiting.'' Powell cleared his throat and readjusted his position behind the desk. "Meanwhile,'' he said, "I'm assigning this case to you. I want you to handle it, but not through the usual channels. This is technically an Internal Affairs matter, but I don't want anyone else in the division to know about it, understood?''

"No problem,'' said Ben, not quite sure what his boss was up to.

"Good,'' said Powell, with a tone of finality. He pulled a pack of Marlboros from his shirt pocket and lit one.

"Francis, my friend,'' said Ben, choosing his words carefully, "the special treatment on this case wouldn't have anything to do with your future political plans, would it?''

"I don't follow,'' said Powell, taking a short pull

from his cigarette, his hand in front of his mouth to cover his smile.

"Right," said Ben. "The fact that you want *me* to handle this case personally, more or less outside of the usual channels—that doesn't have anything to do with the fact that Romero is obviously a Latin name, and that the last thing you're gonna want during the campaign are accusations by Hernandez that you're racially biased against Mexicans."

"Benny, when this case hits the courts . . . *If* it ever hits the courts, it's gonna make front-page news for a lotta months. If the D.A. blows it on this case and Romero walks, the D.A.'s not gonna take the heat, *I* am. That's just the kind of heat I can't afford to take, not in an election year, and not with a Mexican mayor and his cronies breathing down my neck, looking for any sleazy thing they can lay their hands on to use against me."

Powell continued: "I need someone I can trust to handle this thing. If Romero is doing the kinds of things that I think . . . I *know* that he's doing, then he's one dangerous asshole that should be off the streets and behind bars. But until I'm absolutely sure that we can put him there, I've gotta be careful. Hernandez is going to be licking his chops, just waiting to pin the racial-bigot badge on me, in the hope of swaying the minority vote his way. I can't afford to give him that opportunity."

"All right," said Ben, getting up from his chair. He took the picture of Romero from off the top of Powell's desk.

"One more thing," said Powell. "You'll have a partner on this."

"But . . ."

"Joe Curzon."

"You've got to be kidding," said Ben. "Curzon's been I.O.D. for months. He just got out of the hospital from what I heard. Besides, Joe's the original bull in a china shop. I thought you wanted . . ."

"I know what you're gonna say, Ben, but believe me,

I've thought this one out. Joe's a damn good cop, even if public relations is not his strong suit. Besides, I already talked to him.''

Ben gave Francis Powell a look of disgruntled resignation.

"Don't worry, Benny, the Indian will work out just fine. He tells me that he's never felt better since the operation. He's even lost twenty pounds.''

"So now he's down to what? Two eighty?''

"Maybe a little more,'' said Powell, laughing and placing his hand on Ben's back. "Believe me, I won't forget this one, Benny, you know that, don't you?''

"Yeah,'' said Ben. "You know something, Francis, I think you're making the right move with this mayor thing.''

"Thanks, Ben, I appreciate that, coming from you.''

"Yeah, I gotta admit you got all the angles covered. I myself would never have picked Indian Joe Curzon to partner up on this case because the guy's a heavy-handed, slow, overweight, old-time cop, who'd just as soon break a suspect's legs as have to bother arresting him and writing out a report. But then, I'm not as politically *attuned* as you are, Francis. I bet that the fact that Indian Joe looks and sounds like your basic Tex-Mex Mexican had absolutely nothing to do with your selection. I bet that the fact that his last name sounds more Mexican than Indian had nothing to do with your choice. Right, Francis?''

Francis Powell pulled away from Ben, putting his hand over his mouth to muffle his laughter.

"And I bet,'' continued Ben, "that you want me to make sure that Joe's name and picture are prominently displayed in any press coverage that we might receive on this case.''

"Benny,'' laughed Powell, "you're always one step ahead of me. Maybe I *will* make you my V.P.''

"Yeah, right, Francis,'' muttered Ben, as he walked out of the chief's office.

CHAPTER 4 ━━━━━━━━

He found the small bungalow offices in a small, quiet industrial park, detached from the usual hustle-bustle of the main hospital. He'd been concerned about that. Worried that he might see someone, someone he knew who might recognize him. Then there'd be the questions, the inquiring looks: "What ya here for? Hope it's nothing too serious?"

In the waiting room there were two large beige velour couches cornered around a glass-topped coffee table. An assortment of magazines covered most of the table-top, except for a small potted fern that occupied the center, and a plastic container holding brochures for the Kaiser Foundation Health Plan. A young woman, Ben guessed around thirty, sat in the furthest corner from the door, her nose in a paperback book. She didn't look up when Ben entered. She remained intent on the pages of her paperback as Ben looked through the magazines on the coffee table, waiting for his name to be called.

What could she be here for? he thought. Slender, young, her blonde hair cascading over soft, feminine shoulders. A doll's perfect face, beautiful, but obviously secure too. Like some child's mother, the June Cleaver variety. Totally wholesome. And what was that she was reading? So calm, peaceful—in control.

What the hell's she doing here?

Ben cleared his throat, glancing sideways at the young blonde. She didn't look up.

Maybe she's waiting for someone? That could be it. Sure, she's not a patient, just a friend of someone. Much too sane-looking to be one of the crazies. She's probably wondering just how crazy I am. I bet she half-expects me to start hallucinating, maybe tell her I'm the pope or the king of England. She's probably wondering what I'm thinking about her. Or am I the only one that's always worried about what people think of me? Definitely crazy, at least unbalanced. Paranoid, that's the word.

Still, she looks awfully in control to be seeking professional help. Appearances could be deceiving, though.

Look at me . . .

If the guys could see me here, now, they'd probably think I was waiting for a friend. No, not a friend. I wouldn't have any friends that were crazy. No instability in my life, no sirree! If I were sitting in a head-shrinker's office it'd be strictly business. Looking for a suspect, following up on a lead.

"Mrs. Randolph, the doctor will see you now." Ben looked up to see one of the secretaries smiling at the young blonde, who, upon hearing her name, rose from her seat with book and purse in hand and followed the secretary into one of the rear offices.

Ben went back to the brochure, staring at the print but not reading. Thirty visits, that's what the Kaiser Medical Plan covered. Did that mean that if he wasn't cured after thirty visits he was expected to just go through the rest of his life being crazy? He'd have to talk to the doctor about that one. Surely they had some provisions for people with serious problems, truly crazy people—like himself.

"Mr. Green?" The voice was soft, and sweet like the face. When Ben looked up, his first thought was that Dr. Elizabeth Mellnor was beautiful, not in the model-sort of way, but natural. He'd expected old, with heavy out-of-style glasses on a withered face and a frumpy dress. Instead, what he saw was soft shoulder-length black hair framing a delicate porcelain-like face, and deep-set green eyes that appeared genuinely pleased to see him. She wore lipstick in a pale salmon shade, almost natural. No other makeup. She looked to be in her mid to late twenties, but Ben figured she had to be older. He'd heard people talk about women glowing, but hadn't seen it for himself until now.

"I'm sorry to have kept you waiting," she said, like velvet, extending her hand. "One of my patients, on the phone. It took longer than I thought."

"No problem," said Ben, feigning manly self-assurance. Jesus, he thought, that sounds pretty damn stupid. Like I would be here in the first place, ready to get my head shrunk, if I actually had that sort of confidence!

Her office was small and simple. A desk, a credenza filled with file drawers, two oversized chairs, and some pictures on the walls.

"Where's the couch?" Ben tried to laugh, hoping she'd join in. He was starting to think that this wasn't such a good idea.

"Would you feel more comfortable lying down?"

"Oh, no, I was just joking. You know, psychiatrists and their couches . . ."

"Oh."

Ben thought: This is getting off to a bad start. It was his fault. He couldn't be himself. He had to put on some act to prevent her from seeing him—seeing who he really was. God, that was stupid! What in hell was he here for in the first place?

"I see from your records that you've been in therapy before?"

"Uh, yes. About a year ago."

"I have a report here from Dr. Wallace saying that you worked with him for about six months and then were discharged. Depression. An incident involving the death of your daughter."

"She was raped and murdered," said Ben, a little too loudly. It was as if he thought by treating the incident in a normal day-to-day fashion he could render it as such. It didn't work. The same pictures began to run again in his mind. He saw himself at Julie's funeral, the guilt pressed upon him by Sara and the others. He'd been too busy, they'd said. Too involved with his own life to answer his daughter's plea for help. And that had caused her death. He was responsible.

"I have a brief summary of what happened, Mr. Green," she said, interrupting his thoughts. "We don't have to go into that just yet. Maybe we should just use this first session to get to know one another a little better."

"I might need all thirty," said Ben, forcing a smile. She didn't respond, just stared, as if waiting for him to explain. She removed her glasses and placed them on the desk. He hadn't remembered her putting them on.

"You're a police officer, aren't you?"

Ben nodded. "More or less. I practiced law, criminal defense, when all this happened. Recently, after the therapy and all, I started with Internal Affairs at L.A.P.D. The chief is an old friend. It seems to be working out okay."

"Than why are you here?"

Ben looked down at the pale gray carpet, wondering why all of his words seemed so transparent. "I guess it hasn't worked out *that* well," he said. "I had been trying this big case. A death-penalty case. It was taking pretty much all of my time. Julie, my daughter, was having problems at home. My ex and I had been divorced, and Sara, my ex, had taken Julie back east with her. Sara had remarried, and Julie was having a hard time adjusting to life with a new father.

"I did what I could, to help her I mean. The telephone is not the greatest means of communicating, at least with an emotionally upset teenage daughter. I thought everything was going to be okay. Then Sara called to tell me that Julie had run away. That she was on her way to see me.

"I'm sorry." Ben rubbed at his eyes. "You said we'd talk about this later."

"That's all right. Go ahead, if you like. I want to hear this."

"They contacted me. The cops, I mean. Said they'd found her body in some gully near Bakersfield. I found out later that she'd tried to call me, to let me know she was coming. I never got the call."

"And you blame yourself for that, and for her death?"

"There's more. I should tell you more."

"Only if you want to."

"I tried to kill myself. I suppose that's all in there. You'll read about it. I had this case, the one I told you about. I got the guy off."

"That was your job, wasn't it?"

"Yeah, my job . . ." Ben paused. For the first time in a long while he thought about Claire, and his discussions with her about representing the guilty and trying to get them off.

"I did get him off," mumbled Ben. "A month later he killed a whole family, parents and kids, in a robbery. He shot each of them in the head while they were on their knees begging for mercy."

"I see," she said. "And you've taken that onto your shoulders as well?"

"I went on medical leave for over a year," said Ben. "They put me in a rest home. It was a while before they could get me to even talk about it. We tried to work through it, you know. Everybody kept saying it would pass. I went to the therapy sessions. We both did, Claire and I."

"Claire?"

"A girlfriend. She tried to help."

"Do you still see her?"

"No."

Beth Mellnor waited for an explanation, but none was forthcoming. "So," she added, "you terminated treatment with Dr. Wallace."

"I went back to work," said Ben. "I had to. There was nothing else left."

"And you made everyone believe that you were okay. That you'd been through the worst, but had come out all right."

Ben looked down at this lap, slowly shaking his head back and forth. He readjusted his position in the over-sized chair.

She continued: "And now you find that you're really not okay. But you can't admit that to anyone, can you? You've just let it fester inside you."

"I have no choice. I can't go back to the convalescent home, huddle under some warm blanket and stare blankly at the television waiting for the drugs to take effect. I can't do that. I thought I was ready, and this job seemed like the perfect answer. If they found out I was still in trouble it would mean the end."

"So," she said, "you try and cover it up. Put on a good show. Nobody suspects a thing."

Ben remained silent.

"So what's the problem, Mr. Green?" She arched her eyebrows and pressed her head back against the cushion of her chair, gently rocking back and forth. She had the look of a chess master who has just checkmated her opponent.

Ben said: "This is the part where you know the answer and want to hear it from me, right?"

"I'll ask the questions." She smiled. "You give the answers, okay?"

"Fair enough," said Ben. "The problem, as you put it, is that I can't do it any longer. I can't keep up with the act. I thought that the memories would go away, or at least . . . I don't know . . . get less intense. But they haven't. I see things when I'm walking down the street or sitting in the car, stupid little insignificant things, and they trigger a memory of Julie. And then it all starts again. I'm afraid that one of these days I'll just explode. There are times, especially lately, when for no reason, I just feel like crying."

"And your wife—I mean, ex-wife?"

"Sara? We're apart. She's out of the picture. The last thing that would cross her mind is to try and help me."

"And Claire?"

"Claire . . ." For a moment, Ben's mind drifted away from where he was to happier times.

"I forced her away," he said. "When it happened, I mean the biking accident . . . when I tried to kill myself . . . well, she wanted to be there for me, but I couldn't. Can you understand that? Every time I looked at her, I saw Julie, and myself, and the whole goddamn screwed-up thing. Claire grew to recognize that, I guess. How could she not? She's a good-hearted person, but not a saint. Like I said, I pushed her away. It just seemed to happen."

"And you still blame yourself for all of this?"

"No. At least I don't think I do. I don't know. I've tried to think this through, and I don't think I do blame myself. At least, that's not what's causing me to feel this way. It's beyond that now, beyond who's to blame. It's just the overwhelming feeling of loss, of wasted life. It doesn't make sense, doesn't seem right, you know what I mean? And it's not all the time. And that probably makes it even worse. It's like you're just walking along on a sunny day and suddenly fall into the deepest darkest hole in the universe. You think you'll never get back. You're surrounded by total darkness, being crushed by unbearable despair."

She said: "But it eventually goes away, this darkness?"

"Yes. So far."

She got up from her desk and walked around to where he sat.

"Let's call it a day, for now." She smiled. "I would like to see you next week, in the evening's okay. Whenever it's convenient for you. The girls outside have my calendar. If you need to contact me, they'll give you a card with the number of my service. I can be reached day or night for emergencies."

"You must never leave the telephone," he said, standing up.

"It sometimes seems that way." She took his arm and walked him to the door. "I mean it," she repeated. "Call me if you need to talk."

"I just may take you up on that, Dr. Mellnor."

"Elizabeth, or Beth. It's less formal."

"I'll do that, Beth." He paused momentarily, wanting to say something that he'd been thinking about earlier.

"Is there something else?" she asked.

He was thinking about telling her that she was wasting her time. That as far as he was concerned, no matter how good she was, his case was hopeless. Then he looked into those understanding green eyes and thought, Maybe . . . ?

"No," he said. "Nothing for now." He smiled and shook her hand, then headed out the door.

CHAPTER 5 ━━━━━━

Celeste had never seen one quite that big. The thing just hung there, like something she had once seen hanging from the ceiling in an Italian delicatessen, dead to the world. This *had* to be the right guy. After all, she knew she hadn't lost her touch. In fact, most of her clients had just the opposite problem, finishing up before they barely got started. She was good at her work and she knew it. A real pro. And up until now, could straighten even the limpest pecker.

This must be the guy, she thought, listening to him softly moan a low humming noise. What a crying shame. All that meat, like liverwurst without the casing.

"Honey," said Celeste, on her knees looking up from between his legs. "You want me to try something else or are we gonna call it a day?"

He just smiled, slowly throwing his head back, making that soft humming noise again, enjoying himself, like he wasn't the least bit concerned at the lack of action between his legs.

Celeste rolled her eyes upward, still concentrating on the task before her. She could see the slight change in color and texture at the sides of the man's head where the toupee left off and his natural hair took over. She had noticed something odd about his hair earlier, but couldn't quite put her finger on it. From where she was now, though, she had a different angle at it and the toupee seemed to float like some hairy beanie atop the back of the man's head. She smiled to herself, thinking how different things seemed looking up from between some guy's legs. A perspective that, over the years, she had grown accustomed to.

He breathed deeply, taking her head in his hands, gently at first, then harder. He brought her lips over him, breathed deeply again, then looked down at her face.

"Bite the tip," he said, watching her carefully, then added, "Gently."

Celeste looked up, then did what he said, thinking that maybe the old guy was kinkier than she'd thought.

"You'll feel a small bump," he told her. He waited until she had found the button-sized bump, first with her teeth, then with her lips.

"That's it." He sighed. "Now press down on the button . . . slowly, not too hard." He was holding the base of his dick in one hand, the other hand still atop Celeste's head, guiding her in the right direction.

Celeste pressed the bump with her lips, looking up at his face for some sort of confirmation that she was doing the right thing, certain that she was wasting her time. She noticed a thin, pale pink razorlike line running across the man's stomach under a fold in his skin. When he leaned back, the faded line of scarred skin was just barely visible, peeking out from beneath the fold of flesh on his stomach.

She was watching him looking down at her, smiling, his eyebrows raised in anticipation, when what she had been sure was liverwurst gone bad began to arc swiftly upward, like a compass in a magnetic field. Within seconds, the liverwurst had taken on the robust characteristics of a family-sized Genoa salami, which is how it remained after Celeste withdrew a few inches to admire her work.

"Jesus, honey, that's really something," she said, moving to the side to take in the full effect.

"Yeah, I know," said the man.

* * *

Arnie Rosen, previously Leonard "The Kid" Fine, had done it again. He lay on his back, letting his mind follow his body rocking gently back and forth with the water in his water bed. He was within moments of being exactly and completely aware of where he was, that uncertain state of mind between sleep and awakening when dream and reality become hopelessly intertwined. Arnie liked that feeling. He liked it because he would dream about the old days, the old neighborhood in Jersey after the war and before the big money and the big trouble. His dreams would almost seem true. Waking was invariably a disappointment.

His eyes moved mechanically around the room, like a security camera in a bank, clicking off those items, his possessions, with which he was familiar. Mentally checking that everything was still there and where it was supposed to be.

In the same moment, Arnie looked down the length of his stomach and noticed that he was still hard. He saw the girl, what was her name?—he had forgotten—looking in the same direction, making quick stabbing motions at her hair with a small brush.

"I didn't think you had it in ya, hon," she said, still thrusting the brush at her hair, working her way toward the back of her head. She had showered and was wearing one of Arnie's large bath towels wrapped around her.

Arnie thought she still looked good. That was not the way it usually was with him. Over the years, and it always depressed him to think just how many years by this point he was looking over, he found the actual sex act increasingly less satisfying. He was at the point where he got more pleasure out of mentally undressing women than fucking them.

"My God, honey," she said, moving closer to the bed, "that is one hell of a world-class hard-on."

Arnie's eyes followed hers down to where they were focused between his legs. He felt his usual mixture of pride and deceit. The doctor had said that if he wanted it enough he'd learn to get comfortable with it, and he had done just that. The best part now was watching the expression on the faces of all those sweet young things—the ones who always called him "honey"—when he told them to bite the tip. He never told them right away, but like any good performer he'd hold back, waiting until that moment, just before impatience set in. Then he'd set the forces of modern medicine into action.

And prodigious forces they were indeed. His implant had been a special-order affair to accommodate what he liked to consider his larger-than-life contribution to the happiness of the female sex. Arnie smiled as his mind drifted back to the old days, in Jersey, when Tony Ruggerio and the others had called him "Limp Dick." Back then Arnie was one of Big Tony's boys, one of Tony's inside money men. But that had all ended when the feds got involved in Arnie's life.

Dr. Cohen, Arnie's urologist, had told him after the surgery that he could have sold tickets to his office staff to witness the unveiling. The other doctors in the group were curious about whether the modified, beefed-up version of Arnie's penile implant could do the job; a question of torque conversion or something like that, they had said. The nurses and female office staff were interested in the result of Arnie's surgery for different reasons.

Arnie watched as the girl dropped the towel and started to dress. He thought that this was the moment in the old movies when the guy, the bedsheet slung provocatively at an angle down from his waist, covering just barely what had to be covered for the censors, would reach over to the nightstand and retrieve a single cigarette, light it, inhale deeply, then pass it to the woman beside him.

Arnie didn't feel like doing any of that. He had given up smoking cigarettes after Dr. Lubish, his heart specialist, told him his lungs looked like shit and his heart not much better. Lubish said that if he expected to get much use out of his implant he better cut out smoking altogether, which Arnie did, except for the cigars. There were some things even more important than sex.

Arnie pulled himself up so he was sitting almost upright, resting on his elbows. The girl—Celeste, that was her name—was at the foot of the bed, her back to him, smoothing her nylons on legs that seemed to go on forever. Arnie reached down with his right hand and gently squeezed the button valve at the tip of his penis, holding it for a second as the fluid was evacuated from one reservoir into another, transforming him into a mere mortal once again.

"So, hon," the girl said, still working on her stockings, looking away from him, "how you gonna spend all that money?"

Arnie swung his legs over the side of the bed and shuffled into the bathroom without answering. The thought of the money he had recently won in the lottery had disappeared from his mind until she mentioned it. The money made him feel good and bad at the same time. Another mixed blessing. It seemed to Arnie that there was nothing anymore that made him feel totally great. Everything seemed to have its downside, always something that Arnie could grasp on to and worry to death.

And when it came to worrying, Arnie Rosen was in a class by himself. A world-class worrier, as the girl would have put it. Arnie had doctors to worry about his heart, and doctors to worry about his lungs, and, of course, the architect of his most recent sexual triumph, Dr. Cohen, to worry about his dick. What he didn't have doctors to worry about, Arnie did himself, filling the worry void admirably in their absence.

The lottery was one of the things that Arnie worried about. It still bothered him. He had bought the tickets at the Boulevard Mall, where he worked selling timeshares at the Vacation Villas, fleecing suckers out of their retirement. He never expected to win anything more than a couple hundred if he got lucky. It was just his luck that he hit it big. Or at least big enough that he had to go on local TV to collect his check.

He'd told the girl about the prize, sitting in the bar at the Holiday Inn. And she said she remembered hearing about it somewhere and reached over from her bar stool and placed her hand directly on his crotch without missing a beat. Arnie figured, what the hell. This was just an added, unadvertised bonus of playing the California Lottery.

As Arnie peered into the mirror over the sink, trying hard not to think about how he looked even less healthy than he had that morning, he thought about the girl, the bar, the fact that she was now getting dressed in the bedroom of his semi-luxurious condominium, after having what was for him a semi-acceptable orgasm.

Arnie figured it wasn't likely that Tony Ruggerio and his army of thugs had caught his action on TV. The last Arnie had heard, Big Tony was holed up someplace in Miami, an aging gangster like himself, enjoying the last years of his life living off the spoils that running numbers and loan-sharking had provided.

Still, if the girl had actually seen him on TV, who knows who else might have seen him. He placed the tip of his finger to the right side of his nose, then the left, gently pushing while turning to catch his partial profile in the mirror. He then placed his finger on his upper lip so that it covered most of his mustache. There was no getting around it, the surgery had definitely made him look different. Nothing like his former self. Big Tony would never be able to recognize him, even if he were still looking. Yeah, nothing to worry about.

Arnie sat down on the toilet, opening a copy of *Time* magazine to an article he had started the last time he was on the toilet. The *Time* article was about crime and corruption in America, and seemed to focus on organized crime families, the Mafia, and mob ties with well-known entertainers and politicians. The authors of the article quoted anonymous sources—probably mobsters, thought Arnie—as saying that the whole Mafia thing was an exaggeration, that there really was no such thing as organized crime.

Arnie smiled, laughing to himself, a smile of part amusement and part dread. Again that mixed blessing thing. He tried not to strain too much on the toilet, his doctor's orders. This was definitely not good for his system. Arnie knew the answer to the author's question. He knew the quoted anonymous sources were full of shit. And it made Arnie Rosen, previously Leonard "The Kid" Fine—mob snitch and informant for the Federal Witness Protection Program—worry just a little bit more.

CHAPTER 6 ━━━━━━━━━━━━━

It was Monday, late afternoon; a corner table inside the Ventura Room of the Woodland Hills Holiday Inn. The only illumination inside came from three recessed spotlights located in the ceiling near the mirror over the bar. They cast a pale smoky light over the interior of the bar and not much else. The darkness smelled of stale cigarettes and spilled drinks from the night before. The bartender, shirt unbuttoned and bow tie clipped to one corner of his collar, stood, pad and pencil in hand, behind the bar taking inventory.

A waitress in a short black miniskirt and black fishnet stockings leaned on the opposite side of the bar, the back of one of her spiked heels rocking back and forth on the foot rail. She was busy making miniature shish kebob concoctions on plastic toothpicks out of red and green maraschino cherries, chunks of pineapple, and orange slices.

Celeste nursed her white wine spritzer in the booth in the corner, alone. She still wore her wraparound shades, black shiny plastic, making her soft white skin look even whiter. She wore a striped halter top with large plastic buttons for decoration down the front, a pair of tight fleece aerobic pants, and her white Reeboks, no socks. A dark red headband was stretched across the top of her hair, separating the long bangs in front from the ratted blonde portion in the back. Her hair came down to the shoulders where it was flipped

and heavily starched with hair spray. Every time she
moved to take a drink her hair would move only slightly.
She sat looking straight ahead, watching the bartender
making notes on his pad.

When the man in the velour jogging suit entered the
bar and saw her, his first impression was that she looked
like the girl that played Lolita in the movie. She had
changed. He remembered her as a redhead.

The man settled into the booth alongside Celeste.
She didn't look up from her drink. In fact, looking at
her, you'd never know that anyone else had joined her
at the table.

The man in the jogging suit removed a tan envelope
from within his jacket and placed it on the table between them, just out of her reach. He was also wearing
sunglasses: tortoiseshell frames, heavy, thick, and
dark—the prescription variety.

"Talk to me," said the man, low and firm, without
looking at her. He waved off the waitress who was making her way toward their table.

"He's not your man," said Celeste, lifting her glass
to get the waitress' attention.

The man looked only slightly put-out. He motioned
for the waitress to bring another wine spritzer. Up until
then the barmaid appeared in a state of suspended an-
imation, uncertain whether to serve the table or not.

"What makes you say that?" said the man.

"He's not like you said he'd be."

"You're sure?"

She turned her head and looked at the man for the
first time. A small smile came to her mouth, just the
corners, then disappeared. She turned away, back to
looking straight ahead.

"Yeah, I guess you would know," said the man. The
waitress brought Celeste another drink.

"Tell me about it," said the man.

Celeste turned away from her drink to face him again,
somewhat surprised.

"Tell you about it?" she said.

The man reached for the envelope and moved it closer to Celeste, saying, "Yeah, tell me all about it."

Celeste shrugged, as if she were resigned to going through the story but knew it was a waste of time. She told the man about meeting the guy in the bar, about the lottery story, about what happened at the guy's condo, the sex, and that was it.

"That's all?" asked the man.

"What did you expect?"

The man didn't answer Celeste's question. He pulled a large cigar from the pocket inside his jacket, bit off the tip, carefully removing it from between his front teeth with his fingertips, and placed it in the ashtray on the table. He lit the cigar, leaning back, relaxing for the first time since coming into the bar. He placed both his arms on the back edge of the booth for a moment, then removed the cigar, blowing a plume of smoke across the table. The smell from the man's cigar mixed with the smells of the room. Celeste watched the smoke gather in a layer at the low ceiling, like clouds with no place to go and no wind to get them there.

"Tell me more about this bump," said the man.

Again that look of resignation bordering on outright impatience. Celeste wanted to take the envelope in her hands, look inside, count the money, and leave. But she didn't. She knew you didn't act that way with the man.

"Like a small button," she said. "Near the tip." She took a sip of her drink, then wiped the corners of her mouth with a cocktail napkin. "Actually," she continued, "you said the guy you were looking for couldn't get it up. I was sure you had the right guy until he told me to bite down on that button thing. Boy oh boy, I tell you, that guy swung into action like Reggie Jackson in October." She laughed, looking down at the red lip marks on the rim of her glass. "You should have seen the size of that guy's Louisville Slugger!" She laughed again, shaking her head.

The man didn't smile. During her story he had held

the cigar between the first two fingers of his right hand. The ash at the tip of the cigar was about to fall, and Celeste was concentrating on that fact while she'd been speaking.

The man made the next comment. He leaned forward, knocking the cigar ash into the ashtray, then placed his elbow and forearm on the table and turned to face her, still holding the cigar between his fingers.

"You didn't think there was anything funny about the guy's dick?"

"Funny?" asked Celeste.

"Yeah, like this whole business with the bump and him being a limp dick early on. That didn't strike you as kinda odd?"

Celeste shook her head no, as if she hadn't the slightest idea what the man was getting at.

"Incredible," said the man.

Celeste wasn't sure whether he was referring to the guy with the dick, or to her. She couldn't see the man's eyes behind his prescription sunglasses. She just smiled a half-smile, which is what she always did when she wasn't sure what people meant, which happened a lot to her, at least when she wasn't in bed with them.

The man shoved the envelope in front of her and started to slide around to the front of the booth. Celeste watched as he straightened himself at the edge of the table, knocking some errant ash off the front of his jacket and pants. Then he just stood there, looking at her.

Celeste lifted the envelope and peeked inside at the crisp twenties. There were lots of them, more than she had expected. More than the man had first mentioned. She smiled, placing the envelope in her purse.

She was beginning to feel the effects of the wine. Not that she was drunk, just a little light-headed, but feeling good. The edge of anxiety she had felt upon entering the bar had disappeared.

The man was still standing at the other side of the table looking at her. He had removed his sunglasses and Celeste could see the look of expectation in the man's eyes. He just stood there. Waiting.

She fingered the envelope inside her purse.

"Are you in a hurry?" she asked, looking into those eyes, sure she already knew the answer to her question.

"Not at all, honey," he said, a leering smile coming to his face. Celeste noticed that the look of expectation in his eyes had been replaced with something else. Another look. A look she was all too familiar with, like something she had once seen on TV, late at night. The look on the vampire's face, just before he went down on the girl's neck.

Celeste grabbed her purse and started toward the lobby elevator, the man following. Her eyes had adjusted to the darkness inside the bar so that when she entered the lobby she was momentarily blinded by the light from outside. The hotel lobby, like an overexposed photograph, was bathed in bright sunlight, which made the people and furniture inside seem vague and indistinct, pale versions of the real thing. Celeste reached into her purse for her shades before realizing that she was already wearing them.

"Too bad you got the wrong guy," she said over her shoulder to the man as she entered the lobby elevator.

"Yeah," said the man, laughing. He laughed again, then said, "A *real* pity!" He was still laughing as the elevator doors closed behind them.

CHAPTER 7 ▬▬▬▬

It was one of those blast-furnace San Fernando Valley nights when the air was thick with heat, unmoving, and the temperature dropped to a sticky, suffocating ninety degrees with the nightfall. The two window swamp coolers had been pumping away all day with little to show for it. Tiny insects fluttered in the porch light, searching in vain for even the slightest current of air to carry them away. Outside, in the distance, there was the sound of cars snaking their way through the canyon, the pop of an exhaust, and the muted flapping of rubber on pavement as somebody rounded the corner and accelerated toward the top of the hill.

Jonathan Racine sat behind the oversized partner's desk, conscious of the rivulets of perspiration making their way down his back, collecting near the elastic band of his undershorts.

On his desk were stacks of books and magazines carefully piled five and six high, forming a semicircle around the area in which he worked. A cut-crystal highball glass, filled with partially melted ice cubes swimming in a clear liquid, rested within reach. On the desk in front of him, the object of his present attention was the *AB Bookman Yearbook* along with a copy of John Carter's *ABC for Book Collectors*.

Jonathan slowly ran the tip of his finger down the columns listing the booksellers who he thought might carry the volume he was searching for. He had already checked his *American Book Prices Current* in an attempt to fix the price of the Faulkner volume. The listings specified a recent sale at Swann Galleries for a 1927 edition of the novel *Mosquitoes,* but without specification as to binding color.

A client had called offering to sell the same Faulkner novel with a blue cloth binding and in nearly mint condition. Jonathan knew that the color of the binding would dictate the value of the book. A variant binding, or a binding of a color other than the standard, indicated that the volume was probably bound at a different time. It could mean that the book being offered was in its first state. Other minor differences between volumes—like the type of binding, variations in the design of the title page, and errors in the text or print that were later corrected—delineated different states of the same book. The state of any particular volume invariably had some effect, sometimes dramatic, on its value in the bookselling community. The Faulkner that Jonathan was looking for could fetch in excess of $1,500 with a blue cloth binding, while he could expect substantially less if it was bound in a different color.

Jonathan reached for the highball glass, bringing it to his lips without taking his eyes off the list of prices. He heard a stirring outside, just beneath the window. He got up, grabbing the tumbler of vodka, and walked over to the window, placing his face closely against the glass to cut the glare from the room lights. The compressor of the window air conditioner vibrated the glass against his forehead. He liked the feeling, especially after three vodkas. Like a kind of brain-numbing massage that helped block out the hassles of the day.

Two fat black cats rested atop the wooden fence that separated the front of his property from a shallow gully on the other side. Jonathan watched the headlights from the cars on Laurel Canyon flicker on and off on the far side of the gully as the drivers made their way along the serpentine stretch of canyon road.

The canyon was quiet. That was one of the reasons

they had chosen the house. That, and the fact that the side yard was big enough to park the limo.

There was also the anonymity of living in the canyon. Jonathan could walk out onto his front porch, crane his neck around a stand of low-hanging eucalyptus, and barely see his neighbor's porch light seeming to spark on and off between the leaves of the trees. They were close in actual distance, but the way the homes were laid out amidst the overgrowth of foliage, it was difficult to keep track of what was going on in your neighbor's yard.

And that was just fine for Jonathan Racine and most of the other people who made their home in the partially rustic, partially sophisticated canyon that separated the San Fernando Valley from the city. Jonathan looked on Laurel Canyon as a sort of demilitarized zone, a buffer between two distinctly different countries—the San Fernando Valley and the city of Hollywood—the citizens of both professing no identity crisis, certain in their knowledge that each area was preferably different from the other.

The canyon, on the other hand, was an amalgam of people who couldn't make up their minds whether they belonged in the city or the Valley (or, according to some, on the planet, for that matter). There were identity crises of epic proportions occurring daily amongst canyon residents. Sometimes, Jonathan thought that it wasn't really an identity crisis at all, but was, instead, a statement by those who resided there (more or less permanently), that they refused to be categorized or pigeonholed.

He liked that theory because it matched the way he had been feeling lately. Why drag around the baggage of other people's opinions about you and your predecessors just to make it easier for those same other people to avoid dealing with you as a person. *Hell, Blanche,* he could imagine those suburban Valley residents saying, sitting in their BarcaLoungers in front of the TV with a dish of ice cream in their lap, *he's just one of those weird Laurel Canyon cliff-dwellers . . . You know, the people who live in those stilt houses. The ones who are always on the eleven o'clock news, standing in the street, sleepily—probably on drugs, you know—being interviewed by some television reporter while watching the entire canyon go up in flames.*

Jonathan returned to the desk, putting the Faulkner out of his mind for a moment. He kept thinking about the phone call. He'd expected as much. Even in the beginning, when he first borrowed the money, he knew there would be trouble. But he had no choice. All along, he realized that he wasn't going to get a free ride. That there had to be a payback, a reckoning day. There always was a payback, especially with those guys.

Jonathan leaned back in his chair, placing the soles of his shoes against the edge of the desk. He thought about getting a refill on the vodka, then decided against it. He'd need his wits about him if he was going to take care of this thing tonight.

Jonathan gazed at the picture of Danny mounted in the metal frame on the desk. It was an early one of the two of them, just after they got out. All smiles and hope, only better times ahead. The exuberance of being too young to know that most of life's cards had already been stacked against them.

And why shouldn't they be smiling after four years in the joint? Four years of life in a room the size of a closet. A room that served as living room, bedroom, and toilet for two men, sometimes more.

The only good thing about that experience, thought Jonathan, had been meeting Danny Villapando. An unlikely match if ever there was one. Danny, a rough-around-the-edges New York street kid interested in making a buck and little else. And Jonathan, tall and strong, but with a beauty that bordered on the feminine. Despite his size and strength, Jonathan hadn't the experience or the street savvy to know how to use them. If it weren't for Danny, at least at first, Jonathan would have been eaten alive by the system—a pretty-boy pincushion for the hard-timers, who viewed Jonathan as the next best thing to a fuck on the outs.

Looking back, Jonathan liked to think that they had watched out for each other. Danny, taking the lead while they were inside, and himself, once they were released. As efficiently as Danny was able to operate inside prison, he was equally as lost once he stepped beyond the prison walls. Within a week of their release, Danny was back to his old habits, risking new arrest.

It was Jonathan who stepped in and set him straight, who took the lead and let Danny rely on him for most of the decision-making. Danny accepted the new role. They had trusted each other while inside the Big D. That trust had kept them both alive. It was that trust that made it easier for Danny to let Jonathan take over once they were back in society.

Albany was their first stop. After all, it was close and neither of them had much traveling money. The two of them got a place together, but Jonathan realized it was only a stopgap. It wasn't long before he decided that they both had too many contacts, of the wrong kind, back east. Too many people to whom they actually owed favors, and even more who figured that they were owed favors. They were both starting to fall back on what was comfortable—their prison contacts. Guys who could set both of them up with a quick thousand per job, just a favor, a little muscle, no risk—or so they said.

It was the kind of job that came easy for them. Unfortunately it was the only thing they really knew how to do. After four years inside the New York State Prison at Dannemora, the Big D, leaning on people had become a way of life for the both of them. Jonathan figured that if they didn't distance themselves from their past, it would just be a matter of time before they ended up back in the joint.

California, Jonathan thought, would be the clean break that they needed. And Danny, who despite his man-of-the-world swagger hadn't set foot outside New

York City except for their stint at Dannemora, grudgingly came along, more than a little scared at the prospect, though he never admitted as much.

One of Danny's friends from New York fixed it so that Danny got a job driving limo for a small outfit in West L.A. Jonathan was more than a little suspicious about the connection, but after a few months without any trouble his concerns began to disappear.

While Danny would come and go at all times of the day and night, chauffering the wealthy and the near-to-wealthy, the famous and the hangers-on, Jonathan eventually found himself behind the counter as night man at a used-book store just off Melrose.

That's where he started to learn about the business side of books. Old man Cohen, the owner of the shop, took a chance on an ex-con. Jonathan still remembered their first meeting.

The old man was worried about hiring an ex-con. The bookstore was all he had. No family, no relatives. The books and the business were his family, his life. The last thing he wanted was to see it all go to waste at the hands of some hoodlum, as he put it.

Jonathan was up front about his prison record. He decided that he wanted his employer, whether it was Cohen or anyone else, to know that he was an ex-con. He figured that it would avoid problems down the line, and it would give him more of an incentive to prove himself. It was all part of a decision he'd made when they left New York to try and deal honestly with whatever situation he happened to encounter. It wasn't the prison way. Prison had taught him to keep his mouth shut and his eyes closed. Dannemora had taught him not to volunteer anything of himself. To avoid confrontation, but if it came your way, to eliminate its source quickly and effectively. His new plan was proving even more difficult to put into practice than he had thought.

"Prison, you say?" The old man gazed into Jonathan's eyes in disbelief, as if expecting to see some sort of scar, perhaps a number tattooed somewhere on Jonathan's body to indicate that this man had spent time being locked up. That he wasn't one of us.

"Four years, sir," answered Jonathan, figuring he might as well turn and head out the door, that this job interview was over.

The old man looked down at a stack of books near the cash register. The two men were standing on opposite sides of the counter, sizing each other up. Jonathan knew what the next question would be. He had been rehearsing his answer for years, lying on his back in his bunk, staring at the paint peeling off the ceiling of his cell, listening to the sounds of the animals in their cages.

His answer never sounded quite right.

"What were you in prison for, Mr. Racine?"

Mr. Racine, that was promising. Still, as he reviewed it quickly in his mind, the answer still didn't sound right.

"Murder, Mr. Cohen. It was dropped to manslaughter, though."

It would never sound right. As if this old man knew the difference between murder and manslaughter—or cared. It was then that Jonathan thought he had made a mistake in deciding to be up front with the old man. He could see that the old guy was thinking, trying to figure a way to get this ex-con killer out of his store. Jonathan half-expected him to reach for the phone and call the cops.

"Sit down, Mr. Racine." Cohen pointed to a small table and chairs in the center of the store. Jonathan wondered whether this was some sort of ploy to keep him at bay until the cops showed up.

"Mr. Racine," said Cohen, his fingers playing across the fine gray beard stubble on his chin, "I am in a quandary. I've always thought of myself as an honest, compassionate man. I've made mistakes in my life, just like other people. I don't like to dwell on my mistakes, though. I doubt if you do either. But I feel compelled to know a little more about you. I realize this must be unpleasant for you, but . . . there are certain questions that I must ask. You understand, I hope?''

"Ask away," said Jonathan. "But let me explain something to you that might cut short this whole thing."

Jonathan repositioned himself in his chair before continuing. The old man was looking at him intently, his shoulders thrust forward and down so that he seemed small in the wooden chair. His hands were clasped neatly on his lap, like a schoolboy hoping to please his teacher. There was no smile. Just the large pools that were his eyes, looking at him inquiringly, waiting to see what this villain, this ex-con, this defiler of society's rules, could possibly say in his own defense.

Jonathan started slowly: "I killed, Mr. Cohen, because the person I killed would have killed my mother if I hadn't." He paused, gathering his breath, then added, "The person I killed was my father."

Jonathan watched the old man's thin black eyebrows arch for a second in disbelief. Cohen moved uncomfortably in his chair, then resumed his schoolboy position. He had his legs crossed, and Jonathan stared at the old man's thin lower leg bouncing nervously up and down as he spoke. "Back then," said Jonathan, "in that place, beating on your wife was more or less accepted. Things weren't like they are today. Today, they're making all these movies and TV shows about wife abuse. It's different than it used to be.

"Back then, there was no place for my mother to go with her complaints. A poor working-class neighborhood. It was a pretty rough place, Mr. Cohen. The cops at the station just filled out their reports and laughed behind her back. You see, Mr. Cohen, where I grew up the man ruled the house. That meant that if he felt like getting drunk and beating on his wife and kid, which happened a lot not just with me, then that was okay.

"I don't know whether you understand what I'm talking about . . ." The old man had his hand over his mouth, and was slowly nodding his head as Jonathan spoke.

"Anyway," said Jonathan, "the beatings started to get worse. I'd lay in bed at night and I could hear them yelling at each other. Then I'd hear him punching on her, over and over again. She'd be crying, and I'd feel like getting out of my bed and doing something to stop him. But I couldn't. I couldn't do that, Mr. Cohen, could I? He was my father. It wasn't supposed to happen that way."

"You needn't tell me any more, Mr. Racine." Cohen raised the palm of his hand as if to stop Jonathan from continuing.

"No, I've come this far," said Jonathan. "You may as well hear the whole thing. There's not much more to tell. Only that night. The night that it happened."

Jonathan said: "I had thought about doing it for a long time. But I tried to put those thoughts out of my mind. I knew it was wrong. I even tried to convince myself that it would get better. But it didn't. The beatings just kept happening. Getting worse. I couldn't take it any longer."

Jonathan felt his words coming out slower now, and from a place deep inside himself. There was a tightening in his stomach as if something were holding the words in bunches, not complete sentences, and releasing them two and three at a time, forcing him to have to wait in mid-sentence for the rest of the words as he spoke.

"One night, when I couldn't stand to listen to the sounds of his fists anymore, I confronted him. I had a baseball bat from my bedroom. I didn't want to use it. I was afraid of the man, and what he might do to me, and my ma, if I did anything.

"He just laughed when he saw me. My ma was slumped against the sofa, her lip bleeding and her face more swollen than I had ever seen it.

"I started to cry, Mr. Cohen. Seeing my ma that

way . . . I just couldn't help it. Something took hold of me then. Part fear, part anger. Mostly confusion, I guess.

"He just kept laughing. Like his family was a big joke. I . . . *we* were nothing to him. I could smell the liquor as he came toward me, pounding his fist in his hand, telling me I wasn't man enough to use the bat.

"I took one swing and missed. He grabbed me by the hair and threw me across the room. I hit the wall on the other side. When I looked up, he was still standing where I had swung at him, holding up a piece of my hair in his hand and smiling. I could feel the warm trickle of blood on the right side of my face. I wasn't sure where it was coming from. The top of my head was burning.

"He came at me again, but this time, in his stupor, he tripped on the lamp cord and fell over the back of the couch. My first thought was to run, get out of there. But then I remembered my ma, still slumped over on the floor, barely conscious from his punches, unaware of the grisly scene that was taking place right in front of her.

"I reached down and grabbed the bat from the floor. He was reaching for my legs with one giant outstretched hand, still that smile on his face. He was so drunk, I started to wonder whether he could make it to his feet. I don't think he saw the bat in my hands. I felt his hand around my ankle gripping tighter, and knew there was still some pounding left in him. There was only one thing to do, and I did it. I hit him, hard. Then I hit him again, and again, and again. I just kept hitting him until I couldn't hit him anymore."

"But surely, the police . . ." Cohen hadn't moved since Jonathan started telling the story.

"The cops were hardly in a position to admit that they could have stopped it, were they? I mean, they even denied being aware of my ma's complaints. Her reports conveniently disappeared.

"And I was charged with murder, though not even the prosecutor figured it was worth that. They gave me a public defender and he said I should cop a plea to voluntary manslaughter. He said because I was only nineteen that the court wouldn't go too hard on me. So I did what he said. It cost me four years in Dannemora. Now you know everything.''

The old man was silent, averting his eyes from Jonathan, fingering the corner of an old magazine on the table between them.

Jonathan waited for the old man to speak. He had told his story, just as he had thought about it a million times over.

"You can start tomorrow night?" asked the old man, getting up from the table.

"Ah . . ."

"Good, then it's settled." Cohen was already back behind the counter, his back to Jonathan.

"But . . ."

"We'll take care of the particulars tomorrow," said Cohen, turning to face him, "when you start."

Jonathan put out his hand and the old man shook it. The subject of his father and prison was never brought up again.

Old man Cohen never questioned his living arrangements with Danny, either. Jonathan assumed that he thought they were just roommates, nothing more.

In the following months, Jonathan and the old man found themselves spending most of their time together talking books. Mr. Cohen would often stick around after Jonathan arrived for the night shift, instructing him on the basics of the book business, the investment side of buying and selling books. Why certain books increased in value and others did not. And how one could earn a living by providing the collectors with the volumes they wanted . . . It wasn't too long before Jonathan had his own little bookselling business on the side, keeping a list of current catalogs at the house, trying to fit into those specialty areas that weren't flooded with dealers.

As the months went by the old man spent less and

less time in the store. He'd putter around inside while Jonathan took care of the day-to-day operation of the business. When Cohen died, he left the entire inventory to Jonathan. By that time, Jonathan had a sufficient client list not to have to worry about getting business off the street. The lease on the store was almost up, and he figured he could operate his specialty business just as well out of the house without the overhead of the store. So he closed the store, selling part of the inventory to other book dealers, and keeping the more marketable items for himself. He moved everything into the house on Laurel Canyon and began in earnest his own business of supplying books and information to those collectors who, by this time, had come to rely on his special expertise.

During this time, Danny was still driving the limo. He would often be away from the house for days at a time. Business, he said. Some special fat cats who hired him to drive up the coast, or to Vegas for a few days. Jonathan never gave it a second thought. Danny always came back, and their life together had never been better. Everything seemed to be working out just fine. He and Danny, the new book business, even the extra cash Danny was bringing in. For once Jonathan figured things were going his way, making up for all the bad luck before. By the time he found out that he was wrong, it was already too late.

Jonathan changed his mind about the vodka. He made his way down the hall into the kitchen. The television that he had been watching earlier was still on. Jonathan paused by the open freezer door, his eyes on the screen, watching J. R. Ewing throw a couple of ice cubes in a glass, then follow it with bourbon. Jonathan did the same, letting the vodka come within about an inch of the rim, sipping off a little, then adding the two ice cubes that were left in the tray.

Jonathan thought about the episode where J. R. got involved with some Mafia types. He couldn't remember whether it was last season or the one before. Maybe it was part of the dream season, he wasn't sure. Something about using Mafia hit men to blow up Arab oil wells and raise the price of Texas crude. Or maybe that was some other show . . . ?

Anyway, J. R. was going to have the mob guys—these two typical swarthy Mediterranean types in shiny double-breasted suits who went around saying a lot of "dems" and "doze"—do his dirty work for him. Then, if they were caught, J. R. intended on leaving them hanging. He'd deny that he knew who they were, and that he had anything to do with their actions. J. R. eventually thought better of the deal with the mobsters and backed out. Even the great J. R. Ewing knew he couldn't pull that one off.

In October, just before Danny got sick, Jonathan learned that he had gone back to working for the mob. A message directed to Danny accidentally came to Jonathan's attention. Danny's time away from home over the past year suddenly made sense. All the extra cash that Danny claimed was from driving the limo was mob money. The two- and three-day trips for the fat cats to Vegas had actually happened, except Danny was performing other services for his mob connections while he was there.

Jonathan learned that Danny was providing muscle for the mob, helping to collect delinquent debts. It was New York all over again. Anybody late in their payment was paid a visit by Danny, along with a couple of mob thugs, regulars. Either the poor sucker paid up or he spent the next four months in a body cast.

To make matters worse, Danny had mentioned to his mob connection that Jonathan knew all about what he was doing, that Jonathan was one of them—an ex-con—and that he and Jonathan had both done the same sort of work back east after being released from the joint.

When Jonathan confronted him about his discovery, Danny admitted the whole thing, the side trips to Vegas, the extortion, the under-the-table payoffs. But by that time it was already too late. By that time Danny was already showing signs of his illness. It was evident to Jonathan that even without Danny's promises to go straight from then on, he wouldn't be doing any more enforcing for the mob.

The doctors traced it to a blood transfusion Danny had received in the hospital while recuperating from minor surgery over the summer. A goddamn polyp on his intestine. No risk, according to the surgeon. A few days of rest and relaxation after the surgery and he'd be as good as new.

That's why Jonathan didn't make the connection initially. Always tired and suffering from what seemed like a permanent cold, Danny figured he was just run-down. That all he needed was a little rest. He'd always been such a bull, strong and tireless. They both assumed he'd snap out of whatever it was.

But with each week his condition grew worse. Then came the sores and the difficulty in breathing. It was the second time that they took him to the hospital that he was diagnosed as suffering from pneumonia brought about by the AIDS virus.

In Danny's case, once he had been diagnosed, determining the origin of the disease was easy. Danny had been with no one other than Jonathan for years. When another case turned up in a person who received a transfusion at the same hospital, the mystery was solved.

Jonathan brought his vodka back to the study, the TV still blaring in the living room. His mind was on Danny. He was thinking about that year before he died.

They had tried everything. Even treatments that they both knew were useless. Anything to keep on hoping. And so in January, they found themselves in Europe, receiving the latest discovery in a long list of therapeutic treatments and breakthrough drugs that proved to be powerless against Danny's disease.

But it gave them a way to avoid looking at what, to an objective observer, was the inevitable. Yet after all the money and the travel and the false promises, Jonathan wouldn't have done anything differently. He wouldn't have denied Danny, or himself, that one last possible glimmer of hope.

Danny wanted to quit, but Jonathan kept him going. He had already taken most of the money out of the business and mortgaged the Laurel Canyon house, and that money was gone. The little that was left in their bank account represented loans and gifts from their friends.

Finally, after all the doctors in Paris and all the hospitals in the States had done what they could, Jonathan could no longer avoid facing the truth. The bottom line was that he would have to watch Danny die just a little every day, and there was nothing that he could do about it. Nothing anybody, no matter how rich and powerful, could do about it.

Jonathan leaned back in the swivel chair behind the desk and removed the plain white business card from his shirt pocket. The look of the name printed above the small circular seal that was embossed on the card caused him to think twice about dialing the number. He put the card down on the desk and took a long slug from his vodka. He wasn't sure whether he was ready to make that move, not just yet.

In the last few months of Danny's illness they had run out of money. Jonathan would have done anything to ease Danny's pain. Danny's contact, his connection, offered them money, no questions asked, no forms to fill out, no security and no waiting. Jonathan gave it only a moment's thought, the time it took to look at his friend's suffering. Then he took the money.

From then on the money came in regularly. Jonathan lost track of the total amount, his mind being consumed with trying to maintain a sense of dignity and comfort for Danny during his last days.

Now there was the phone call. It was time for the payback. He expected the call. They at least had waited until after Danny died before demanding their money. But then, they would, wouldn't they?

Jonathan swirled the cubes in his glass, then finished off the vodka, and placed the glass against his forehead. It was cool, and he thought he could almost feel the steam coming off his forehead when he pressed the glass to his skin.

He picked up the business card again, staring at the name. The loan shark had made it hard for him. He expected that they'd want their money and that he'd be unable to pay. What could happen? They could break his legs or his arms, or both. Or they could kill him. At least he'd know, being broke, that he had no choice in the matter.

But this new twist started him thinking. They were making him an offer, a deal. He could get out from under the Big Boys once and for all. Maybe they'd never catch him. After all, the cops were notoriously lazy when it came to hoods hitting hoods. Maybe he could just get away with it.

Jonathan flicked at the corner of the business card with his fingernail. The clicking noise provided a cadence for his thoughts. He tried to run through it, the whole plan, piece by piece, keeping up with the cadence.

He wasn't sure how many times he had gone over the plan in his mind before he picked up the phone and dialed the number on the card.

CHAPTER 8 ━━━━━━━

Deputy Public Defender Harold Stein placed his brief-case on the counsel table in Division 104, steadied himself on the arms of an old wooden swivel chair, and sat down. He could hear the clanging of metal and the whirring of motors as the bars in the courtroom lockup were being opened. He thought about his client, swallowed hard—as if trying to get rid of the bad taste that his thoughts had given him—and removed his notepad.

His mother had wanted him to become a doctor. "Your brother Ronald's a dentist," she would harp, "and look how happy he is, with a nice big house and a practice in the Valley, so what's to complain?" But he was never that good at science in school, and to tell the truth, it bored him. Just like his older brother Ronald had bored him. So he joined the staff of the college newspaper and participated in political rallies to end the war in Vietnam and managed to get through four years of college in five years with a degree in political science and a part-time job as assistant recreation director at the local park.

After college Stein figured that he'd worked hard enough and deserved to see the world, so he used what little of his park earnings and bar mitzvah money was left, and hitchhiked across Europe for three months, finally arriving home with a bag of dirty laundry over his shoulder, bearded, scruffy, and penniless, and into the waiting arms of his mother. He started law school the following month, and now, at the age of thirty-nine, was beginning his fourteenth year in the Los Angeles Public Defender's Office.

The whirring motors of the lockup had stopped. All the security doors between the courtroom and the custody tank had been slammed shut. For a moment, it was uncharacteristically quiet in the courtroom. Harold Stein looked up and saw the bailiff escorting his client past the witness stand and into the courtroom. The bailiff was expressionless as he went about his duty, though his client had the usual shit-eating grin on his face. An expression midway between a smile and a smirk. Like the arrogant smile that flashes on the face of some boxers, who grin, trying to convince the world that they remain unharmed by the onslaught while being pummeled senseless by their opponent.

"How you be doin' this fine mornin', *Mistuh* Stein?"

Stein didn't bother giving the client an answer. A quick smile and down to business.

Shapiro Darnell LeGardy was being accused of possessing cocaine with the intent of selling same. He had a four-page rap sheet of primarily juvenile offenses ranging from assault with a deadly weapon to various narcotic-related charges, burglaries, and strong-arm robberies.

Stein quickly reviewed LeGardy's rap sheet and an earlier probation report. Identified as a member of the Pacoima Pierce Crips, LeGardy had been a gang-banger since the age of eleven. Now, at twenty-four, he had been arrested, but not charged, with two gang-related shootings—insufficient evidence—and was on probation for a robbery that had been reduced to a misdemeanor grand theft person when the witness refused to positively identify LeGardy at the preliminary hearing.

The present drug charge turned on an arrest by a rookie cop, who just happened to be driving by when he saw something pass from LeGardy's hand into the hands of a young black woman. The cop had written in his report that he recognized the small package as being a small manila coin envelope, which, he wrote, he thought was typical of the manner in which rock cocaine or crack was packaged.

Stein knew that the case against LeGardy depended on the legality of the arrest. The young black woman had disappeared as soon as she spotted the patrol car. Stein's client, being more experienced in such matters, calmly started to walk away from the rookie officer, until he was ordered to stop, which he did. A small amount of cocaine was found on LeGardy, and a manila envelope containing two small rocks of cocaine, similar to the envelope seen by the cop, was found within a few feet of where the sale had gone down.

The D.A.'s theory was that the envelope found on the ground was discarded by LeGardy upon seeing the cops. LeGardy's prints were not discovered on the envelope, because the rookie cop neglected to order a fingerprint analysis. The D.A. was relying on the legality of the arrest and subsequent search to get past the preliminary hearing. Once the coke found on LeGardy's person was admitted into evidence, the cop's observations of the apparent sale would elevate a mere possession charge into a possession with intent to sell, and it would mean state prison for Darnell LeGardy.

Harold Stein cradled the yellow legal pad in his lap, made a few notes to himself in the right-hand margin, and blanked out the young black man, his client, from his thoughts. Just another academic exercise in the administration of justice, he told himself. He'd represented LeGardy before on drug charges, but he also blanked that from his mind for now. For a split second, as always, he thought about his brother with his office in the Valley, and his house and swimming pool in the hills, and his Wednesday golf game, and his European vacations, and his Mercedes 480 SL. And for a split second, as always, he suffered a twinge of self-doubt about the choices he'd made and what he was about to do in the name of justice. Then, as quickly as it had come over him, the feelings of uncertainty disappeared.

He immersed himself in the police report as the witness began testifying, and began furiously scribbling notes for his cross-examination.

Ben Green had arranged to meet Bryan Talley at the Criminal Courts Building. Bryan had the morning free and suggested that prior to having lunch at the studio, he'd like Ben to show him around the courts, maybe pick up some ideas for future Jake Stone scripts.

Bryan discovered Ben seated in the audience section of Division 104 of the municipal court. Other than the court personnel and a couple of attorneys, the courtroom was empty.

Bryan took a seat next to Ben, who smiled, shook his hand, and pointed toward the counsel table. The judge was on the bench looking disgruntled and impatient, fidgeting with his pencil and looking at the D.A. with daggers in his eyes. The defense attorney, a public defender who Ben recognized from having represented codefendants together years back, was arguing his case before the judge.

"You're just in time to see the prosecution go down in flames," whispered Ben. "Ya see that cop over there?" He pointed to a clean-cut, dejected-looking young man in a leather jacket and blue jeans seated in the front row of the audience section.

Bryan nodded.

"That defense lawyer just made cow shit out of him on the witness stand." Ben waved his hand in the air. "It's his own fault. The kid didn't do his homework. Figured he'd wing it or something." He shook his head. "That P.D. just crucified the poor bastard."

The public defender had finished his argument and was seated next to his client at the counsel table. The judge briefly explained his ruling on the illegality of the young cop's arrest, saying that there was insufficient probable cause for the cop to stop and search the defendant, Darnell LeGardy; that the subsequent discovery of the cocaine on LeGardy's person was illegal, and thus the cocaine was inadmissible as evidence. Without that evidence, the D.A. had no case and declared the same to the judge. Grudgingly, the judge dismissed the charges.

Bryan and Ben stood as the judge strode off the bench and into his chambers, obviously unhappy about what had transpired. Darnell LeGardy was all smiles. He stood at the counsel table, then slowly turned toward the audience, winking at Ben.

"You know the asshole?" asked Bryan.

"Never seen him before," said Ben. When LeGardy smiled, Ben noticed that the young black man had something wrong with his upper lip. Some sort of deformity, maybe a harelip. Yet it wasn't the harelip that held Ben's attention, but a reflection, a sliver of bright light that flashed from LeGardy's mouth when he smiled. Ben at first thought LeGardy was wearing metal braces and that the overhead lighting was being reflected off the metal. Moving closer to the front of the courtroom, Ben saw that the reflection was not from any braces, but was instead from something shiny in one of LeGardy's front teeth.

As the bailiff led LeGardy back into the lockup, Ben found himself standing at the railing that separated the audience section from the front of the courtroom. He watched as the young gang member, that same glassy, shit-eating grin plastered across his face, was led through the security door into the rear lockup.

It was party time in the Van Nuys lockup. Darnell LeGardy flashed his diamond smile at his homeboys, giving them the hand sign of the Pacoima Pierce Crips, an offshoot of the larger Rolling 60s Crips from downtown. In Darnell's holding tank all the brothers were Crips, some from the Pierce Street projects, some from other areas of the city. The sheriff's department kept the Bloods, their rival gang, in a separate lockup.

The central jail was full of Crips and Bloods, but the sheriff kept them apart. The gang affiliations from the street transferred completely to the jail. A sign outside the attorney conference room told lawyers and probation officers the separate times when Crips and Bloods would be available for interview. The two gangs ate meals separately, went to the yard separately, showered apart, and slept in separate units. To bring them together meant certain violence.

Darnell had been jumped-in to the Crips when he was eleven, and except for a few short stints in juvenile hall and probation camp, he hadn't attended school since the sixth grade. He didn't care about school. That was just so much bullshit to him. As long as he had his homeboys, his fellow Crips, he could party, have a good time, maybe off some Bloods—show them who was really bad.

Darnell said to his homeboy, flashing his smile after exchanging high-fives: "Man, you be lookin' at one free brotha."

"You shittin' me, blood! You beat that rap?"

"Damn straight. Cops fucked up." Darnell was giving high-fives, moving around the inside of the holding tank.

"Shee-it, man," said the homeboy, "don't you be fuckin' wi' me now."

"Why I be doin' that, blood? You just watch, man. I be out onna streets soon as we back at the county. That judge, he say those rocks are . . . *tainted evidence,* that's what he done call 'em. Yes sir, them rocks are done *tainted evidence.* Tol' the fuckin' Man his case weren't worth shit!"

Darnell sat on the concrete bench that spanned the inside perimeter of the holding tank, thinking about the first thing he was going to do when he got out. He thought about getting himself some more rocks, have a little party. Maybe get himself a little pussy. Yeah, for sure a little pussy. Three weeks without it had made him jumpy. He could have joined in the fun at the county, maybe a nice white boy to fuck, but he wasn't really into that shit.

He'd hear the groans and screams coming from the other bunks at night and it only made him more anxious to get out and find himself a woman. It was hard for him to put those thoughts out of his mind, and now he wouldn't have to. Tonight he'd be on the street, selling his shit and getting off, just like before.

Darnell caught a glimpse of his own reflection in the shiny piece of metal that was riveted to the wall over the toilet in the holding tank. Somebody had scratched their gang name in the metal, then somebody else had scratched over it and written the words *Fuck the Crips* underneath.

In the corner, some of his homeboys were going through the pockets of an old drunk, telling the old man that they would be just borrowing his three dollars and did he mind? The drunk had seen it all before and just smiled, shaking his head. "No problem, man," he said. "It's a loan, right?"

The old man reminded Darnell of the grandfather in the house where his mother used to work. The Shapiros. Big fancy house in the hills. His mother would take him and his brother with her sometimes. Especially in the summer when it was hot and the Shapiro kids were using the swimming pool. Sometimes he and his brother could sit on the edge, dangle their feet in the water to stay cool.

His mother really loved those Shapiros. When Darnell was born, she named him after the family, she loved them so much. Just like with his older brother, Levine. You'd think she would have learned that cleaning house for some family doesn't make you one of them. But she didn't. Now he and his older brother both had Jew first names, and his momma had gone off somewhere with some dude, leaving them without so much as a letter.

Darnell turned his head slightly to one side, trying to see what his harelip looked like in the scratched metal. His momma had told him that he was special because of his harelip. She said that he shouldn't pay no attention to the other kids teasing him about it, 'cause it was just God's way of showing him that he was special. He believed her, for a while. That lasted until the first kid he had to beat up in school for teasing him. From then on nobody said anything about it.

Darnell smiled, thinking about the kid he'd beat up, and thinking he really was one bad dude that didn't take lightly to being fucked with. The bare overhead fluorescent light reflected off his front tooth when he smiled. He liked the effect it had, throwing beams of light off the shiny metal setting when he moved his head from side to side.

He fingered the hard smooth surface of the diamond in his front tooth, remembering the dentist putting it in and his having had to talk the guy into doing it. It finally came down to money, plain and simple. Money and a little nose candy he had picked up at the same time as the diamond, in the bedroom dresser of the house that he'd ripped off.

He was going to keep the diamond. Maybe put it in a ring or on a chain. Or just keep it loose and trade it in on some good dope. But then the idea hit him. He'd do something to make himself look really cool. Something that nobody else had. Something *bad*.

So he had the diamond embedded in one of his front teeth. Now when he smiled everybody looked at him. It was like his momma had said, only his way. He'd stand in a room full of people and watch the looks on their stupid faces as the light reflected off the diamond. They didn't know what to make of it, but they knew he was special.

Just like his momma had told him.

Yeah, don't fuck with Darnell LeGardy. Like the brother, Michael, says in the song: "I'm *bad!*"

Ben picked at his omelette with the corner of a piece of wheat toast. It was all he could manage to keep down lately, eggs. He'd have to remember to mention that to Dr. Mellnor. Bryan and Ben were sitting at a small circular table in the Blue Room at the studio where Bryan's TV show, "Jake Stone, Private Eye," was filmed. Ben was having difficulty finding a comfortable position for his six-foot frame on the small bentwood chairs. The Blue Room was a small restaurant on the lot that catered exclusively to studio employees and their guests. A larger room next door served as a cafeteria for those actors and stagehands who found the Blue Room prices a little too steep for their incomes.

"Ya see, Ben, nobody wants to watch a show about cops sitting behind desks moving papers from one side to the other." A large, juicy hamburger sat on the plate in front of Bryan, oozing a greasy red liquid into his French fries.

Bryan took a bite of his hamburger and continued, speaking with his mouth full. He held the hamburger in front of him over the plate with both hands. "That's why we have to . . . *embellish* a little, ya know what I'm talking about?"

"The car," said Ben.

"That's right. A good example."

"I don't know any cops, or any private cops for that matter, who drive around town in a Lamborghini Countach. First of all, none of them could afford it. And even if they could, those things are always breaking down. Why is it that when I watch Jake Stone, his car always starts, it always works, never breaks down? Don't you think that's kind of unbelievable?"

"Jesus," said Bryan. "If you only knew what kind of work we've had to put into that piece of shit. I mean, it's a beautiful piece of machinery and all, but Jesus, it's totally unreliable. Studio's had to hire a special mechanic, from Italy, to keep on staff just to make sure that thing starts up."

Ben chuckled, then pushed away his plate of barely eaten eggs. Bryan seemed comfortable, in his element, smiling and waving at people as they walked by. Thirty and single, his straw-blond surfer's hair made him look even younger. Ben wondered how his friend had lucked into such a great-paying job. It was Jake Stone's first season, but according to Bryan, the ratings were there and it was a lock that they'd be renewed for another. He was already looking at houses in Laurel Canyon, already spending next season's thirty-thousand-dollar-plus scripts.

The wall behind Bryan was covered with photographs of movie and TV stars. There was a picture of Tom Selleck sitting behind the wheel of his "Magnum, P.I." red Ferrari. Ben wondered whether Bryan's Italian auto mechanic took care of that one too. Just to the right of Selleck's photograph was a picture of Dustin Hoffman and Warren Beatty in some sort of camel-jockey getup, with a desert backdrop. Ben couldn't remember the name of the movie.

"Take that case this morning," said Ben. "That's about as exciting as it normally gets. A kid gets busted for selling crack, disappears for a year, then gets arrested on a warrant and shows up in court and drags the case out for another year. Meanwhile, the cops who arrested him move on to other assignments, quit the force, or otherwise become unavailable. The delay works for the bad guys. It's hard to remember details two years later just reading an old police report."

"I tell ya, Ben, between your experiences and my imagination I think we could come up with some great ideas."

"For TV?"

"Sure, why not? You must have heard hundreds of stories over the years. We could just embellish a little here, add a little there. Nothing major, just enough to keep the viewers' interest. Whadya think?"

Ben saw the waitress approaching with their check. Bryan looked up, flashed a smile, causing the young girl to giggle, then scribbled his name across the face of the bill.

"Internal Affairs is even more boring than working the street," said Ben. "Cops investigating other cops.

Besides, the department would can me if you put that stuff on TV.''

"Yeah, but you just started there, right? I mean, you handled plenty of cases before that. You must have lots of stories—big drug busts, smuggling coke in airplanes. And what about the yachts and stuff that I see the cops confiscating every night on the evening news. That's interesting stuff, Ben.''

"That's mostly the feds,'' said Ben. "It's kind of hard to sail a fifty-foot yacht down the L.A. River.''

Ben thought about what Bryan had said. All the stories over the years. The times when he and Sara had lived in that small one-bedroom apartment in Culver City. When Julie was born. Just the three of them. And that was all he had needed, all he ever thought he'd want out of life. He felt it happening again—his mind floating, drowning, in memories.

Bryan said, "Listen, Ben. You think about what I said. We'll talk about it some more over the weekend. You're going to be home, aren't you?''

Ben nodded, thinking that he'd stopped planning that far in advance.

"Good. We'll pop open a few brews, maybe sit around the pool and get some color. I've been spending too much time cooped up in an office behind a typewriter.'' Bryan pressed a finger on his forearm. "Jesus, will you look at that! I look like I've just spent the winter in a Siberian prison camp. No damn color at all.'' He got up from the table and gestured with outstretched arms. "Hell, this is Hollywood, man. Home of the beautiful people.''

CHAPTER 9 ━━━━━━━━━

Ben hadn't seen Indian Joe Curzon in years, since back in the early days, fresh out of the police academy, when they pulled a couple of assignments in Narcotics together. He'd heard bits and pieces about him, though, mostly rumor. Weird stuff, like Joe having gone off the deep end, nearly killing a suspect in a child molest case.

He'd also heard stories that Curzon had been found prowling the hills near his trailer in Topanga Canyon, stark naked except for an Indian headdress. Ben wasn't sure how much of that was true. Things had a tendency to get blown out of proportion when they had to do with Joe. Probably, Ben thought, because Curzon himself was out of proportion with the rest of the world.

Standing near to six feet, eight inches, and weighing every bit of three hundred pounds, Indian Joe Curzon was known to almost everybody in the department, and was the butt of more than his share of jokes.

That's what was curious about Francis Powell's selection of him as Ben's partner. Despite a certain absence of police decorum when dealing with child molestors, dope dealers, and the other low-life sleazoids, Curzon was a good cop. He got the job done, and due to his size was usually a welcome sight to any officer in the middle of a potentially violent confrontation. Still, low-profile Joe Curzon was not.

Sitting behind the wheel, heading west, letting the car drive itself along the Ventura Freeway, Ben started thinking about his conversation with Francis Powell, and about why Powell didn't want to bust Romero immediately. If it were *his* decision, Ben thought, he wouldn't have chanced Romero doing further harm. He would have picked him up, at least long enough to have him questioned by Internal Affairs. If that hurt the investigation against Romero, then so be it. As it stood now, the guy was still on the loose, and who knew what additional damage he could do while Ben and Joe Curzon were trying to build an airtight case against him.

It was the political reasoning that bothered Ben. Francis Powell had always acted with an eye toward benefiting himself. Yet, despite Powell's interest in advancing his own career, Ben had never known him to take serious risks with the public's safety in order to gain political advantage. This decision to wait on Romero, and, to a lesser degree, in selecting Joe Curzon, seemed to Ben to be ill-advised, tainted by Powell's political agenda.

As he wound his way through Topanga Canyon, occasionally glancing down at the small piece of paper on the passenger seat containing the directions that Curzon had given him over the phone, Ben continued to try and make some sense out of what Francis Powell had said.

He began to think just how little he had seen of his old friend in recent years. Maybe he was reading him wrong. Maybe Francis Powell had changed. For a split second it occurred to him that perhaps this whole thing with Romero and Indian Joe was just some huge joke that Powell was playing on him, trying to see just how far Ben would take the hook before realizing that he was playing the fool.

He passed a number of old wooden signs, relics of the various sideshow businesses that existed in the canyon for a short time and then died, the proprietors packing their bedrolls and moving on, leaving their ramshackle houses and lean-tos dotting the hillside along the canyon.

In Topanga Canyon, there were also those well-to-do urbanites, who had taken all they were willing to take in the form of abuse from their fellow city dwellers, forsaken their split-level homes in the suburbs or their office-building condos, and pulled up stakes, calling home a concrete pad carved into the hillside. Trying to get back to the simple life, or so they claimed.

The canyon was filled with such homes, traditional and otherwise: geodesic domes and trailers, nudist colonies, palm readers, Hell's Angels, aging hippies, movie stars, and an assortment of self-proclaimed Temples of Human Realization, all creating a hodgepodge of building styles.

It was on one such hillside that Joe Curzon had his trailer, mounted atop a concrete pad, overlooking the canyon road below.

Ben eased his way up the series of short switchbacks, careful to avoid damaging his car on the jagged boulders that had been washed off the hillside onto the dirt road by the recent rains.

The trailer was on jacks, elevated about a foot off the concrete pad. Under the trailer were various forms of debris, weeds, beer bottles, old auto parts, a rusted fender, part of a toilet seat—what most people would consider junk—thrown carelessly in piles. The aluminum trailer had a flat roof which extended out over the front door, creating a sort of shaded patio. Ben could hear the sound of a motor, a cooler of some sort he guessed, whirring and banging in the back.

The aluminum panels on the trailer had been painted a bland shade of institutional green. The paint was chipping in large flakes all over, giving the trailer a mottled look. One of the three small windows in front still had a screen on it, rusted black and torn in the center. The screens for the other two windows lay twisted on the ground, partially covered by the garbage and weeds that together constituted Indian Joe's land-scaping.

The door to the trailer was open, except for a screen which hung loosely over the door frame, one of its hinges missing.

"Hello, anyone in there?"

Ben was answered by the flushing of a toilet. Ben could hear the sound of rushing water in the pipes that fed the trailer from underneath. One of the stories about Curzon, before his surgery, was that he had had a bowel problem which made it difficult for him to do stakeout duty. He'd always have to run to the bathroom to relieve himself, leaving the subject of the stakeout unobserved. It got so that the other guys in his division started calling him "Chief Running Bowel." Not to his face, of course.

Ben heard a slamming noise, then Joe Curzon's voice saying, "God damn it! Hold your goddamn horses, I'll be right there!"

Curzon came to the door wearing a pair of worn chino slacks, stained at the crotch, and a pair of scuffed black cowboy boots. The pants were held up by a wide piece of thick leather—his belt—connected in front by a tarnished silver and turquoise buckle with a picture in the center of an Indian seated atop a horse. He had on an old plaid Pendleton shirt buttoned up to the top, with two flap pockets in front, and a string tie with a silver clasp that more or less matched the belt buckle.

His thick black hair was slicked with a greasy shine, pulled straight back from an oversized forehead, coming to a short ducktail at the back of his neck. The first impression he gave inside the small trailer was of one of those giant humans in bad science fiction movies: horrible giant chemical mutations walking through town lifting cars and people as if they were insects. A giant head on a giant man.

The fierceness in his eyes that Ben remembered was no longer there. In its place were two milky pools, like small opaque marbles set inside dark rings, unfocused. He had just shaven, and there were still some remnants of white shaving cream on his neck, just above his shirt collar.

As Curzon leaned forward to shove open the screen door, Ben felt the entire trailer move slightly under the Indian's weight. Once inside, the trailer continued to sway as Curzon moved to the breakfast nook and sat down at a small collapsible table, motioning for Ben to do the same.

A cigarette was half-smoked, balanced over the rim of an old coffee cup. There were ashes on the table just under the edge of the cup. The first thing Joe did after sitting down was to pick up the cigarette, flick it quickly with his thumb, put it to his lips, and inhale deeply, as if trying to suck out its entire contents. He paused after inhaling—Ben wondered what happened to the cigarette smoke—then made his lips into an *O* shape, and with the aid of his tongue, exhaled four perfect small circles of smoke into the already sour air of the trailer.

"So, Mr. Green," he said, watching the rings of smoke disappear. "Tell me about this case that our friend, the great Francis P. Powell, thinks is so important that he calls me personally at home, and me just out of surgery. It smells a little funny, don't you think? Can I get ya a drink?"

Ben waved him off. He wasn't sure whether Curzon was referring to the smell of the air inside the trailer or the Romero case.

The Indian said, "I think I could use a little belt to get the morning off to a good start." He slid out from behind the table, in the process lifting it a few inches off the metal pole that supported it. He opened a cupboard and removed a bottle of Johnny Walker Red Label and two small jelly glasses.

"Just in case you change your mind," said Joe, placing the bottle and glasses on the table. He poured from the bottle into one of the glasses and, without looking at Ben, drained its contents in one swallow, smacking his lips and then wiping his mouth with his shirtsleeve.

"You know us Indians," he said, pouring himself another. "Can't make do without our daily ration of firewater."

Ben smiled, thinking about Francis Powell and how he felt like strangling his good buddy right about now.

"Listen, Joe," said Ben, deciding that the normal small talk with Curzon would be a waste of time, "it's like I told you on the phone. Powell wants us to partner on this case, but to keep it low-key until we're sure we got the guy. I got a set of reports, the whole package for you to go over. Meanwhile, I think we oughta get moving on this thing as soon as possible."

"Guy's a cop?" asked Curzon, lifting the photograph of Vincent Romero from off the top of the stack of papers that Ben had placed on the table.

"Yeah."

Joe Curzon sipped at his scotch, his eyes boring into the photograph of Romero.

"Why me?" he asked, still looking at the photo.

"Powell thought of it."

"And you're not crazy about the idea, right?"

Ben didn't answer right away. Curzon had a grin on his face—to cover his real feelings, Ben thought. The Indian just sat there, all smiles, as if as long as he kept grinning he'd have the upper hand.

"Joe," Ben finally said, "it's not up to me to pick my partners. To tell the truth, I think this whole thing kinda smells, like you said. I have my own ideas about what's going through Francis Powell's ambitious little brain. But it doesn't really matter, does it? He's the boss man, right? He says jump, and you and me are both thinking, How high? It's the same old bullshit."

"I knew there was a reason I always liked you, Green."

"Yeah, well, hold that thought," said Ben, reaching for the bottle and pouring himself a glass. "We're gonna be seeing a lot of each other for a while, so it's best we set a few ground rules right now, in the beginning.''

"You afraid old Indian Joe's gonna fuck up your case or something? Maybe knock a few heads that shouldn't be knocked?''

There was that grin again. Ben realized Curzon was hiding behind it. The Indian distrusted everybody in the department, and for good reason. Over the years he had been left languishing in the worst assignments without promotion, while other, younger, less experienced guys were being promoted to cushy desk jobs. Part of it was no doubt due to Curzon's innate streak of brutality when dealing with suspects. But part of it was because Joe Curzon refused to kiss up to anybody. He'd just as soon tell some young lieutenant to fuck off as follow an order or directive that he thought was ridiculous.

"That's not what I meant," said Ben. "Powell wants you to be up front on this case. Wants your picture and name in front of the camera." He paused, enjoying the other man's look of disbelief, then asked, "Does that surprise you?''

"What kinda scam does he got going?''

"No scam. There's talk about him running against Hernandez for mayor. This cop we're investigating is named Romero. Powell's afraid that if he doesn't tie this guy up and make it stick, he'll be accused of being anti-Mexican. That's why he wants it kept low-key until we're sure we got him.''

"Then," said Curzon, "Powell tells everybody how he wrapped this case up with the use of one of his crack officers, whose name happens to be Curzon—not Mexican, but close enough.''

"And they say you're stupid," said Ben. This time it was his turn to grin.

Curzon lifted the small jelly glass in one of his huge hands and poured from the bottle. Ben couldn't see the glass inside the giant paw. It looked like the Indian was pouring the amber liquid directly into the top of his cupped hand, like some sort of magic trick, with the liquid disappearing inside.

"Lazy," said Curzon. "And maybe a little short-tempered with the dipshits," he added, then drained the entire glass of scotch. "But *never* stupid."

CHAPTER 10

"Don't you think that all of us, at one time or another, act out a lie? I mean, we're all putting on some sort of show to varying degrees, not displaying our deepest feelings."

They were both silent for a moment, thinking about what she said.

"And now," she continued, "it's gotten to the point that you can no longer be certain that your inner feelings are going to stay in check. That feeling of despair that you spoke of in our last session is taking over."

Ben glanced at her, then back at the wall. He was seated opposite Beth Mellnor in one of the club chairs. He found it easier to speak his mind if he didn't look right at her.

"It seems," Ben said, "that it's no longer connected to any specific incident. I know in my heart that it all stems from Julie's death, and the way I handled, or rather, mishandled it. I know that to be the case, and when the depression comes over me, I can think about that, you know, think it through. And usually, that pulls me out of it. You know what I mean? What I can't seem to control is the feeling, the depression coming on me in the first place. It's not like I'll be sitting somewhere, perfectly okay one moment, then start thinking about Julie, then get depressed. It just suddenly falls on me, like a heavy black curtain, covering me in darkness. I could be anywhere, doing anything when it happens."

As he spoke she jotted notes on the inside of a file that she balanced on her lap. He was having difficulty concentrating, except when he directly answered one of her questions. But she seemed to want him to do the talking. Bits and pieces of his conversation earlier that week with Francis Powell kept jumping into his head, distracting him. He tried to focus on a picture, a watercolor of a lake scene, that hung on the wall behind her.

"You said before that you don't blame yourself for your daughter's death. Do you really believe that?"

"Yes, I think I do . . . believe it, I mean."

"And this depression that comes and goes is something else. Something not caused by any sense of guilt or blame, but more a result of the loss?"

"You tell me. All I know is that I've tried to think it through about a thousand times. At first I blamed myself, but that's passed. What's happening now is that I'll see her face, not always on that day, but the face, the expression, is always the same. Little scenes, like a blink of the eye. And that'll trigger it all over again. I just start spiraling downward until it seems like nothing's worth it anymore. I'll be sitting at my desk at the station and it'll happen. And somebody, one of the guys, will ask me a question or something, and I'll just sit there, totally out of it. At first, I tried explaining it as not enough sleep, which was partially true. I told them I was working a night job for some extra cash. But lately I've been getting some weird looks. I don't know how much longer I can keep up the charade."

"You took some time off," she said, flipping through his file. "I gather you feel that taking some more wouldn't help?"

Ben shook his head. "Just give me more time to stew in it," he muttered. "Besides, I couldn't get away with it again. They'd know that something was up. Now that I'm back, everybody looks at it as if I've had my time to mourn and my time to recuperate. If I took off again,

I have the feeling they'd just give up on me, and maybe they'd be right."

"But these things don't always resolve themselves according to schedule."

"Tell them that. They'd smile and say, 'Sure, take whatever time you need. Call us when you're ready.' And that would be the end of it. I'd never get back. That's the way people work. Believe me, I've seen it."

"Is there anybody you see? A close friend in whom you can confide, someone you can talk to?"

Ben thought for a moment. "There's a guy in my building," he said. "A young guy. He's a screenwriter for TV. I sometimes talk with him. But he's not what you'd call a close friend. I've only known him since I moved into the building. Besides, he thinks all cops are straight from the pages of some Elmore Leonard shoot- 'em-up. Tough guys talking tough, burying their fists in the face or solar plexus of some bad guy, or crashing through windows and breaking down doors, that sort of thing. He's always after me to provide material for his screenwriting. And when I tell him how basically boring and tedious most police work is, he doesn't want to hear it."

She smiled. "I have to admit," she said, "that I've always thought that way myself. I thought most police work was action-packed. I guess I've been affected by your screenwriter friend. I don't watch that much television, but what I do see seems to portray a pretty dangerous, romantic sort of life-style."

"Jake Stone and his red Lamborghini Countach."

"What?"

"Nothing. I was just mumbling to myself."

She closed the file and placed it on the desk. It was atop a stack of similar-looking files, the rest of the evening's appointments, Ben surmised.

"Tell me about Internal Affairs," she said, crossing her legs and clasping her fingers around her knee.

"Cops investigating other cops," he said. "When some cop goes astray, commits a crime or gets in trouble, Internal Affairs comes in and investigates. Sometimes the cop's prosecuted, sometimes he's fired. Usually there's an investigation and if I.A. can't turn up an actual crime, the report gets filed in the cop's personnel folder and that's the end of it.''

"And your job there, in Internal Affairs, is the same as a regular officer? I mean, I imagine, given your background as a defense attorney, that you're not exactly considered one of the guys?''

"I fit in okay. Francis Powell, my friend, the chief, set it up so that I have an office and secretary. They all know that I'm more of an independent contractor for special cases. I work under the auspices of Internal Affairs. Actually, though I'm not limited to I.A. cases, most of what I've been involved in are investigations of crooked cops.''

"So you play police department for the police department? I imagine that doesn't make you the most popular person at work.''

"Sometimes. There's a sort of circle-the-wagons mentality among cops. Cops tend to hang with their own kind and protect their own. Internal Affairs is on the outside of all that. You're right, sometimes it's hard even for us to get truthful information. And sometimes we're looked on as outsiders, not to be trusted.''

"And that doesn't bother you?''

"Not really. I used to work Narcotics when I was a rookie cop, before I went to law school. There's a lot of stuff that goes down in Narcotics that's not according to the book. You start to close your eyes to that sort of thing. It's not as bad as on the East Coast, but it's getting there. Anyway, I was satisfied with what I was doing. If the other guys wanted to skim that was their business. I played it straight.''

Ben's mind flashed back to the photographs of Vincent Romero and the dead woman. He focused on pushing it out of his mind and concentrating on her questions.

"What about hobbies?''

"Hobbies?"

"Sure. You must have something that you do with your free time. Fishing, sports, something along those lines?"

"I don't know if I have any. I used to ride a bike, but . . . Well, I like to listen to music, if you can call that a hobby."

"What kind?"

"Mainly jazz. Jazz singers. Anita Baker, Phyllis Hyman, even a little Sade once in a while. And . . ." He stopped himself, hesitating a moment. Seeing the look of expectation on her face, he continued: "I like to read. I read a little poetry now and then."

"Poetry?" she exclaimed, then quickly added: "I'm sorry. You just didn't strike me as the type. Most cops, I mean . . . well . . ."

"You're right. There's not a cop on the force that knows, or ever will know, that I read poetry. Talk about unmacho!" They both laughed.

"It relaxes me, though. Takes my mind off what's bothering me, to another place, another mood. It's nothing deep with me. I probably miss half the technical niceties. I used to hate reading poetry as a kid. Fought it tooth and nail. It's funny how things get turned around."

Beth Mellnor furrowed her eyebrows, then tilted her head and smiled, as if momentarily confused or mildly surprised. She saw that the lights on her telephone were lit bright red, signaling that the waiting room was filling with the rest of the evening's patients.

"Time's up, huh?" Ben forced a smile.

Beth Mellnor closed her file. "For now," she said, standing and moving toward the door.

"Uh . . ." Ben stood, not sure whether to ask for another appointment.

"Let's meet again next week," she said. She held the door partially open. Ben was aware of faces in the waiting room staring at him.

"I'll call," he said. She nodded.

Ben moved hurriedly through the doorway into the waiting room. He could feel Beth Mellnor's eyes on him as he walked straight to the door, then out to his car.

Once outside, he was surprised to find himself sweating profusely. He removed his coat and placed it on the back seat of his car. He loosened his tie.

"She hasn't a clue," he whispered to himself. "Not a fucking clue."

Ben slipped behind the steering wheel, gazed at his reflection in the rearview mirror, then dropped his chin to his chest and began to cry.

CHAPTER 11 ━━━━━━

Darnell LeGardy was lying on his bed, propped against the wall, eyes closed. His head and shoulders kept beat with the heavy bass rhythms blasting from his box. It soothed him. He didn't have to think as long as he kept moving with the rap, especially if he had some good shit, a little crack, to let his head play nice little tricks on him. Man, that was good!

He was getting fed up with all the little assholes out in the street selling their shit to his regular customers. Fuckin' twelve-year-olds! Too much rock in the wrong hands, he thought, that's what the problem was. Sure, he could make the little suckers understand that this was his turf, that they could peddle their shit down the street. But that wouldn't last. In a few days there'd just be some other dudes doing the same thing. There was just too much shit to be had, and too many guys willing to cut the price to make a buck.

Darnell rolled out of bed and checked himself out in the mirror that was propped up against the wall of his bedroom. He played with the zipper on the jacket of his shiny Fila jogging suit, seeing which way he looked the best. He liked the look and feel of the heavy gold rope around his neck, the one he had ripped off that fat dude in front of the market with L.A. the other night. It had started him thinking that there was good money to be made off the white folks. And it was so easy, all he had to do was give 'em the look, his *bad* look.

L.A. said all white folks weren't worth shit. That it was okay to kill whites, 'cause they all deserved it. L.A. was crazy, but that's what Darnell liked about him. Lavelle Morris, or L.A. as he was called, had been a member of the gang when Darnell was jumped-in. L.A. and Darnell got along because Darnell did all the thinking and kept L.A. in drugs. Darnell noticed over the years that every time L.A. got out of juvenile hall, or jail, or prison, he was always just a little meaner and a lot more stupid. Darnell figured it was the drugs. L.A. would do anything for drugs.

Darnell checked himself out in the mirror again, and thought he looked bad, all in black, except for his white leather high-tops, unlaced. That was a good look, his Run-D.M.C. look. He put his hard look on the mirror, checking it out again, then laughed to himself, throwing his head back and turning as if to leave, then whipping back around and pointing at himself in the mirror.

"You are one *bad motherfucker!*" he said in his best Michael Jackson imitation, pointing at his reflection, checking out his diamond smile in the mirror.

L.A. was still in the living room watching TV. Three people, two white girls and a black dude, were fucking each other on the screen.

"Shit, man," said Darnell, "how many times you gonna watch that fuckin' tape? You just 'bout wore the fuckin' thing out already."

L.A. didn't answer. He had his hand inside the front of his pants and Darnell could see he was in his own little world watching those naked white girls getting fucked on Darnell's twenty-seven-inch Sony.

"I'm takin' the car, man," said Darnell. He reached for the keys on the coffee table. L.A. glanced at Darnell, then back at the television, his hand still moving, never missing a beat.

"I'll be back, man. You want I should pick you up anything, like some nice white pussy or something?" Darnell laughed, watching his friend watching the screen, then walked out the door. L.A. was talking to the TV now, telling the black guy what to do.

"Stick it to 'em, man," yelled L.A. "That's it. Oooh, that do feel fine, don't it? Mighty fine! Ooohwee!"

Too bad, thought Darnell as he eased the '81 red Fleetwood with the white leather interior and the primer spots on the front panel into a corner spot in the parking garage next to the Boulevard Mall. L.A. would have liked this one. All white bread. Daddy and Mommy out for the evening, and rich white kids from the Valley, loaded with money just waiting for someone to take it. Shit, this was gonna be real easy.

Maybe it was better without L.A.—the guy was crazy when it came to white folks. Darnell figured it was okay if they were just driving by in the Fleetwood and L.A. felt like capping off a few rounds, just for fun, watching all those white faces looking real scared, not knowing what was happening, thinking, *This sounds different than on TV.* But that wasn't what Darnell had in mind, not tonight. Cool was what he needed tonight. Just a look, to show 'em that they better not fuck with him. That would do it. Easy.

Darnell had been waiting for less than a half hour when he spotted the tall guy with the blue windbreaker. He was making his way from the mall, through the pass-through tunnel that led to the underground parking area.

Darnell waited near the stairs, behind a concrete pillar, watching the tall man as he approached. Big guy, he thought, with a pretty-boy white face. But dressed like he had bucks and looking like the last thing he expected was to get shaken down on the way to his car.

Darnell let the man pass, keeping his eyes on the man's back as he moved quietly behind him. The man was moving toward a limousine parked a few rows down from where Darnell had parked the Fleetwood.

Shit, the dude's probably loaded, what with the limo

and all. It was just his fucking bad luck that the guy would have a driver inside. Too dangerous to hit the guy, not with the driver waiting for him.

Darnell slowed a little, still watching the tall man who was at the trunk of the limo now. He watched as the man left the trunk lid open and walked to the driver's door, then back to the trunk.

"Well, ain't that somethin'?" Darnell whispered, seeing that the man was alone, that the driver of the limo was gone.

Darnell came up behind the man, already thinking about taking his money.

"Say one fuckin' word, motherfucker, and I'll blow your pretty white face all over the back of this nice car you be drivin'."

Darnell had grabbed the taller man and had spun him around, throwing him against the back of the limo. He had the man by the throat with his left hand, while pressing the barrel of the 9-mm hard against the man's nose. He could smell the man's breath on his face and saw moisture begin to form on the tip of the barrel of the gun from the man's quick breathing.

"Give me your fuckin' money," yelled Darnell. "Now!"

"Just relax," said the man. "You can have what I've got. Just take it easy with that thing. I'm not going to give you any trouble."

Darnell liked that. He would have liked it even more if the guy had been so scared that he shit in his pants. He'd had guys do that before, right there in front of him, they were so fucking scared.

The man pulled out his wallet and slowly handed it to Darnell. Darnell backed away a few inches, trying to open the wallet with one hand, the gun in his other hand still pointed at the man's face.

It was when he glanced down at the man's wallet that he felt the blow right below his left eye. He heard the 9-mm explode in his hand, then felt something grab his wrist and heard the clank as the gun hit the pavement and skittered off underneath the limo.

The man was all over him now. Darnell reached up trying to punch the man, but hit only shoulder and air, clawing at the taller man's face.

Darnell wrenched himself away from the man and dove for the gun. Just as his fingers gripped the steel barrel, trying to find the handle, he felt a numbing thud between his legs, radiating pain down both legs and making him dizzy. He could see the bumper of the limo spinning above him. Then another blow, a little higher this time, and everything started to blur. He groaned and rolled onto his back. The tall man was kneeling over him, breathing heavily. Darnell could see a gash on the man's cheek, midway between his ear and the corner of his mouth.

Darnell closed his eyes, then blinked, trying to clear his head. He put one hand between his legs, hoping to ease the pain. He was surprised when he heard himself crying and felt the warm tears streaming from the corners of his eyes.

Darnell saw the man stand up. He thought it was over. He knew he needed to get out of there, back to the Fleetwood, but he couldn't move. The pavement of the parking lot felt cool on his cheek but his head was still spinning. Out of the corner of his eye he saw the man bending over to pick up his wallet, placing it back in his pants. Then he walked closer to Darnell, so close that all Darnell could see was the man's shoe and lower leg swing back and then forward, toward his head. Darnell turned his head, taking the first kick in the back of the neck. If lifted his head like a football off a tee, making a cracking sound as it bounced off the pavement. He heard the man grunt and then felt the sharp pain of the man's shoe in his lower back, sending electric shocks through his body.

For a split second, in a blur, his head under the bumper of the limo, Darnell thought he saw something,

someone, in the distance, then it was gone and everything was darkness.

He spotted the black kid hanging around the parking
lot and figured he was up to no good. Not that he was
paid to guard the garage. It wasn't part of the Boulevard
Mall, even though a lot of people that shopped in the
mall used the covered lot to park their cars. It was just
a short walk from the lot to the south end of the mall
near Sears.

The two-tiered garage was owned by the city of Los
Angeles. Each of the stalls was metered. They never
had any security down there, even though a few people
were mugged every year getting in and out of their cars.

Vincent figured if you were stupid enough to park
down there at night then you got what you deserved.
He usually parked in the open lot so he could keep an
eye on the Beemer, except when it looked like rain.
Then he'd park in the covered structure, near the thru-
way to the mall.

That was where he was when he saw the black kid,
leaning against the driver's door of that old Fleetwood,
just standing there doing nothing. Couldn't bust the kid
for that, even though Vincent knew he was up to something. He made sure the kid heard him turn on his
alarm, the two chirps echoing in the almost empty
structure. Then he walked away, like he was off to the
mall to do some shopping.

Just on the mall side of the pass-through he stopped,
taking a position near the front corner door of Sears
where he could keep an eye on the kid. Vincent stood
there for a few minutes, just watching. The kid didn't
move. Vincent thought he might have been wrong about
the kid, that maybe he was waiting for somebody.

Then the kid did something that reaffirmed Vincent's
lack of faith in his fellow man. He had to give the kid
credit, the mark he picked was no old lady with a purse
dangling off an arthritic arm. But then again, the tall
guy, the one the kid picked, seemed to have his mind

elsewhere, not even noticing the kid and the old Fleetwood parked there as he walked past.

With his eyes focused on what was happening in the garage, Vincent zipped open his duffle and reached inside until he felt the plastic grips of his off-duty .38, the one that he used for show at the mall. He placed the duffle on the ground near some bushes and quickly moved closer.

The kid was following the guy in the jacket, and the guy, by the looks of him, had no idea that he was about to join the city's long list of crime victims.

Vincent was near the kid's Fleetwood now, about twenty yards from where the kid was coming up behind the man in the windbreaker.

When it happened, it happened so fast that Vincent was frozen for a moment. From behind the kid, who had already pointed his own gun at the mark's face, Vincent could see the man's lips moving, speaking calmly, then the wallet being slowly removed from his back pocket and handed to the kid. Vincent watched as the kid, his face animated with an almost crazed agitation—the gun waving back and forth near the mark's face—fumbled with the wallet.

Before Vincent could take another step toward the action, the mark moved quickly, like he was used to these kinds of situations. A quick, short punch to the kid's face, then another, and the kid hit the ground, groaning and reaching for the gun. The mark, still calm, took three steps to where the kid lay—his hand barely gripping the gun—and kicked the kid hard in the lower back.

Vincent thought the man had paused, as if on purpose, waiting to give the kid a chance to go for the gun before he came over and finished him off. Then the last two kicks to the kid's head—after the mark had picked up his wallet as if nothing had happened—when the kid was just laying there, out cold. Vincent heard the thud and saw the kid's body jump an inch or so off the ground.

Vincent put his gun to his side and backed away behind one of the concrete pillars, keeping his eye on the man, who, after brushing himself off, slid behind the wheel of the limousine. The sleek black Lincoln, its rear windows tinted dark gray, slowly pulled away and down the aisle, turned, then headed back toward the exit.

From behind the concrete pillar Vincent caught a glimpse of the driver as he stopped momentarily at the base of the driveway, then slowly pulled into the service road that led away from the mall. A calm, cool face, handsome like some soap-opera actor on TV, except for the bright red slash on his cheek as he drove by.

Ben thought it might be funny to let Bryan and the rest of them at "Jake Stone, Private Eye" get an eyeful of a real cop. He only hoped that studio security wouldn't sound the general alarm when they spotted Joe Curzon pulling onto the lot in his beat-up '62 Impala with the empty bourbon bottles on the floorboard in back.

The Indian had said that he had something to report, which was welcome news to Ben, who hadn't been able to turn up anyone close to a witness in the Romero case. It seemed that Officer Romero had been very careful to cover his tracks, leaving no loose ends to connect him with any criminal wrongdoing.

Ben knew that this one would probably be a little harder to crack than usual. After all, Romero was an experienced cop, who knew all the stories and scams, all the ins and outs of the petty and not so petty criminal.

He'd also know that cops don't have an easy time of it in the joint, whether they're segregated from the general prison population or not. Romero had every inducement, and all the necessary experience and knowledge, to make Ben's job a difficult one.

"Who the hell is that?" It was one of the lighting

technicians, standing on a ladder adjusting a bank of lights, who first spotted the Indian.

"I'll take care of it," said Ben, gesturing toward the light man, along with the rest of the crew, whose focus had been turned away from the set and in the direction of the Indian.

He got Joe's attention, motioning for the Indian to join him at the edge of the set. Joe was hard to miss. He had on his standard-issue greenish plaid Pendleton with the flap pockets (buttoned to the top), tucked inside a pair of denim bib overalls, the kind farmers and hippies used to wear. He had on a pair of lizard-skin Tony Lama boots with silver toe tips, which made him seem even taller.

"Nice boots," said Ben, surprised that the Indian could look out of place and bizarre even on a studio set where bizarre and unusual were the norm.

"Okay," somebody yelled, not the director, but one of his assistants. The director was standing in the center of the set. [Ben could tell he was the director because he didn't seem to have anything to do except to walk around looking at his watch and shaking his head.]

Ben and Joe watched as Jake Stone went through his paces. The scene took place in an alley behind some old warehouses. The crew had roped off a small area of one of the narrow streets inside the studio lot, and stationed people at either end to prevent passersby from unknowingly walking into the line of fire during shooting.

Off at one end of the street the stunt people had parked Jake's red Lamborghini Countach. A young girl with a clipboard and walkie-talkie stood leaning against the driver's door of the Countach. Ben could see the stuntman talking with her from behind the wheel.

The director had already given directions to everybody so that when his assistant yelled, "Action," Ben heard a rumbling noise coming from the door area of one of the warehouse buildings, followed by the high-pitched screeching of wheels. The Countach began accelerating down the street at high speed right at Jake Stone.

Jake, being the macho television hero that he was, instead of jumping out of the way, firing off a few rounds and maybe disabling the car, assumed the Jake Stone position: feet apart, knees slightly bent, both outstretched hands holding the handgun pointed at the bad guys, or in this case, at one hundred and forty thousand dollars' worth of Italian automotive engineering.

He then began firing at the Countach, which by this time had gathered enough speed so that even if Jake had been lucky enough to have the one round that he was able to fire off actually hit the driver, the momentum of the car alone would have crushed and permanently altered the career of the famous TV sleuth.

Ben was unsurprised to see that Jake was able to take the driver of the Countach out with one shot. A shot so well-placed that it killed the driver, causing him to turn the car away from Jake and up onto the sidewalk where it collided with a trash truck, then came to rest between two parked cars.

"Pretty exciting stuff, huh?" said Ben. The Indian didn't comment. Ben added, "Just like you and me, right?"

"Ya know," said Curzon, "I see this stuff on TV all the time. It's why I don't watch cop shows. Jesus, that guy coulda been killed, standing there firing that little thing at that car. Jesus, it's just plain stupid. Why didn't he jump outta the way, then try to pick the guy off?"

"Camera angle," said Ben, as if he were some sort of expert.

"What?"

"I said, it has to do with the camera angle. It makes for a better shot to have the camera behind ol' Jake there while he's firing at the Lamborghini. The people at home feel more like they're right there with him. That they're in danger of being run over by this speeding Italian road rocket unless they can fire off the perfect shot and save the day. Which, of course, since this is the next-to-final scene of the show, everybody knows is gonna happen anyway. It's all got to do with ratings.''

Joe grunted.

''Ya see,'' said Ben, ''if Jake's car crashes don't beat out the other networks' car crashes, then ol' Jake Stone there ends up being replaced mid-season by some situation comedy about an extraterrestrial who comes to earth, becomes a stockbroker, then gets sent to prison for insider trading. It, of course, becomes a big hit on the Fox Network, and is probably moved to Sunday night, right between 'Married . . . with Children' and 'Women in Prison.'

''And then,'' Ben concluded. ''Jake Stone gets to go to television detective heaven, along with Mannix and Barnaby Jones, and about a hundred others I could mention.''

''Which one's your friend?'' asked Joe.

''Over there. Near the director. Just a sec, and I'll get him over here.''

Ben motioned for Bryan to join them.

Bryan approached, giving the Indian an uncertain glance, then shaking Ben's hand.

''Great action, Bry. I especially liked the part where Jake challenges the Lamborghini to a game of chicken. Really realistic, you know.''

''Why is it that I get the distinct impression you're giving me a ration of shit?''

Ben laughed. ''Who, me?

''Listen, Bry, we only have a few minutes before we have to get back. I'd like you to meet a friend of mine. Bryan Talley, meet Joe Curzon.'' Ben watched the two shake hands.

''Joe's gonna be my partner for the next few weeks.''

''Partner?'' Bryan slowly looked the Indian up and down, then raised his eyebrows and smiled.

''Yeah,'' said Ben, enjoying his friend's obvious chagrin. "Joe's been out for a while. Injured on duty. Anyway, he's back in the saddle now. Isn't that right, Joe?"

Joe grunted again.

They watched as the giant Indian ambled away, hands in his pockets, tilted slightly forward on his Tony Lamas, looking more the cowpoke than the Indian.

"He's not as dumb as he sounds," said Ben. "Actually, he's pretty damn sharp."

"Yeah, but . . ."

"I know. He doesn't exactly fit the Jake Stone mold, does he."

"The last thing I would have guessed was a cop," said Bryan. "But then, I guess that's why you brought him by, right?"

"Well, anyway . . ." Ben laughed, not answering Bryan's question. "We gotta get going. I just thought since we were in the area, you know, that we'd stop by."

"Sure, Ben. Anytime. Hey," Bryan added, "maybe we can get your partner there a part as an extra. I hear they're talking about bringing back 'Gunsmoke.' Who knows, maybe . . ."

"Yeah," said Ben, "I'll be sure to mention it to Joe, make sure he wears his headdress and squaw boots next time." He began walking toward his car.

"What was all that bullshit at the studio? You didn't have to bring me by. Shit, a lot of young dumbshits running around giving orders. They actually pay those little shits good money for that?"

They were seated outside at a small table under an aluminum umbrella eating hot dogs and French fries.

"Hell, Joe. You'd be surprised. All those TV guys are young nowadays. Millionaires by the time they're thirty."

"No shit! You and me are in the wrong line of work, man. Busting our butts for thirty years just so we can spend the next thirty, if we're lucky, working as some sort of rent-a-cop at the Alpha Beta."

Curzon stuffed the rest of his hot dog in his mouth and washed it down with Coke. They were at a small food stand with a patio that looked out on Topanga Canyon Boulevard. Bryan had said that the place had the best chili dogs in the Valley, and after tasting one, Ben couldn't argue with that—though, after the first, he was concerned with how many days the taste would stay with him.

"So, fill me in on Romero," he said. "What were you able to dig up?"

Curzon finished chewing, took another swig of his Coke, and wiped his mouth with a small white paper napkin.

"Interesting sort of security job he's got over there at that mall," he said, stuffing the paper napkin into an empty plastic cup.

"I tailed him from his place into the Valley, just like we discussed. He usually works that night job at the mall three or four days a week, so I followed him there the other night. He pulls into the covered parking, with me not too far behind. He goes below, and I take the ramp to the roof. I can see him, ya know, from the edge of the roof parking. Him with that silver car of his and all."

"BMW."

"Whatever. Anyway, I'm just about to take the stairs down to the ground level and follow him into the mall, when I see him stop, just the other side of this little tunnel-like thing they got that connects the parking area to the mall. So I stop on the stairs where he can't see me, but I gotta pretty clear shot at him. I see him just watching something going on somewhere below.

"Then I see him start walking, real slow at first, straight back from where he came. He's got a gun, drawn and down near his side. I figure something's up, but I don't know what. I don't wanna screw the whole investigation so I stay put, at least until I can get a handle on what's going on.

"I move down a little on the stairs so I can see what's

happening. Romero is down there too, just watching some black kid trying to shake down a white guy who's driving a limo.''

"A limo?"

"Yeah. Long, but not stretch. Black Lincoln. Anyway, the black kid goes after the white guy with a gun.''

"What's Romero doing?"

"Just standing there, watching, at first. Then he starts moving toward the black kid. Then he backs off. I can see the white guy and the black kid going at it, and the white guy is kicking the holy shit outta the black. I mean, really laying into him.''

"And Romero's just watching all this?''

"Yeah. He's standing behind one of those supports that holds up the roof. The whole time, just watching.''

"Then what?"

"Then the white guy—once he's finished with the black kid, who's laying on the ground near the bumper of the limo, out cold—he gets back into the limo and drives away like nothing happened. And Romero, he's just standing there, smiling. Can't say that I blame him for that, though. The little shit had it coming. Looked like one of your typical gang-banging assholes. I enjoyed seeing the kid get the shit kicked outta him, myself.''

"Did you get the kid's name?''

"Nah. I followed Romero into the mall and kept an eye on him for a while. Nothing exciting. The usual stuff, just walking around letting the public see he was there.''

"What happened to the kid?''

"Hell if I know. I got tired of flat-footing it around behind Romero, so I came home, had a few beers, caught the tail end of the Dodger game and hit the sack.''

"Still, it's a little funny that Romero didn't lift a finger, don't you think? I mean, the guy's still a cop.''

Curzon didn't answer. Both sat silently, watching the beach traffic starting to mount up.

"Hell," said Ben, getting up and throwing his trash into the swinging lid of a nearby garbage can. "I guess following up on the kid would've been useless anyway. Probably no connection with Romero. Just some asshole out for a score."

"That's what I figured," answered Curzon. "The way I look at it, the guy was doing a public service by taking the little shit outta commission. Too bad he didn't do the job permanently."

Ben smiled, wondering what Francis Powell would say if he could hear their conversation.

"Listen, Joe," he said, "don't bother doing a report on what you saw. Not just yet, anyway."

The Indian smiled the same mischevious smile Ben had seen earlier, back in the Indian's trailer when they were talking about Francis Powell.

"Hell, Ben," said Curzon, serious now. "You know me. I don't bother with no reports unless there's something real important, like a homicide or something. Like when I try to make an arrest and the suspect resists. Then I just change his name from 'suspect' to 'victim.' It's easier that way."

CHAPTER 12 ━━━━━

Osborne was avoiding him.

"I gave Mr. Osborne your message, *Mr. Rosen,*" his secretary would say, probably while doing her nails and chewing on a piece of gum. Arnie could just picture it.

Something was wrong. Somebody was tailing him. The guy showing up at the mall, then at his place . . .

Osborne was having some lackey return his phone calls, like Osborne was too busy tossing down double scotches to answer his calls.

Something was definitely wrong.

Now he'd have to try and handle it himself, which he figured was probably better than Osborne and those government assholes screwing the whole setup. Besides, Osborne had acted a little funny the last time; like he wasn't worried because he either knew something that Arnie didn't, or he just didn't give a shit.

He'd deal with Osborne later. Arnie put D. David Osborne out of his mind as he pulled on the brass handles to the large oak-and-glass doors that led into T.G.I. Friday's.

The first thing that hit him was the ear-piercing din of human voices: laughter, babble, drunken revelry—everything that passed in this meat-market pickup joint for conversation. Arnie could see people talking, but couldn't hear a word being said. It was like a large sheet-metal press set at super-high speed, the banging of metal against metal becoming a deafening hum, drowning out all individual sound. This was Romero's place. Where he had told Arnie to meet him.

From his table in the corner Vincent immediately spotted the worried look under the bad toupee. He got up, stepping around two guys in suits whose hands were filled with small plates of pizza hors d'oeuvres. He waved Arnie over. The guys in the suits were standing in the aisle trying to pick up two young women who looked like they had been through the whole scene before.

That's what Vincent loved about this place: it was a supermarket of young, firm bodies. He could sit back, have himself a nice vodka martini, and go shopping. It was fucking great, just great. And everything was for sale, for the right price.

"Jesus," said Arnie, removing his sports coat and quickly sitting down at Vincent's table, as if not wanting to be spotted. "I can barely hear myself think in here."

Vincent smiled, noticing the gray rings of perspiration at the underarms of Arnie's shirt. "Relax, Arnie," he said. "I like doing business here. The place is so noisy that you can't hear normal conversation. Jesus, you practically gotta yell just to give the damn waitress your drink order. Makes for more private conversation, ya know what I mean?"

Vincent liked the way the little man looked: real nervous about something. That worried look that meant he needed Vincent to do something for him. Vincent liked to feel wanted, especially when it came to other people paying him money. This one looked like easy pickings, Jew or not.

Vincent sipped at his martini. Yes sir, the little Jew was thinking real hard about something. Rosen had sounded that way, anxious and maybe a little scared, at the mall when he'd practically begged to set up this meeting. Vincent told himself to be careful with this one. He'd probably start to kibitz (wasn't that what they called it?), maybe try and get Vincent to do him a favor, something for free. Just like those suckers Rosen ripped off over at the Vacation Villas, taking their money for some pie-in-the-sky retirement time-share condos. Vincent knew all about the little Jew's action.

Yeah, he'd try and hit Vincent up for favor. He'd have to play the guy cool, at first—see just how bad he was hurting.

"It's your dime," said Vincent, letting the little man know that he had better things to do.

"I hear you do a little moonlighting," said Arnie.

Vincent looked at him like he didn't know what Arnie was talking about.

"Besides working at the mall," Arnie added.

"Who'd you hear that from?" asked Vincent.

"I just heard. It's not important."

"And if I do?"

Arnie looked around, adjusting his position in the bentwood chair. The two guys in suits had taken up seats right behind him at the table with the women. The guys were looking at each other, raising their eyebrows and smiling, while the two women sipped at tall pink drinks through plastic straws, trying to act barely interested.

"I might have a job for you," said Arnie. "Actually, it's no big thing. I kinda need a favor. Something you might be able to help me with."

There it is, thought Vincent. Just a little favor, no big deal. *Bullshit.*

"Ya see, there's this guy's been hounding me. Pissed off 'cause I been seeing his action. Ya know what I mean?"

Arnie laughed. Vincent didn't.

"Anyway," said Arnie, "the guy must've found out where I live, 'cause he's been stopping by when I'm at work. My housekeeper told me. And the other day, he came by the Villas, ya know, like he was gonna buy something. Acted real interested. Well, shit, I didn't know he was the same guy that's been comin' 'round my place, so I talk to him. Seems okay. Doesn't buy anything though. Then I get back and talk to Carmen, that's my taco housekeeper. She don't talk too good English, but she describes the guy to me. It's the same one."

"So what do you need me for?" asked Vincent, knowing exactly what Rosen wanted. He decided to let the taco remark slide, at least for now.

"I don't know . . . I just thought, maybe we could scare the guy. You know, nothing serious. Just lean on him a little, get him to back off."

"We?"

"Well, that's where I figure you come in. Shit, I'm sure the guy's just doing a macho number on himself, ya know? Like I'm dipping the ol' stick into his private reserve and he's gotta do something so he can think he's still a big shot. Ya know what I mean?"

Vincent looked at the little man's smile, concentrating on the two crooked yellow teeth in the front. A nervous smile. Vincent figured the business about the girlfriend was just so much shit. An old guy like that, with that stupid-ass rug of his . . .

"What'd you have in mind for the guy?" asked Vincent, wanting to end this conversation and maybe take a seat at the table where the two women were in the process of giving the guys in the suits, with their shit-eating grins, the brush-off.

"Just a word to the guy oughta do it." said Arnie. "No big deal. Hell, the guy'll probably shit in his pants."

Yeah, thought Vincent, you'd like that, wouldn't you. Fucking shyster with your fucking rug and fucking gold jewelry. Trying to act like a big man, just as long as someone else—some *taco*—provides all the muscle. Shit.

"Twenty-five hundred, in cash," said Vincent, evenly, looking away from Rosen, toward the bar.

Arnie put both hands, palms down, on the table. For a moment his mouth hung open, then he quickly closed it as if suddenly realizing that he looked surprised. Arnie looked away from Romero, who he could see was watching him without wanting him to think he cared.

"Ah . . . And what'd you plan to do to the guy?" asked Arnie, trying to buy time to think. He figured the Mexican wouldn't charge him, not cash anyway. Maybe a favor for a favor. But the Mexican was cold, like he had done this before, like he was used to it. Arnie realized he'd underestimated the man.

"Like you said, that's up to me, right? No rough stuff. Just enough to get the message across."

"Ah . . . Yeah," said Arnie. "That sounds good."

Vincent looked straight at him, saying, "Fifteen now, and a thousand when it's done."

"Ah, I'll have the fifteen tomorrow. At the mall. That okay?"

"Cash."

"Of course," said Arnie, trying to sound sure of himself, and doing a bad job of it. He was having second thoughts about the Mexican, the cop. He figured it was worth fifteen hundred to find out about the guy who was hassling him. If it was what he thought, the Mexican wouldn't be coming back for the thousand, and Arnie would camp out in Osborne's office until the feds did something.

If it turned out to be just some joker who was pissed off about something, maybe a former client or something like that, then Arnie would figure a way to handle the Mexican. Maybe Arnie would tell the Mexican about the guy from the insurance company asking him about the computer store rip-off in the mall. That would put a lid on the Mexican for a while. Arnie toyed with the idea of telling the Mexican about Ruggerio, but decided he'd hold that one back, at least until he had a better handle on who was following him.

Vincent knew the little Jew would try and cheat him. He wasn't worried. The little man would underestimate him. *Just another stupid Mexican,* that's what he's thinking. Probably ask me to mow his fucking lawn next.

"What's this guy look like?" asked Vincent.

"Tall. Good-looking. Big, but young. Baby-faced. Black hair."

Vincent asked, "What if he doesn't come back? What makes you so sure he hasn't shot his wad already?"

"Oh, he'll be back. He acted like he was real interested in one of the villas, but I know that's just so much bullshit. He said he'd be back real soon, as soon as he got some money together."

"So you'll let me know when . . . *if* he shows up again."

"Yeah."

Vincent made like he was getting up to leave, hoping that Rosen would get the hint. One of the two women was eyeing him over the rim of her pink drink. Vincent gave her one of his quick smiles, just a flash of teeth to set the hook.

"Oh, yeah," said Arnie, after making it halfway to the door, turning around and coming back. Vincent was already at the edge of the table asking the pretty young things if he could buy them a drink and did they wanna go for a little ride in his Beemer.

"I almost forgot," said Arnie. "The guy's got a cut on his face, right here." He traced a line down the left side of his cheek from ear to chin.

Vincent watched the little man turn and walk away. He was aware of the two women looking at him, but his eyes were still on the front door, long after Rosen had left.

"A friend of yours?" asked one of the women, finally breaking the silence.

"What? Oh, yeah," mumbled Vincent, still thinking about what Rosen had said. He thought about the black kid in the garage, and the tall guy, the one with the baby face, coolly pulling the limo past him onto the service road.

Vincent thought: A jealous lover? Yeah, right. Sure. Interesting.

What's the little Jew got himself into? Maybe get the dumb Mexican to find out, huh?

Vincent looked at the young blonde seated next to him, giggling at her friend across the table. She was wearing a low-cut pink Lycra aerobics top, a second skin showing the outline of two firm nipples, like bull's-eyes, grazing the wooden tabletop as she bent over to sip her drink.

"Ya know something, honey?" Vincent smiled. "I can't help but think you'd look real good sitting inside my 633 CSi."

CHAPTER 13 ━━━━━━━

D. David Osborne took one look at the marble fountain spewing water in front, the people lined up with their suitcases at the curb, and the two funny-looking doormen in their fake Beefeater uniforms, and he knew that he had been right about Rosen. The little weasel was just making sure the safety net was still there. He wasn't really worried, not like Osborne knew he should be. Too bad.

Osborne eased his Taurus past the parking attendant, almost taking part of the kid's leg off in the process, and pulled past the valet park to the employee parking in the back.

It had been a while since he had last seen the little weasel. He guessed that the lottery business was what this was all about. Rosen said a telephone call wouldn't do, he needed to sit down and talk. In person.

Osborne entered through one of the back doors of the hotel, near the ballrooms, so he wouldn't have to walk past the parking attendant that he'd nearly maimed. The place had a nice feel, if you were into lively, bright, and shiny, which D. David Osborne definitely was not.

He followed the sound of a piano—past two hookers holding up the wall in the hallway, smoking their cigarettes and waiting for some businessman with an afternoon to kill—into the main lobby of the Woodland Hills Marriott Hotel. He could see the parking attendant outside waving his arms up and down, demonstrating how he was almost run over by some asshole. Osborne could read the word on the attendant's lips. *Asshole.* He said it more than once while pacing back and forth, waving his arms and thrusting the fuck-you finger in the direction of where Osborne's car had disappeared. Osborne thought it was funny. From where he stood inside the lobby, it was like watching an X-rated mime in an usher's uniform.

Osborne slipped past the front door when the attendant wasn't looking, and found himself standing at the entrance to the bar. At least he thought it was the bar. Once inside he realized that it was the hotel dining room, which was closed, but it did have a small bar off to the side, separated from the eating area by a Plexiglass divider that didn't look much like stained glass.

He felt a little more at home, even though the bar was empty. At least it had a normal ceiling, low, with a couple of recessed spots over the cash register. The rest of the hotel, at least the part that Osborne had seen, rested like a human greenhouse under a high glass ceiling. Various species of people were being fed and watered, coddled and pampered in an atrium the size of a football field.

Osborne preferred to do his drinking in the customary darkness of those inconspicuous little corners of old hotels and restaurants (invariably furnished in booths of tuck-and-roll red vinyl and Formica, with flickering red glass candles), normally reserved for those inebriated denizens of the afternoon darkness, to which D. David Osborne had pledged his allegiance many years ago.

Osborne knew this was not one of those places. The bar was like an afterthought. Someplace they figured might get used at night, while the restaurant-goers waited for their tables. There were no inconspicuous booths in dark, tucked-away corners. Hell, there *were* no corners. The place seemed to open up into the kitchen on one side and the atrium lobby on the other. In fact, the little tables and chairs near the bar were placed to encourage people to take their drinks into the lobby instead of standing around blocking the entrance to the restaurant.

There was that small bar though, and Osborne took a seat on one of the six stools, the one nearest the kitchen and away from the lobby. He ordered a double scotch and waited for the weasel to make his entrance.

Leave it to Rosen to pick a goddamn fish bowl like this, he thought. About as inconspicuous as a third tit on one of those high-priced hookers out in the lobby. Shit, that little fucker was probably upstairs getting laid this very moment—it would be just like the little weasel.

Just like that lottery crap on TV. The stupid shit couldn't resist. Then, after the thrill of winning the twenty Gs wears off, he calls and says he's worried! Says he's been getting some funny phone calls and could we check it out. Shit! Just who the fuck does that little weasel shithead think he is?

Osborne sucked the liquid from the glass, swallowed hard, and motioned for another. He drained half of the next one before putting the glass back on the bar and letting himself relax, just a little.

Arnold Rosen, Leonard Fine—what did it matter? Once a fucking hood, always a fucking hood. If those assholes wanted to waste each other, then Dave Osborne said, Let 'em at it. Just one less sleazy crud to have to worry about. Not that he spent much time worrying about Rosen or any of the other snitches in the program.

Twenty-seven years in the bureau, Osborne thought, and what did he have to show for it? He had gone as high as he was going to go, they had made that perfectly clear. Now he was taking orders from some snot-nosed Ivy Leaguer whose father was in tight with a couple of senators. Well, fuck the bureau and fuck Randall Morrell III. He'd show that snot-faced little shit where he could stick his ambition.

The kid behind the bar was already there, pouring him another. Osborne thought the bartender had a smart-ass, condescending look to him. Like the punk wasn't going to say anything, but he sure as hell wanted Osborne to know that he had him pegged.

"Fuck you, too," he whispered.

"Pardon?" said the bartender.

"Nothing," said Osborne. "Just daydreaming."

He tried to organize his thoughts. No use getting mad. He'd done that before and it hadn't accomplished anything. Just ate away at the inside of his head, little by little, until the alcohol was the only thing that would make it better.

Now he had a new idea: If you can't beat 'em, join 'em. Isn't that what they said? Yeah, and it worked. Just a few more like Rosen and David Osborne would be able to walk away. Say good-bye to the bureau and all the crap.

Gotta keep playing the game though, he thought. No sense blowing it now. Figure out what the weasel expects to hear, then give it to him. He started thinking about Arnie Rosen: a protected informant in the Federal Witness Protection Program. One of the early ones, before Osborne's transfer into the department.

He'd inherited Rosen, along with the rest of the snitches, as the bureau's second man on the West Coast, working under Randall Morrell III, the head of the department. He was supposed to make sure that Rosen and the others weren't wasted by some mobster. Personally, he couldn't give a shit what happened to them. He'd just as soon see all of them in concrete shoes at the bottom of some river, after they testified and served what he considered their only useful purpose.

He finished his third scotch, then stared at the bartender, daring the punk to give him that holier-than-thou sneer. The bartender backed down, pouring another drink with his best here-you-are-sir smile.

By the time Rosen stuck his head in the bar, Osborne had the punk eating out of his hand with stories of daring close calls in the bureau, which he made up as he went along.

"Ah, Rosen," said an obviously tight Osborne, extending his hand and momentarily losing his balance. The bartender reached across the bar and placed a hand on Osborne's shoulder in an effort to prevent him from falling off the bar stool.

"A little dark in here," said Osborne, as if his near-fall had nothing to do with the four scotches he had consumed and the fifth, a double like the rest, that he was presently working on.

"I see you started without me," said Arnie, looking from Osborne to the kid behind the bar, who gave Arnie a knowing wink, cleaned the bar where Osborne had spilled part of his drink, and asked Arnie what he was drinking.

"Club soda," said Arnie.

"Club soda!" exclaimed Osborne. He acted as if Arnie had just casually announced that he had shot the president.

"Can't take the hard stuff anymore," said Arnie. "You get to be my age, you gotta watch yourself. Every once in a while I'll have a beer. But nothing stronger than that, not anymore."

"Jesus, that's a hell of a thing," slurred Osborne, looking at Arnie for a moment as if he truly cared about the man. Then, as quickly as his compassion had hit, it disappeared.

"Kevin, ol' boy . . . How 'bout another. This one's getting a little runny."

Kevin, the kid bartender, looked at Arnie, then moved toward Osborne with a fresh glass.

"Kevin here's a good kid, Arnie. Workin' his way though college, ain't that right, kid?"

Kevin didn't answer. He smiled, nodding to Osborne, then turned away, rolling his eyes.

Arnie took a good look at the man who held his very life in his hands. It didn't make him feel too comfortable. Osborne was a little guy like him. Nothing wrong with that. Except Osborne was the type of little guy who never quite got used to being a little guy. He was always the first to run off at the mouth when he thought he had a chance to look tough. The guy who always had to out-macho every other guy at the bar.

And once at the bar, D. David Osborne gave new definition to the term "obnoxious drunk." Which, considering the percentage of the day that Osborne was unquestionably sloshed, meant that D. David was more or less permanently obnoxious. That didn't make Arnie feel very comfortable either.

Arnie sipped at his club soda, catching his reflection in Osborne's glasses. He could see the small beads of perspiration on Osborne's scalp, along the edges of the bald part at the top of his head where the skin met the two squirrelly-brown fenders of thinning hair on the side.

"So tell me, Rosen. What's so important that I gotta drive all the way out to this place with all these old broads running around in their tennis outfits? Couldn't ya've picked a different spot?"

"Whatsa matter, you don't like it here? Not enough old guys in worn wing tips and crumpled suits sitting around getting sloshed and telling war stories?"

That got his attention. Arnie knew it, because Osborne stopped drinking in mid-sip, and carefully placed his glass on the bar before speaking.

"Ya know something?" said Osborne in a garbled, accusatory tone. "You got a real attitude problem, that's what you got. Shit. I come all the way out here, not because I wanna *partake* of the buffet over there by the pool, and not because I get my rocks off watching a bunch of tourists taking pictures of the exotic birds.

You get me? I come out here because you *asked* me to, 'cause you don't wanna talk about it on the fucking telephone. That's why I'm sitting here listening to some asshole playing Barry Fuckin' Manilow on the fuckin' piano in the lobby, and gettin' fucking down-the-nose looks from some pretty-boy kid bartender that's waiting to get discovered or something.''

"Just take it easy," whispered Arnie, placing a hand on Osborne's forearm, trying to get him to lower his voice.

"I'm *taking* it easy," answered Osborne, removing Arnie's hand, but not lowering his voice.

"Listen, I'm sorry about the crack," said Arnie. "It's just that things have been happening lately. I guess I'm a little jumpy."

"Whatsa matter, you run outta lottery money or something?"

"You heard about that?"

"How could I help it? Your face was plastered all over the TV and most of the fucking newspapers. Some kinda way to keep a low profile, that's all I can say."

"That's what I need to talk to you about. I've been getting some strange calls at the office. Just breathing on the other end, like some kind of pervert or something."

"Maybe some guy's got the hots for you, Arnie." Osborne laughed.

"It ain't funny. Now I'm getting the calls at home, too. Whoever it is must be following me around. He knows where I work *and* where I live."

"So what makes you think it's anything but some crank? The world's full of them. Hell, this city is the crank, asshole, *and* pervert capital of the world."

"I can see you don't give a shit what happens to me."

"Now come on, Arnie. You know that isn't true." Osborne paused, feeling like telling Rosen that it was, in fact, true, that he couldn't give a shit what happened to the old fart. Then he decided against telling him that. Rosen would go to Morrell and that bastard would have his ass in front of a review board. He'd find himself assigned to some office in New Mexico counting the Indians, making sure the bureau was ready for the next uprising.

"Listen," said Osborne. "You gotta expect something like this when you have your face out there for every asshole to see. Hell, some jerk probably saw you on the tube and figures he'll try to score some of that lottery cash. I'm sure that's all it is. The Big Boys don't work by making crank phone calls, you know that."

"Yeah, I suppose you're right."

"Sure I am. Just some crank, nothing to worry about. If you want, I'll look into the calls, see if we can trace the guy or something."

"Nah, don't bother," said Arnie. He finished his club soda and threw a twenty on the bar. He'd decided that it was time to level with the Mexican about Big Tony. What did he have to lose. He needed someone to look out for him and it was damn obvious that Osborne couldn't give a shit.

"I gotta get outta here," said Arnie, getting off the stool and looking at his watch. "I got an appointment."

"One of those tennis matrons out there?" asked Osborne. "You gonna check 'em for scars, see if you can find the nip-and-tuck lines?"

"Yeah, sure," said Arnie, not paying much attention. "Listen," he said, "I'll stay in touch."

"Yeah, you do that," muttered Osborne.

Arnie waved in Osborne's direction and headed out of the bar.

Osborne smiled to himself, thinking about their conversation. It was like he thought. The little weasel was worried, but not very much. Not like he should've been. He still didn't suspect a thing. Osborne thought it was funny how guys like that got lazy, like they could really afford to be careless.

The weasel should know better, thought Osborne. It's his own fault, him being such a careless fucker and all.

Osborne laughed out loud, getting the attention of the bartender.

"Kevin, my boy," he bellowed, "hit me again!"

CHAPTER 14 ━━━━━━━

Darnell got there early, so he pulled out his Magic Marker and sat on the ground near the brick wall. Carefully, he drew the picture he had in his mind, the one he'd been thinking about all day. It was starting to get dark, but not so dark that he couldn't see what he was doing if he got close to the wall as he drew.

First, the outline of the Blood, sitting in a chair, hands tied behind his back, wearing his red hat and jacket. But the Magic Marker was black, no color. Darnell drew arrows to the cap and the jacket and wrote the word "red" at the end of the arrows.

There, that was good. He wrote the word "Blood" right over the guy's head.

Standing opposite the Blood in the picture was Darnell, bigger, holding his piece, pointed at the Blood motherfucker, laughing. Then some flash-marks coming out of the muzzle of the gun. That was good.

Then some blood, dripping from the guy's head.

There, that looked good.

He thought about the white dude in the mall. The one that kicked the shit out of him. For a moment, he saw the white dude sitting in the chair getting his fucking brains blown out. He'd do it, he thought. Pretty soon he'd even the score, fuck up that asshole real bad.

Darnell drew L.A. and some of the other brothers

standing behind him, pointing at the Blood and laughing. Stick figures, but they'd get the idea.

Now, the words on the bottom: *Crip Or Die.*

Perfect.

Darnell stood back to admire his work. In the distance he heard voices and instinctively reached toward the pocket of his jacket, making sure the 9-mm was ready. He saw a few of the brothers making their way to where he stood near the wall. All dressed in blue, ready to strut their colors, see if they could get into a little shit tonight.

L.A. pulled up in the Fleetwood, turning his head their way but not getting out of the car.

"Hey, bro!" Darnell yelled. No answer. "You be stoned in there? Shit. Come over t' here and take a look at what I got."

L.A. didn't move, just bobbed his head to the music that Darnell could hear blasting from the car stereo.

"Hey, Crip," yelled the others.

L.A. still didn't get out of the car.

One of the others said, "Shit, man. He be stoned for sure. Come on, Darnell, let's get in."

"You be holdin' out on us?" asked Darnell, as they all piled into the Fleetwood. L.A. continued to move to the music, oblivious to the others.

"Done used it all," said L.A.

"Shee-it!" said one of the two in the backseat. "You be holdin' out on us, you stupid-ass nigger. Man, you better not be foolin' with me. That's all I can say, man. You better not be fuckin' with us."

L.A. smiled, as did Darnell. They were all laughing now, cruising down Lake View Terrace Drive, past the 7-Eleven and the Terrace Liquors.

Suddenly, there was a *crack,* then another. Darnell felt splinters of broken glass hit his cheek, and looked up to see that the window on the passenger door of the Fleetwood was gone.

L.A.'s first reaction was to step on the gas. The car

plunged forward with its tires squealing, throwing the others backward inside the car.

"Turn around, man! Turn around!" Darnell was yelling at L.A., his head torqued around trying to catch a glimpse of who was firing at them.

One of the guys in the back reached down underneath the driver's seat of the Fleetwood and came up holding a sawed-off shotgun.

"Shit, man. You be careful with that fuckin' thing, blow my fuckin' head off!" L.A. was yelling now, seeing the sawed-off in the rearview mirror, suddenly alive with the excitement of the others in the car.

L.A. eased the Fleetwood back up the street, tracing their route. Darnell had the 9-mm in his right hand, the barrel resting on the edge of the door where the window used to be. Three inches of the sawed-off protruded out from the left rear window, covering the other side of the street.

Nothing.

They drove back and forth another time, then stopped at the Terrace Liquors and picked up a couple six-packs of Colt 45 and a bag of pork rinds.

Kicking back in the parking lot behind the Terrace Liquors, working on the second six-pack of Colt 45, Darnell said, "Just like that guy, what's his name? The Hammer! Yeah, that's right. The Hammer. The guy on the TV." Darnell was on his third tall can.

"That ain't the right dude," said L.A. "You done got the wrong brew, man. That's Cobra, man. Cobra is what that Hammer dude drinks. That asshole's some sorta fuckin' football player, ain't he? Man, that guy really pisses me off. Shit, like he's so fuckin' tough, with all that pussy hangin' around him. Shootin' pool with all that fine pussy. Man, he ain't nothin'."

"Nice fuckin' pussy," came a voice from the backseat.

"Shit, man," said Darnell, spilling beer on his jacket. "You be right there. Wouldn't mind havin' some of that. No sirree, that be mighty fine pussy that Hammer's got. Mighty fine!''

They were still arguing about the beer commercial when the Olds came slowly down the street in front of the 7-Eleven. Darnell could see the red baseball caps inside the Olds as it passed in front of the store.

"Fuckin' Bloods," he said, getting the others' attention.

L.A. started the Fleetwood, backing up a few feet to clear the back wall of the store, then eased down the alley behind the 7-Eleven and out onto the street.

The Olds was visible at the end of the street, still moving slowly away from them.

"Go around," yelled Darnell, agitated. The 9-mm and the sawed-off were out again. They were all yelling at L.A. to go after them.

"Go around the fuckin' block," yelled Darnell. "This way, man, this way. Over here." He was pointing to his right, trying to get L.A. to follow his directions.

"Yeah, that's it. That's it. Yeah. That's good. Keep goin', man." Darnell was whispering now. "Keep goin'. Turn up there, at the light."

The Fleetwood kept pace with the Olds, paralleling the other car, a block apart.

"Wait here," said Darnell. "When they come by, pull alongside. Jamere, come on over on this side. We'll fuckin' blow them away when we come by."

The Olds passed through the intersection.

"There! There! Now easy, man. Just come up behind, then come around."

L.A. did as he was told. They caught the Olds by surprise, shattering both windows on the driver's side of the car. The Olds veered sharply to the right, away from Darnell and the others, up over the curb, and collided with the corner of an apartment building. L.A. stomped on the accelerator, and the Fleetwood sped away.

"Go back!" yelled Darnell. "Go back, let's finish those Blood motherfuckers!"

"Shit, man, you crazy or somethin'?" L.A. said. "Fuckin' cops'll be all over. You finished 'em, man. Ain't nobody gonna walk away from that, man. Nobody."

"Go the fuck back, man," demanded Darnell. "I wanna see."

When they came past the apartment building the Olds was gone. They could see where the stucco in the corner of the structure had been cracked off the wall, revealing the wood framework underneath. Two deep tread marks on the lawn leading from the curb to the apartment were left as a reminder of the Olds.

"Down the street," directed Darnell. "Keep goin', man. Keep goin'."

They were headed back toward the 7-Eleven now, with L.A. riding low in the seat, arms outstretched on the wheel. The smells of the night came through the missing passenger window.

"Slow," said Darnell. "There, over at the driveway." Darnell pointed to the driveway leading into the 7-Eleven parking lot. Leaning against a car, not the Olds, were three young men, drinking from cans of beer.

"That ain't them," said L.A.

"Shut the fuck up," snapped Darnell. "Pull close, man."

L.A. eased the Fleetwood up alongside the three men, rolling slow, not looking at the men—waiting for the sounds.

There was a tinny thud, a can of beer dropping from one of their hands, then someone said, "Hey, what's . . ." Then four quick bangs, metal on metal, reverberating in the night.

"Stop the fuckin' car," yelled Darnell. "I wanna look."

"You *are* crazy, man."

"Stop the fuckin' car, you *hear* me?"

Darnell got out of the Fleetwood and walked back a few steps to where two of the three young men lay on the ground near their car.

"Don't fuck with Crips," he yelled, holding the 9-mm at his side. He looked up, seeing the faces inside the 7-Eleven looking out the window, afraid to come out.

Darnell smiled, then pointed the 9-mm at the 7-Eleven like he was going to fire a round at the glass front. He liked to see the looks on their faces, all scared and scrambling for cover, as he lifted the 9-mm from his side and pointed it at the window.

"Now don't be talking to no riffraff, you hear me, girl?"

"Yes, Mama."

Dayna Adams put on her white sweater, the one her mama had knit for her last Christmas, and headed for the door of their apartment.

"Dayna, you make sure I gets my change, you hear? Just two quarts of milk. I swear, you kids go through this milk so fast, I can hardly keep up." Her mother was in the kitchen of the one-bedroom apartment feeding her baby brother.

"Don't you go buying any candy," she said. "And tell Mr. Galindo that I'll be in to see him tomorrow morning as soon as the young ones are off to school."

The young ones that her mother mentioned were Dayna's younger brother and sister, who were sound asleep on the floor.

"Yes, Mama," she answered, walking out of the apartment onto the walkway that looked down upon the central courtyard of the Lake View Apartments. They had lived there for almost a year, the five of them, surviving on her mother's monthly welfare and AFDC checks. Dayna, at eleven, was the oldest of the four kids. She and her sister had the same father. Dayna's oldest brother, Jerome, had come during her mother's second marriage. Dayna didn't know who her baby brother's father was.

It was only about a half block from the apartment to the 7-Eleven. Dayna had made the walk many times, even at night, so it didn't surprise her to see the car with the three boys parked near the driveway in front of the store. She was used to seeing the boys, talking loud and drinking beer out in the street. Usually they paid her no attention, and she acted like they weren't there, keeping her eyes straight ahead, not stopping to smile or even to look. Like her mama told her.

Her mother had told her that she was at the age where the boys would start talking to her. Say things about the way she looked. Dayna knew about that already, even before her mama told her. At school, the older boys were already starting to act crazy like that. She kind of liked it, and so did her girlfriends at school.

But these were older boys, almost men. And they were drunk. They had that hard look that the boys at school didn't have. She passed by, not looking at them, listening to them call to her, making noises like animals, and laughing.

Mr. Galindo and his son were inside the store.

"Your mama know you're out this time of night?" he asked, smiling and handing her a cookie from a large plastic container that sat atop the counter.

"Thank you, Mr. Galindo," she said. "Mama needs some milk."

"Yes, I imagine she does," he said, "with that baby brother of yours. Here, let me get it for you." The store owner walked over to the bank of glass doors and opened one.

"How many?" he yelled over his shoulder, bent over, his arms and head inside the refrigerator box.

"Two quarts, please," said Dayna, smiling at Mr. Galindo's teenage son. He smiled back, shyly, then continued sweeping the floor in front of the counter.

"There we go," said the owner, placing the two

quarts of milk in a brown bag. She handed him the money and waited for the change.

"And tell your mama that these are for the young ones, all right?" He handed Dayna three more cookies from the same container, after placing them in a smaller paper sack.

"Thank you very much, Mr. Galindo," she said, smiling.

"Now you go straight home, you hear?" he said.

"Yes, sir," she said, turning to leave the store.

Outside, the three older boys were still there. They looked at her as she walked toward them, the large paper bag clutched to her chest with both hands. The milk felt cold against her hands, but her sweater kept the rest of her warm.

One of the boys turned to say something to her. She saw his face, smiling, and could smell what they were drinking and what they had spilled on themselves and the ground. Then the other two turned. She gripped the bag tighter to her chest and kept walking.

The one closest to her said something, and started toward her. Then she saw the headlights of the car, a different car, in the street. It was stopped, no, moving slowly. And one of the older boys turned around, toward the car. The smile had disappeared from his face.

Then there was a flash from the window of the moving car, and a terrible loud cracking sound, and she saw one of the older boys thrown up against the fender of the parked car, then slump to the street. Then three more flashes from the window. After the second cracking sound she only saw the flashes, she heard nothing. The other two boys had disappeared. She thought she had seen them fall, but wasn't sure, didn't care.

Dayna felt a burning in her chest. She looked down and saw a white watery liquid draining from the soaked paper bag, over her sweater and pants. She felt her shoes and ankles getting wet and looked down to see a puddle of dark liquid where she stood. Then she looked at her sweater. The white liquid had changed color, staining her sweater and the paper bag a dark pink, then red. The first thought that came to her mind was that her mama would be very angry that she had ruined her beautiful Christmas sweater.

She dropped the paper bag, looking at her chest, seeing her sweater darken to a dark blackish-red color. The burning felt deeper now, and her head felt light, dizzy. There was a fuzzy edge to what she was looking at. She took a step, then fell to her knees. Everything turned dark, silent.

Her mama would be mad, that's what she was thinking. Her head rested on the sidewalk, still warm from the day's sunlight. She tried to focus, keep her eyes open, figure out what happened. She couldn't. Everything she looked at was tilted, moving.

She could see one of the older boys from the moving car, a black man, standing in the street near the curb, smiling. A funny smile, like those cartoons about movie stars. Electric teeth, with a flash, like from the gun. Then the smile was gone.

It was the duty that Vincent liked the least. Taking a new guy, just out of the academy, on routine patrol. Give him a little training so he didn't get himself shot the first night out.

It cramped his style, having to have this young white kid follow him around, asking questions.

"You stay with the car, kid. I'll be right back."

"It's Rick, Sarge," said the kid, who was sitting in the passenger seat of the patrol vehicle.

"Yeah, right. Sorry. I forgot. Terrible with names." Vincent walked into the Doughnuts 'n' Cream and ordered a couple of jelly-filled and two cups of coffee.

"This is a good place," he said, back behind the wheel of the patrol car, blowing on the surface of his coffee. "Usually pretty quiet, and the owner gives us a break on the food. I used to come here when I worked Foothill Division.''

Vincent stopped eating for a second, looking at the kid. ''Whatsa matter, something wrong?'' he said, noticing that the kid hadn't touched his jelly-filled.

''Nah, no big deal. I hate jelly-filled.''

''Oh. Sorry 'bout that.''

''I'm not hungry anyway,'' said the kid.

Vincent had just about finished the kid's doughnut when the broadcast came over the radio. ''Shots fired, man down, possible 187, gang-related.'' And then the location.

''Shit, that's us,'' said Vincent, stuffing the remainder of the doughnut in his mouth, starting the patrol vehicle, and backing out of the parking lot.

They arrived to the usual crowd of onlookers. Women in bathrobes, wearing curlers and smoking cigarettes, like they had just gotten out of the shower. Lots of kids who should have been in bed. Guys, old men, in work pants and sweat-stained V-neck T-shirts, wearing slippers. Everybody staring at the bodies on the pavement and shaking their heads.

''Stay close, kid,'' said Vincent. He parked the patrol car in the 7-Eleven lot, then pushed his way through the crowd to the sidewalk where an older man sat, crying, holding a young girl's head in his lap.

''Let me take care of that,'' said Vincent, crouching at the man's side and gently lifting the girl's head. He could hear some wheezing coming from the girl, but her eyes were closed.

''She just came for milk,'' said the man, sobbing, looking up at Vincent.

Vincent said, ''Kid . . . Rick, take this gentleman into the store. Let him calm down a little, then try and find out if he saw anything. Call for an ambulance first. And call for some backup, okay? See if we can clear some of these people out of here. But find out if anybody saw anything.''

Vincent was sitting on the sidewalk now, the girl's head resting on the pants leg of his uniform. He stroked the hair from her face, listening to the wheezing noise coming from her chest.

"Anybody know this girl?" he asked. The people in the crowd pulled a few steps back, shaking their heads.

Vincent put his hand on the girl's neck, searching for a pulse, and felt a faint rhythm, indicating that she was barely clinging to life. He could hear the wail of the ambulance sirens in the distance.

The girl's eyes fluttered momentarily, then closed, then opened slightly.

"Honey," whispered Vincent, close to the girl's face, "what happened? Tell me what happened."

The girl was looking straight up, not at Vincent. Her lips moved slowly, without sound.

"Who shot you?" asked Vincent. He moved over her now so that she was looking at his face. He could feel warm liquid saturating the trousers of his uniform.

"Who did it, honey? Who shot you?"

"Boys." The words were barely audible.

"What?" said Vincent. "Boys?"

"Uh huh."

"What boys? Come on, honey, hang in there. What boys shot you?"

"Mama. Where's my . . ."

"Honey, listen. The boys . . . the ones that shot you . . ."

"My sweater, it's . . ."

"What? What about your sweater? Come on, honey, tell me. *Please!* The ones that shot you . . . Tell me."

"Shiny smile," she whispered, then closed her eyes, her lips still mumbling words, incoherent.

"Shiny smile," said Vincent. "That's good. What else?"

"Shiny . . ."

"Black or white? Honey, were they black or white?"

The girl's eyelids opened so slightly that Vincent

could barely see her eyes. She said, "Shiny smile . . .
Black . . . Bad boys . . ."

"Bad boys?"

"Mama . . . I'm sorry, Mama."

Then her eyes closed, forever.

CHAPTER 15

"What brings you hotshots from Internal Affairs down here? Believe me, all those complaints are pure bullshit, I only beat up half of those people."

A smiling Detective Richard Curtis was standing at the front desk, behind the counter, extending his hand to Ben Green.

"Dick," said Ben, grasping the other's hand and shaking it. "How long has it been? Five, maybe six years?"

"Too long, Benny. I heard you decided to join forces with the good guys. I won't miss going up against you in court, that's for sure. Listen, Ben, I just wanna say that it's an honor, no, it's a *fucking* honor, for you to grace us here at West Valley with your presence."

Ben laughed. He glanced over at the rookie manning the phone at the front desk. The kid looked like he didn't know what to make of their conversation, whether to laugh or not.

"Come on back," said Curtis. "They mentioned something about your being interested in one of our gang-banger shootings."

"Not so much the shooting," said Ben, following Curtis back to the homicide desks in the back of the detective room. "I need to see the reports."

"Ah . . . As usual, checking out the cops, not the bad guys, huh?"

"Sometimes they're one and the same," said Ben. "You know what I do, Dick."

"Here's the file," said Curtis, handing Ben a manila legal-size folder. "Three or four cops involved in the statements. More in the preliminary investigation. I won't ask which one you're interested in."

"Thanks," said Ben, opening the folder and quickly flipping through the paperwork.

"Captain says to give you the file, I give you the file. None of my business who you're after."

"Listen, thanks, Dick. Can I get a copy of this?"

"Sure. Take it to the front. They'll Xerox a set for you. Just leave the file up front, I'll get it later."

Ben had the file copied, then headed for the parking lot. He had asked Joe Curzon to stay in the car, not wanting to raise any more eyebrows than he had to.

"Hot off the press," said Ben, sliding into the passenger seat and opening the folder between them.

"Any problems getting it?"

"Just the usual bullshit. I know one of the detectives handling the case, so it was okay."

The two men pored over the reports.

"Looks like our boy was first at the scene," said Curzon, slowly going over the initial crime report.

"Yeah," said Ben, distracted by something he had just noticed in one of the supplemental reports. "Jesus Christ," he exclaimed. "I don't believe it."

"What?"

Ben handed Curzon the supplemental report. Curzon read the two-page report detailing the investigation of the Valley Gang Unit, and the conclusion that, based on the statement of the victim and statements from various gang members, the primary suspect was one Darnell LeGardy, a hard-core Pacoima Crips gang member.

"You know this LeGardy asshole?"

"Sorta," said Ben. "I'll tell you about it later. You see any problems with what we got so far?"

"Yeah," said Curzon, sifting through the pages of reports, looking for a particular page. "I see one very big problem. Here it is,'' he said, lifting a sheet from the folder. He started reading from the report:

'' 'Officers arrived at scene, where Sergeant Romero found victim, Adams, on sidewalk in front of location, bleeding profusely. Sergeant Romero attempted to question victim as to identity of assailants, at which time victim stated a few words about the assailants being black. Victim stated to Sergeant Romero that assailant had a ''shiny smile.'' Victim then expired at scene and was pronounced dead by paramedic unit No. 72.' ''

Curzon looked at Ben, who was resting his head against the side window, his eyes closed.

Curzon asked, ''How did they make this guy, LeGardy?''

''The supplemental says that besides the victim's I.D., they got some info from some other gang-bangers that LeGardy was the shooter. Word on the street. The gang unit's out looking for him now.''

Curzon said: ''You know what that gang-banger information is worth.''

''Yeah.''

''And all they got, once those gang assholes don't show up for court, is some little girl talking about a black guy with a shiny smile.''

''It's a dying declaration,'' said Ben. ''It's an exception to the hearsay rule, and it's admissible in court.''

''It may be admissible,'' said Curzon, ''but it sure ain't the strongest evidence I ever seen. Besides, they're gonna need our boy Romero in order to get it in. The way I read this thing, he's the only one who heard the girl's dying declaration about the shiny smile. He's gotta testify, if the D.A.'s gonna use her statement to finger LeGardy. Without Romero, there ain't even a bad case. And what in hell is Romero doing patrolling Foothill's territory anyway? He was assigned to West Valley night watch. Jesus, it's just our luck that the guy's driving around where he's not supposed to be.''

Ben didn't respond. He read the supplemental report

over again, trying to figure a way around what Curzon had said.

"That's West Valley's problem," he finally said. "Hell, maybe they can have Romero testify on this thing before we have to bust him. That would solve everybody's problems. With a little luck, the way things are going, they'll get the girl's murder wrapped up, Romero will testify, then we'll bust him with what we've got."

"I sure hope so, Ben. 'Cause you know damn well he ain't gonna testify once he finds out he's been indicted. The last thing he's gonna want to do then is to help us out."

"Yeah, I know." Ben's mind was on other things. He was thinking about Julie, and the newspaper pictures of the little Adams girl. The mental images, the pictures, seemed to be superimposed on one another. As if one were the shadow of the other. It was crazy. He told himself that what had happened to Julie had nothing to do with Dayna Adams. That both murders would likely remain unsolved, and even if they got lucky and found the killers, it would do nothing to bring either girl back to life.

So why couldn't he rid himself of their images? He thought he'd put that one to Beth Mellnor in his next session. Then realized that he wouldn't be seeing Beth Mellnor again, at least not in the near future. It came to him that finding Dayna Adams' killer would have to come first. That without that, all the Beth Mellnors in the world wouldn't be able to help him.

CHAPTER 16 ━━━━━

Word on the street had it they were looking for him. The cops, the Bloods, and every other asshole trying to cut a deal for information.

Shit.

He hadn't seen any girl standing there. Shit. How they gonna pin that one on him? They had nothing, leastwise, nothing that would hold up in court. Some dead girl's talk about a guy with a shiny tooth. Man, that wasn't worth shit. If they picked him up he'd give them some story, say nothing. Yeah, ask for his lawyer and don't say shit. They'd have to cut him loose. Insufficient evidence, that's what they'd call it. Not the same as *tainted evidence,* but just as good, maybe better. He wouldn't go down on this one. No way, man. No fuckin' way.

Couldn't go home, not now. Stay with a friend. Maybe Cassandra's pad, get some sweet ass while he waited. Then he remembered all the assholes that dropped by Cassandra's place. Guys who'd do anything for a hit of something. Anything . . . No. That was too risky, they'd be happy to give him up for a little crack.

He came back to the Valley, to the mall where he'd hassled with the white guy. Far enough away and easy pickings, he thought. Money was what he needed now. Enough to keep him going until things blew over. He'd score a few white assholes, maybe get lucky and pick up enough cash to carry him north. Maybe San Francisco. Yeah, that sounded good. He'd always wanted to see that bridge they had up there.

When he got off the bus at Ventura and Sepulveda, Darnell was already feeling better. He had a plan. He'd get him some money, then make his way north. In San Francisco, he'd kick back a while, check things out, then maybe Crip-it with the brothers up there. Pick a new name. Maybe fuck over some of them Bay Area assholes. He'd heard they were all queer, anyway.

Darnell figured maybe he picked the wrong night. The mall was pretty empty. A few folks coming in and out of Sears, that's all. He decided to take a look, see what was available. It was then that he saw the white dude. The limo guy with the pretty face. He was walking fast, down some stairs, away from an office on the second floor, right toward Darnell.

Darnell ducked behind the corner of Sears and watched the guy go by. He was running now, away from Darnell, but Darnell was sure he was the same guy. The guy from the limo.

Maybe he should go after him?

It was too late. Darnell saw the limo, the same one, parked down the street just to the side of the garage. He heard the sound of the limo's engine revving—the high-pitched metallic noise of the starter. There were red taillights, then the squeal of tires, and the limo was gone.

Back on the second floor, Darnell found the office. The one the pretty-face had come from. An open door. Nobody around. Lights on, like they left for a few minutes to get coffee or something. Maybe it was the pretty boy's office. Like he had some emergency or something and was going to be right back but couldn't lock up. Darnell smiled. Steal the white guy's money, he thought. Yeah, it couldn't have worked out better.

He looked both ways then went inside, clearing his throat loudly to see if anyone was in the back. Nothing. No cash register either. Maybe a safe. Yeah, in the back. These places had safes, maybe only a metal box where they kept the money. He glanced back outside, then went through the door leading to the back room.

Holy shit!

He heard himself say it, then he said it again.

Someone had already robbed the place. That was his next thought. Then, moving closer, thinking: Ooo-wee! Somebody had really done a job on this guy.

Darnell looked back, toward the front door, then to the old man slumped on the floor in the back room. There was something funny about the guy, besides the puddle of blood he was sitting in and the fact that his slacks had been stained dark gray.

It was that thing on his face. Like hair. That's it, thought Darnell. It's hair. A fuckin' wig, or something.

He came closer and lifted the piece of hair off the front of the man's face.

"Oh, shit!"

He jumped back, dropping the wig to the floor.

"What the fuck!"

He thought: This white dude's got somebody's dick stickin' out of his mouth.

"Je-e-sus!

"Man, will you look at *that.*"

Darnell knelt down in front of the old man to get a better look, make sure it was for real. The old guy was just sitting there, eyes wide open, staring at the wall behind Darnell.

Darnell started to laugh because he thought the old guy looked pretty funny, sitting in that pool of blood, someone's dick hanging from his mouth, like some sort of limp cigar.

He was curious. About the old guy, and about the guy in the limo. The pretty boy running. From what? Something in his head was telling him there was a connection. It wasn't clear to him yet, but it would be. A way to get back at the pretty boy. Really fuck him up. And Darnell wouldn't have to do a thing. Maybe he'd even cut him some slack with his own case. He'd just keep it in mind for now, until it was deal-making time.

Suddenly the old man moved.

Darnell jumped up, ready to run. Then he realized that the guy had to be dead. Darnell looked back. The old man had slumped further down, his face now resting partially on his chest and partially on some boxes of office supplies.

Darnell laughed at himself.

Jesus, man. This guy's makin' me real jumpy.

Then he saw the thing—the cock—in the dead guy's mouth start to get bigger. Right there! Between the dead guy's lips, like he was blowing it up or something!

Holy shit! The dead fucker was getting himself a monster hard-on!

The fuckin' thing was *alive!*

CHAPTER 17

Chick Hearn was interviewing Larry Bird, who was saying how tough he thought the series would be and that it would probably go seven, with the last game up for grabs depending on which team wanted it bad enough.

Ben had a TV tray set up so that he wouldn't miss any of the action. The Lakers and the Celtics, as usual. A tape that he'd saved for just such an occasion. A steak and pepper sandwich, hot, from the Italian deli down the street, and a cold beer, with more in the fridge.

Ben was set. His ideal way to spend an otherwise uneventful evening.

Then the phone rang.

Joe Curzon was on the other end, saying, "Hate to bother you at home and all, but I just thought you might be interested in some paperwork that came across your desk. It said 'Confidential,' but I opened it anyway 'cause I saw it was from your friend over at West Valley. That's okay, ain't it?"

"Sure," said Ben, watching the Laker Girls go through their routine at center court.

"They got another body over here. Some guy over at the . . . let's see . . ." Ben could hear Curzon shuffling papers. "Here it is. The Boulevard Mall, over near Ventura and Sepulveda. Seems the deceased was found in the back room of the Vacation Villas office on the second floor of the shopping mall around twenty-one hundred hours. Some kid who works at the yogurt place saw the light on when he was closing and went up to see what was going on.''

''That's where Romero works, right?''

''Yeah. And it seems the deceased knew our friendly sergeant, 'cause they found a slip of paper in his wallet with Romero's name and phone number on it.''

''Anyone talk to Romero yet?''

''No chance. I figured I'd check with you first. Find out whether you want the homicide guys to bring it up.''

Ben paused for a moment, thinking. Danny Ainge was on the free-throw line complaining about something. Boston had their all-white-guy team in the game, with Robert Parrish playing center.

''Tell West Valley,'' said Ben, ''not to mention anything to Romero about the piece of paper. If they want to interview him because he was on duty or something, then go ahead. But nothing special.''

''Okay, that's what I expected you'd say,'' said Curzon. 'I should tell ya that this one's pretty gruesome.''

''Whadya mean?''

''Seems like whoever did this guy was trying to send someone a message. When the yogurt kid found him, the guy had his dick and his balls stuffed in his mouth.''

Ben heard the short gasp, like air from a balloon: his own voice amplified over the receiver.

''Jesus.''

''Yeah,'' said Curzon. ''I haven't seen one of those in a long time.''

''The guy connected?''

''Who knows? The homicide guys over at West Valley are checking it out.''

''Maybe we should find out what Romero was doing last night.''

"I already did," said Curzon. "He was on a night off, according to the watch commander at West Valley. I wasn't with him yesterday."

"And the people at the mall?"

"Nobody saw him last night. Some other guy was on duty. Says it was Romero's regular night but that they switched, at Romero's request."

"Mmm. See what you can find out about the victim. See how well he knew Romero. You might wanna run the victim and see if he's got a rap."

"And Romero?"

"We can't afford this part-time surveillance any longer. He's switched to days now, right?"

"Yeah."

"So it's mainly after his shift that he's likely to pull anything, agreed?"

"Probably. That kinda guy, you never can tell for sure."

"Well, let's go with the idea that he's more likely to pull his shit when he's by himself. Between the two of us, I want him covered when he's off-duty."

"No problem, except it would make things a whole lot easier if we could get us another body, ya know what I mean?"

"Yeah," said Ben. "I'll work on it. Meantime, you take him tonight, and we'll alternate nights. That okay with you?"

"Yeah, no sweat," said Curzon. "I got nothin' better to do anyway. The cooler's out in my trailer. The damn thing's like a fuckin' sauna."

"All right, I'll touch base with you later."

"Ah, there's one more thing," said Curzon. Ben didn't like the sound of his voice. He'd already missed most of the first quarter of the game, and he was having a hard time trying to both keep track of the score and think about what the Indian was telling him.

"Captain says for me to tell you that you got a very

important message. Those are his words, not mine. Seems there's a couple of guys from the FBI who wanna talk to you about this guy who bought it at the mall.''

"FBI? What in the hell could *they* want?"

"Dunno," said Curzon. "Captain just says for you to call them back. Important, he says. I figure it can only mean one thing."

"Yeah," said Ben. "The guy with his balls in his mouth is—*was*—connected."

"You got it. What I can't figure," said Curzon, "is how Romero fits in. I mean, if Romero's involved with the Big Boys, then we got some serious problems leaving him out on the street. You gotta admit, this kinda hit has wiseguys written all over it."

Ben didn't answer. He was visualizing Francis Powell in his office, telling him that he couldn't afford any screwups on this case. Now, with what the Indian had told him, Ben was beginning to doubt whether that was possible. Things were getting more complicated, and they weren't any closer to pinning anything on Vincent Romero that would stick in court.

Ben got the phone number of the FBI agents from Joe Curzon, then hung up. What could the FBI want with him? And why him, and not the detective handling the murder? And how did they get on to this so quickly? There was only one reason that he could think of, as he drained half of his Heineken: Vincent Romero.

He picked up the steak and peppers with both hands, shoving the end of the sandwich into his mouth.

You're getting a little paranoid, wouldn't you say, he told himself, chewing on his sandwich, trying to figure out whether Boston was winning or not.

Maybe it's got nothing to do with Romero. And maybe Romero's got nothing to do with the dead guy with his balls in his mouth.

Yeah.

Sure.

And maybe the Lakers would blow Boston out of the game in the first quarter.

CHAPTER 18 ━━━━━━━

The sign on the door said RANDALL MORRELL III, SU-
PERVISING AGENT. Ben and the Indian were seated in
the waiting room. They had been kept waiting for over
thirty-five minutes, reading the ads in the year-old
Yachting Life, with the name of Randall Morrell III
printed on the mailing label exactly the way it was
printed on the door. Ben had already pictured this
guy, and didn't much like what he saw. As he followed
Morrell's secretary into his office, Ben still had that
picture in his mind.

"Ah, gentlemen," said Randall Morrell III. He was
standing behind a large mahogany desk with a glass
top.

*Gentlemen? What's with that bullshit East-Coast-
preppy fake English accent?*

Morrell wore a double-breasted blue-and-white
pinstripe seersucker suit, a white shirt—his initials
monogrammed on the cuff—a paisley bow tie, dark
brown leather belt, and oxblood wing-tip slip-ons with
tassels. A pair of tortoiseshell owl-like glasses sat on
the tip of his nose, not the bridge. His hair was short,
and golden (not merely blond), and was perfectly in
place and definitely Ivy League. He was younger than
Ben had expected.

Without making an effort to shake hands, Morrell
said, "Randall Morrell the Third here. Glad to make
your acquaintance."

Come on, Randy. Drop that "the Third" business. And what's this "acquaintance" bullshit?

"This is my assistant, D. David Osborne." Morrell extended his hand toward a man in a plaid sports jacket and slacks seated on a couch to the left of his desk.

At least this guy looks normal. Not like you, Randall—Randy—Morrell the Third. You look like you're a finalist for the "Mr. Preppy" title at some hotshot rich kid's Ivy League academy or something. And who the hell reads Yachting Life?

"Glad to meet you," said Ben. He shook Osborne's hand, then introduced the Indian, who had already taken a seat opposite Morrell's desk and was staring at the FBI man, as if Morrell were Custer trying to tell the Indians before the Battle of the Little Big Horn that he really did have their best interests at heart.

"Gentlemen," said Morrell, "I'm not certain the exact extent of what you have been told to date. Suffice it to say that I am in charge of the Federal Witness Protection Program on the West Coast. Mr. Osborne here is my second in command.

"It has recently come to the attention of the federal government that certain individuals, whose names must remain confidential—for national security reasons, of course—that certain individuals . . . What shall I say . . . ? Ah . . . may have become *involved* in criminal acts on a lower level." Morrell was pacing slowly behind his desk, a finger pointed toward the ceiling, periodically jabbing the finger upward, not looking at any of the other men in the room. It was as if he were a don at some exclusive English boarding school, lecturing to first-year students, and resenting having to do so.

Ben thought: This must be some kind of joke. He moved around in his chair, trying to find a comfortable position. Trying to control his temper.

Just who does this asshole think he is? "Lower level," my ass.

"In any event," said Morrell, removing a black Montblanc fountain pen from his coat and using it to poke holes in the air as he spoke, "it will be necessary for the federal government to have access to your files regarding a recent homicide. Further, it will be necessary that we *(The royal "we," Ben was thinking)* be provided with all reports and memoranda dealing with said criminal acts."

"Now just which criminal acts would those be?" asked Ben, knowing exactly what Morrell was talking about.

The younger man didn't flinch. He merely paused an instant, looked at Ben directly, and smiled a quick smile that said, *You're right, flatfoot, I'm pulling rank.*

Morrell said, "I expect the reports on my desk as you receive them. I also expect to be kept informed of any pending arrests in the Rosen case. Is that perfectly clear?"

"Now wait just one minute here . . ." said Curzon.

Ben put his hand on Joe Curzon's arm to keep him from coming out of his chair.

"I suggest," said Morrell, reaching for the phone as he spoke, "that if you have any problems with what I've said, that you contact Chief Powell from your department. You know who *he* is, don't you?" He spoke into the telephone: "Janice, these gentlemen are just leaving. Please send in my next appointment, would you?"

Ben had learned a long time before that when he got this angry with someone, it was usually better to put some distance between himself and the source of his anger before doing anything that he might live to regret. He got up, directing the Indian ahead of him and out the door.

"Jesus Christ, Ben," said Curzon, once outside. "Do you *believe* that asshole?"

They were in the hallway now, waiting for an elevator.

Curzon went on, "I mean, shit! I'd like to have five minutes, five fucking minutes with that little bow tie.

I'd show him what he could do with his goddamn federal government!"

"Take it easy," said Ben. He was saying it as much for himself as for the Indian. "I'll talk with Powell, find out what the story is with this guy. Meanwhile, just forget about it. I'll handle Morrell myself."

The elevator doors opened and the two men started inside.

"Mr. Green!"

Ben held the elevator doors from closing, as Osborne approached them and stepped inside.

"I'll ride down with you, if you don't mind," said Osborne, trying to catch his breath. "I just had to find you guys before you left. I was afraid that you might have got the wrong impression back there."

Ben said, "You mean your boss?"

"Yeah, well, he can kind of get off on the wrong foot, if you know what I mean. He's young, a political appointment. Dad's some big mucky-muck in the party. Lots of dough. Anyway, you guys really won't have to worry about him. He likes to strut around, make people think he's important, but I'll be the guy you'll be dealing with on this thing."

They reached the first floor and the elevator doors opened. Ben and Joe stepped out. Osborne remained inside, holding the doors open.

"I don't stand on formalities," he said. "I know what it's like being in the trenches myself." He smiled, waiting for a response.

Nothing.

"You guys need anything," said Osborne, relaxing his grip on the elevator doors, "you just come to me first. No problem. We'll work it out so everybody's happy. Okay?"

"Yeah," said Ben, watching the elevator doors close and D. David Osborne disappear inside.

"You thinking what I'm thinking?" asked Curzon.

"Yeah," said Ben, walking to the car. "Except these

guys aren't smart enough to pull a good-guy/bad-guy number on us.''

Ben shook his head, smiled, then looked at the Indian. ''At least not Randall Morrell *the Third.*''

CHAPTER 19 ━━━━━━━━━━

"Oh, yeah, Officer," he said, leaning to the right and opening the glove box. "I keep it right in here. I'm sure I was goin' the limit."

Except it wasn't. And he wasn't.

And the Highway Patrol officer who stopped Shapiro Darnell LeGardy for traveling sixty-five in a fifty-five zone was not impressed when Darnell said that the midnight-black Mercedes 450 SL was loaned to him by a friend of a friend. Darnell said he wasn't sure of the name. Bubba, that was it. The owner's name was Bubba. Didn't know his last name.

The Highway Patrol officer said, "Please step out of the car and put your hands on the roof, sir."

These Chippies were just so nice about it. But Darnell spotted the cop's hand on his gun while he was smiling and saying "Please."

"This is an outrage, Officer." Darnell talking to the roof of the 450 SL while the Chippie was running his hands down Darnell's torso and between his legs.

"You ain't even run the car yet. How you know it's stolen?"

No answer.

Handcuffs.

Brought back to the patrol car and a thirty-minute wait (the equipment was down temporarily, they said), while the Chippie called in for a computer check on the 450 SL.

Then, Darnell from the back of the patrol car: "You're violatin' my constitutional rights, Officer. This is truly an outrage. You're gonna pay for this, man. Gimme my attorney. I demands my attorney!"

The Highway Patrol officer's report would read:

—That at approximately 2005 hours, Reporting Officer Thomas stopped a male Negro suspect operating a Mercedes 450 SL northbound on 101 traveling at an excessive rate of speed. Suspect indicated that his name was Johnson, William.

—That after discovering that the suspect had no identification on his person, he asked said suspect to step from the vehicle onto the side of the road, which the suspect did.

—That reporting officer then returned to his patrol vehicle in preparation of issuing a citation for excessive speed and operating a motor vehicle without a license.

—That reporting officer then ran a vehicle check on the subject Mercedes 450 SL via the patrol vehicle's on-board computer.

—That said vehicle came back a Los Angeles stolen (DR No. 88-39825), stolen 6-15-88.

—That said unidentified male Negro suspect was then placed under arrest at 2045 hours and advised of his constitutional rights prior to booking.

At 0800 hours the next morning, Darnell Shapiro LeGardy was led from his cell at the Ventura Men's Jail to a small interview room that had no windows, except for a small one in the door. He was placed in a wooden chair, his wrists handcuffed to the back. The chair, was pushed as close as Darnell's body would allow to the table. He was still tired and sleepy from the night before, so he didn't complain—not immediately, anyway.

The second person Darnell saw that morning was a young cop in a suit. The cop asked him if he was okay, and was there anything that he needed, like coffee or a cigarette. He'd get his phone call later, the cop said.

"Yeah," said Darnell. "I'd like some coffee, ya know. Lots of sugar. And maybe a cigarette, too. Yeah, a cigarette would do just fine."

The young cop motioned to someone outside, and then turned to Darnell. "You know why you're here?"

"Honestly, Officer," said Darnell, in his best, most law-respecting tone of voice. The one he had used about a thousand times already. "Honestly, Officer. I gotta tell ya, I don't have the slightest idea why you dudes done arrested poor little me. Now, I don't wanna think this, and I know you'll say it ain't so, but I can't help but thinkin' that if I were some white dude toolin' down the freeway in my Benz, that nobody woulda said boo.

"Officer, I ain't never been in this predicament before, I want you to know that. I ain't one of your street niggers, ya know. My people is good people, brought me up right to respect the law and all. But I tell you . . ." He emphasized each of those words, liking the sound of his own voice. He was on a roll now, and the young white cop was just sitting there, listening.

"I tell you," said Darnell, "it's things like this that give law enforcement a bad name. Why, that cop out there that arrested me, he just figured there's some jive-ass nigger drivin' that expensive white man's convertible, something's gotta be wrong. Maybe I'll pull him over, see what kind of trouble I can give the jive-ass nigger. It just ain't fair, man. I gots my rights, just like you white folks."

The cop said, "And you had no license, no vehicle registration, couldn't remember who *gave* you the car, and were driving what turned out to be a stolen vehicle."

Darnell couldn't help laughing at that one.

The coffee arrived, a cup for each of them. The young cop gave Darnell a cigarette, then lit it for him.

"You can take off the cuffs," the cop said to the jailer who brought the coffee.

After watching the jailer close the door behind him, the young cop turned to Darnell. He took a sip of the hot coffee and winced, then put the cup on the table. He smiled at Darnell, then crossed his legs and said, "Now, I don't know whether you actually think that all this bullshit you're laying on me is being believed. I don't know that, 'cause how could I? You could even be more stupid than I thought. All I can do is tell you, from the absolute bottom of my heart, that I don't believe a word of your horseshit.

"But listen," said the cop, putting up his hand to stop Darnell from arguing. "You just keep on talking. It's been at least a week since I heard a ration of bullshit from some jive-ass nigger from the big city."

Then the cold look, with that little smart-ass cop smile, the one that Darnell didn't expect from the nice young cop out here in the sticks.

Darnell said, "I want an attorney."

"Damn straight," said the young cop. "If I were you, I'd want a lawyer myself. Hell, this ain't no big-city lockup where we got so many cases that we can't afford to mess around with a little joyride. Hell, no. Out here, man, you're right up there at the top of the ladder of criminal assholes.

"Judges out here are going to take one look at your black face and then stop listening. You know GTA maxes out at three years, don't you? I mean, if you were white, the judge might give you the mid-term, which is two. But, as we both can see, that's out of the question, isn't it? Man, if I was you, I'd want the best fucking lawyer money could buy."

The young cop took a sip of coffee, watching Darnell, then again gave him that quick smile.

"Ah, but we have a problem there, don't we," said

the cop. "You don't have any money, do you, Mr. . . . ? Well, name doesn't matter. You'll get the public defender. Maybe they'll have enough time to take your case to trial, maybe not."

The young cop pulled the cigarette from Darnell's mouth, dropped it on the floor, then put it out with his shoe. He stood up and knocked on the door for the jailer to take them out.

"Wait a second," said Darnell.

"You talking to me?" The young cop turned around, hands in his pockets. To Darnell, he suddenly didn't look so young anymore.

Darnell said, "What if I was to do you a favor?"

"What kind of favor?"

"Information about a case. An L.A. case."

"Well," said the cop, waving the jailer away. "That depends, Mr. . . ."

"LeGardy," said Darnell. "Darnell LeGardy."

CHAPTER 20 ━━━━━━

He heard the music as he neared the door. Janie's music. He'd wanted to take care of his business with the cop before Janie came on stage. Shit, now that cop, or whatever he was, was gonna be sitting there, looking at her. And from then on, every time he thought of the cop he would see him looking at her that way.

All because the goddamn radiator hose broke, spraying the inside engine compartment of his Continental a rust-colored brown, and causing him to wait at the gas station until the engine cooled off.

Now Jesus Esquivel was late for the meeting that his friend Timmy Gallegos had set up. The cop would be thinking about that when they met. And the cop would probably be thinking that he was dealing with a couple of flakes, one who was late for their first meeting, and the other who was too stupid to know that shaking her tits in a dive like the Honey Pot Room was the beginning of the end of the line.

Jesus pulled his windbreaker over his T-shirt, the one that said BODY BY DIRK CONRAD on the front. He didn't need the cop making fun of anything else. Besides, he knew the cop would ask him, *Who's Dirk Conrad?* and then he'd have to explain to the cop that he was Dirk, but that he couldn't put "Body by Jesus" on his T-shirts because his exercise clients would think he was some kind of religious freak or something.

Timmy had said the cop was good at what he did.

Jesus hoped that Timmy was right. Janie's old man had one foot in the grave already, and Jesus had thought about doing the job himself. Still, it was cleaner this way. Let the cop kill the old guy, then he and Janie would ride off into the sunset with old man Rickert's money and the insurance payoff.

Thinking about spending Janie's old man's money raised Jesus' spirits as he entered the club. From his table near the stage, the cop—the one with the silver hair, "like a movie star," Timmy had told him—turned and looked his way. The cop put his hand up so as to hush Jesus, then turned back and stared at the tits jiggling on the stage right in front of him. Jesus looked at Janie. He wanted to let the cop know that he didn't like being hushed, and liked even less his looking at the girl that way. But he didn't. Instead, he took a seat at the cop's table, wondering why Janie's act seemed to be taking longer than usual.

Vincent Romero decided he'd set things straight right off the bat. Vincent thought: If this muscle-bound greaseball thinks I got nothing better to do than sit around some shithole like this waiting for him, then he's got another thing coming.

He made like he was interested in the girl dancing on the stage—test the greaseball, maybe find out how much of a prick the guy really was. Just sit there and look at the girl, the greaseball's girl, like she was the fucking reigning Miss Universe and Vincent had just gotten out of the joint after fifteen years without a fuck. See how the greaseball handled that.

Vincent asked, "Your girlfriend?"

Janie had just left the stage and Jesus was waiting for her to come and join them at the table.

"Yeah," he said. "I guess you could call her that." He'd caught the sneer in the cop's voice. Things were already starting out badly, he thought. All because of his fucking radiator hose.

"What I don't get," said the cop, "is how it doesn't drive you fucking crazy, having your girlfriend up there buff naked in front of everybody, shaking those tits of hers?''

Yes, things were starting out badly. The fucking cop was playing with him, knowing that he could get away with it. What did all this have to do with the job? He'd known guys like the cop before. In the joint. The joint was filled with guys like that, playing mind games because it made them feel good. Like this cop, trying to get Jesus to bend over and take it.

Jesus didn't say anything to the cop, just smiled. Janie arrived, wearing a cotton robe that was tied in front and a pair of red sequined high heels. When she sat, Jesus wished she had tied the robe tighter in front. The cop's eyes were looking down between her legs as he spoke.

"I liked your act," he said, monotone, still looking at Janie's inner thigh a few inches above the line where her nylons left off. The cop picked up his drink and brought the glass to his mouth without moving his eyes. Before taking a sip, he said, "Luanda Elvisua, that's an interesting name . . ."

Jesus Esquivel thought: Oh, shit! Now Janie's gonna tell him how she got that stupid stage name. It wasn't bad enough that he was late and that the cop started off pimping him. Now she's gonna tell him. The whole fucking story about *Lou* Rawls and *Elvis* Presley. Shit, things were *really* starting out badly.

But she didn't. Janie just smiled, like she had decided to let Jesus handle the talking. Good girl. It was time to get down to business.

Jesus said, "Timmy says you're a handy guy to have around . . ."

Jesus watched, waiting for the cop to say something. He didn't. Just kept looking between the girl's legs.

Jesus said, "Ah—he told you what we need, right?" The cop turned to face Jesus.

"Some," he said.

Jesus said, "Can you handle it?"

"Depends."

"We got some money, not a lot."

The cop said, "What's 'not a lot'?"

"Ah . . . maybe fifteen hundred, a couple grand. That's about all we could come up with now. Later," and Jesus started whispering, "when the old man's out of the picture, well, I guess you could say that money would be no problem then."

The cop smiled at Jesus, then at Janie. He pulled a pack of cigarettes from his front shirt pocket, then a gold lighter from his pants. Jesus watched him light a cigarette and put the pack of cigarettes back in his shirt pocket, leaving the gold lighter on the table for Jesus to see. The mind games again: not offering them a smoke, but letting them get a look at his gold lighter.

"I can see that Timmy was right," said the cop, inhaling deeply and then blowing the smoke in Jesus' face. "You two don't have the slightest idea what's involved here, do you? I mean, you expect the best, and believe me, I *am* the best. But you're talking about getting something for nothing. I don't work for charity. You want the best, you gotta pay." He took another drag on his cigarette and stubbed it out in the ashtray.

The cop said, "It's gonna cost you ten G's up front, and another ten when the job's done."

Jesus looked at Janie, who was rolling her eyes.

"That's a lot of money," she said.

The cop laughed, then shook his head, looking at her like she was a child.

Vincent got up, grabbing his gold lighter from the table and putting it back in his pants pocket. He said, "Well, I guess I'll leave you two to think about it. You know how to reach me." He started to leave.

"Wait," said Jesus. He looked at Janie quickly, saw nothing but blank in the girl's face, then turned to the cop.

"Sit down," said Jesus. "I think we can do business."

Janie started to say something, but Jesus hushed her with his look. The music began again and Janie got up from the table. She smiled at the two men, then went backstage, wondering where Jesus was going to come up with the ten thousand dollars.

When she came on stage for her next number, Jesus and the cop were gone. She went through the motions, like she always did, this time thinking about how she was going to spend the old man's money. She'd buy a convertible for herself and something for Jesus, and maybe they'd drive back to her high school in Ware Shoals and throw some money around, really stick it in their faces.

She was thinking about that as she moved to the music, removing her panties, then her black lace bra on cue, thinking about Ware Shoals and being rich, and Jesus Esquivel with his hard body on top of her. She wasn't thinking about the audience now. She didn't even notice the regulars from the ABC sitting near the front. Nor did she notice the glow of a cigarette in the back of the room, barely illuminating the face of the Indian seated in the darkness.

CHAPTER 21

"What about the Ventura cops?"

Ben and Joe Curzon were seated in one of the glass-enclosed interview cubicles inside the attorney room of the Los Angeles County Jail.

Joe Curzon answered, "Homicide says they just want a crack at him when we're finished. Probably won't bother if the guy goes down on anything serious. All they got is a joyride, maybe GTA at best, with an L.A. victim who probably ain't gonna be too thrilled at having to come up to Ventura to testify."

Ben said, "What about the Dayna Adams case down here? Any more information?"

"Nope. Seems if anybody saw this LeGardy pull the trigger they ain't talking. Gang detail's sure he's the shooter, but none of their information is admissible in court."

"Can't get one of those gang-bangers to finger the guy on the record, huh?"

"You know the answer to that, Ben. Those assholes would just as soon blow each other's brains out as look at one another, but there ain't no way that one of them is gonna take the witness stand and testify. Code of the streets and all that bullshit."

"So now," said Ben, trying to think the situation through, "we have LeGardy, who we know's gonna stay in custody, at least on the Ventura caper, right?"

Curzon nodded.

Ben continued, "He's not going to be able to make any bail in the near future, and if it looks like he is, we can file the Dayna Adams case and hold him without bail. That'll buy us a little more time. Meanwhile, we'll find out what he knows about the killer in the Rosen murder. LeGardy doesn't have a lawyer yet, does he?"

"Public defender in Ventura," said Curzon. "Nothing on the case down here. Probably can't afford his own lawyer. Anyway, LeGardy says he'll talk about what he knows without a lawyer."

Ben said, "Well, he hasn't been charged with anything down here, not yet, anyway. But you can be sure he'll start screaming for a lawyer if he thinks he's looking at a murder beef."

Curzon said, "And what do you got planned for Romero, assuming LeGardy I.D.'s him?"

"Not sure yet," said Ben. "We don't even know whether LeGardy will I.D. someone else as Rosen's killer. As I see it, if LeGardy knows we need his testimony to make Romero, or whoever killed Rosen, then he's going to hold out for some sort of deal for himself on the Adams murder. And if it turns out that he can I.D. Romero as Rosen's killer, then we have a problem. Once LeGardy finds out that we need Romero's testimony to make the Dayna Adams case against him, and that Romero's been arrested and isn't going to testify against anybody, then Darnell LeGardy's going to just sit tight. He won't say a word. He won't have to, knowing that he'll skate on the Adams murder because without Romero's testimony, we won't even have the girl's dying declaration to use against him."

"Meanwhile," said Curzon, "Romero's out capering, doing God knows what, and we gotta just sit around doing nothing. I mean, it seems to me we gotta make a choice, Ben. Either we go after Romero, and put LeGardy on the back burner, or we go after LeGardy for the Dayna Adams murder, use

Romero's testimony about the girl's dying declaration to convict LeGardy, then arrest Romero, and just hope he hasn't caused too much trouble while we were waiting.''

"That's going to be Francis Powell's decision," said Ben, pointing toward the lockup entrance of the attorney room, where Darnell LeGardy now stood, being checked in by the deputy sheriff on duty.

"That's great," said Curzon. "I can just imagine the political bullshit that'll go into that one."

Ben thought about it too. He didn't want to give LeGardy up. He wanted to see him go down for every year that he deserved for killing the little girl. Still, the decision was not up to him. Ben knew he'd have some convincing to do with Francis Powell about not rolling over on Darnell LeGardy's case, regardless of how much they needed his testimony in the Rosen murder.

Ben glanced over at Joe Curzon, wondering what the Indian would say if he knew what he was thinking. Whether the Indian would understand how the Adams girl had, in Ben's mind, become inextricably identified with his Julie. Whether the Indian could appreciate just how crucial it was for Ben to bring Dayna Adams' killer to justice. Or whether the Indian would tell Ben what he already knew—that it was both dangerous and crazy for him to think that way.

Ben watched as Darnell LeGardy swaggered over toward the interview booth. That same cocky grin, that same way of looking around, making sure that everybody in the attorney room saw he was about to negotiate with the Man. And there was that stupid diamond Ben had spotted earlier, with the reflection coming off LeGardy's front tooth.

"Gentlemens," said Darnell, taking a seat opposite the two cops. "So nice of y'all to come down here and pay me a visit."

Joe Curzon said, "Cut the shit, LeGardy. You ain't in a position to be shitting us, not today."

Darnell smiled, unimpressed, and said, "Touchy, ain't ya?"

"Listen, Darnell," said Ben, taking over the interrogation. "We're here to hear what you have to say. If you have something to tell us, then spit it out."

"Well, I don't know about that," said Darnell. He was smiling again, gazing up at the ceiling and then over his shoulder into the attorney conference room. [He was straining to look relaxed.] "What can you gentlemens do for *me?* I ain't stupid enough to just be sittin' here talkin' wit' you for free. What about this murder beef you be tryin' to tag on me? That little girl. You gonna do somethin' 'bout that?"

"Depends," said Curzon.

Ben watched LeGardy smile at the Indian, like he had the situation totally under control, when Ben knew Darnell was thinking real hard about what his next gambit should be.

Darnell said, "S'pose I got some information. Important information 'bout a murder."

"Yeah," said Ben, monotone, disinterested.

Darnell asked, "What's that gonna be worth to you?"

"Depends," said Curzon, enjoying the impatient, pissed-off look on LeGardy's face when he said it.

"Listen," said Ben. "Why don't we stop trying to bullshit each other. You say you got some information about a murder. From what Ventura has already told me, it's about the murder of the guy over at the mall in the Valley. Now, you know we're interested in finding out who offed that guy. And if you have some information that'll help us find out, we're willing to do something for you."

"Like what?" asked Darnell.

"Well," said Ben, not wanting to give up too much too soon. "You got the Ventura case, we could talk . . ."

"That's bullshit, man," said Darnell, leaning back in his chair and laughing. Then he spoke loud enough

for the rest of the inmates in the attorney room to
hear: "That's total Mickey Mouse, man! They ain't
gonna be able to pin that one on me. Shit, it ain't
worth much anyway." Darnell paused, then lowered
his voice, saying, "I ain't gonna give some guy up on
a murder for no fuckin' joyride. You gotta be crazy,
man."

Ben put up his hand to calm LeGardy, saying,
"Okay, okay. What about the shooting of the little
girl?"

Darnell said, "Now you be talkin' somethin' that
just might interest me."

"Of course," said Ben. "We haven't advised you of
your rights since we weren't talking about anything except you giving us some information about the guy in
the mall. Now . . ."

"Don't bother with that, man. I been advised so
many fuckin' times, I know the fuckin' thing by heart.
Shit, the cops in Ventura already done that."

"All right," said Ben. "Let's do it this way. You
tell us what you know about the guy in the mall, off
the record, ya know what I mean? And we'll listen,
knowing that it's totally off the record. If we like
what we hear, then we'll get together with the D.A.
and your lawyer, and see if we can work something
out to help you in return for your testimony against
the guy that killed the old man in the mall. No guar-
antees. You still got the little girl's murder hanging
over your head. But we'll see what we can do to help
you on that. Meanwhile, if you say something to us
that hurts you, well, like I said, it's off the record
and no way we can use it against you in court. Sound
okay?"

"Yeah," said Darnell, pausing to look each cop
straight in the eye, worried, but not wanting to show
it. "That sounds good."

"So start talking," said Curzon.

Darnell told them about the evening at the mall when
he saw the baby-faced guy running, then discovering

the old guy with the toupee in the office with his dick in his mouth. He also told them that he remembered the license number of the baby-faced guy's limo, but didn't mention he remembered it from the time he was beat up.

"So," said Curzon, "you didn't actually see this guy with the baby face coming from the office where the dead guy was?"

"I saw him runnin'," said Darnell. "He was runnin' from upstairs, and the door to the office was wide open when I got there. I tell ya, man, he's your killer."

"And you didn't see anybody else hanging around there, right? Like an older guy, maybe Mexican, with a mustache?"

"Nope. Just the guy in the limo, man. He be runnin' real fast from something. He's your killer, man. No fuckin' doubt about it."

Ben figured that even if LeGardy were telling the truth, they still couldn't eliminate Romero as possibly being involved in Rosen's murder. Rosen did have Romero's name and number on him when he was killed. Nothing was taken from Rosen's office, so they could eliminate robbery as a motive. Given what Ben already knew about Romero, it was still too early to rule him out.

Ben said, "All right, Darnell, that's real good, what you told us. We have to check a few things out first. Make sure that everything you said fits in. We'll get back to you if we have any more questions." Ben and Joe got up to leave.

Darnell stood, saying, "Hey, man! What about my deal?"

"Like we told you," said Ben, "we're gonna check out your story. If it all checks out, then we'll get together with your lawyer and see if we can work something out. You got the P.D. down here, don't ya?"

"Hell no, man," said Darnell. "I'm gonna get myself a *real* lawyer. I ain't gonna let no fuckin' *pubic* defender dump-truck my ass.''

"That's real good, Darnell,'' said Curzon, chuckling to himself as he and Ben headed for the door.

CHAPTER 22 ━━━━━━

It was the size and thickness of the package that surprised him. Ben had expected a thin manila envelope containing a letter, maybe a single-page computer printout, telling him that there were no entries under the subject's name in the files of the Department of Justice.

Instead, there was this thick yellowish envelope, with extra tape on its flap to keep the contents from spilling out. Ben lifted the envelope before opening it, as if weighing the contents, thinking about what could be inside and whether Darnell LeGardy could possibly have been telling the truth about the baby-faced guy in the mall.

Ben had already run the license plate supplied by LeGardy. Luckily, a California personalized plate: DANNY V. Easy for LeGardy to remember and not likely to be the subject of some minor mistake in transposing a number or letter.

Still, not a very low-key vehicle to use in the commission of a murder. Bad enough, Ben thought, to use a limo, let alone one with an easily remembered plate like that.

Ben had little faith in the truth of LeGardy's information. Even less when he had run the personalized plate and it came back registered as a limo in the name of a Danny Villapando, with a subsequent transfer of registration and ownership to a white adult male by the name of Jonathan Racine.

Racine's address and vital statistics appeared at the top of the computer form in shorthand, and looked like the standard information. Just the usual traffic offenses, an illegal turn, and the typical statistics on Racine's physical description.

Ben had run a CII report on both Villapando and Racine, checking for criminal history in California, and found nothing. Both men appeared squeaky clean.

As a last resort, knowing that it was unlikely that either man would have any record of criminal history in California unless they had been arrested in the state, Ben had requested a criminal history summary from the U.S. Department of Justice. It was that package that he now held in his hands as he stared at the formal Department of Justice seal on the mailing envelope.

Ben ripped the top of the envelope and removed the contents, his eyes falling on a cover letter that was paper-clipped to the pages of computer printouts from the agent at Justice who had prepared the information:

July 21, 1988
Mr. Benjamin Green
Los Angeles Police Department
Internal Affairs Division

Re: Daniel (Danny) Villapando and
      Jonathan Racine

Dear Mr. Green:

Enclosed please find the information requested regarding the above-mentioned subjects. You will note that while neither subject appears to have any criminal history in California, both men have served time in prison in New York State.

I have enclosed a copy of the information in our files pertaining to their incarceration at the Dannemora Correctional facility in New York, along with

*any paperwork we received from the probation offi-
cials in New York, and the parole records from Dannemora.*

*I trust that the enclosed will be of some use to you
in your pending investigation. Should I be able to
assist you further, please do not hesitate to contact
me.*

> Sincerely,
>
> Thomas M. Morley
> Keeper of Records
> Bureau of Criminal Identification

Ben put the letter aside and picked up the printout
on Danny Villapando, which was four pages long and
chronicled repeated arrests, with some convictions, for
various misdemeanors and felonies leading to his even-
tual incarceration at Dannemora for felonious assault
with violence.

The probation and parole records on Villapando
painted a picture that was all too familiar to Ben. Villapando was the typical mean-streets kid, getting into
trouble at an early age, going through the juvenile court
system, then the adult criminal justice system in New
York. The records showed Villapando going in and out
of jail for theft and violence offenses culminating in a
commitment to state prison.

There was a paragraph in Villapando's final probation report in which the probation officer expressed his
opinion that Villapando had become involved in running numbers, in addition to his work as an enforcer
for the mob. Yet the probation officer stressed that Villapando steadfastly denied the allegations that he was
linked to any sort of organized crime activities.

The final report from Villapando's parole officer was
dated one year after his release from prison. It indicated
that Danny Villapando had successfully completed his
period of parole after his release from Dannemora at
the age of twenty-nine. Whatever might have happened

to Villapando after his parole was terminated was not mentioned in the documents sent to Ben by the Department of Justice.

Jonathan Racine, on the other hand, was a different story. A one-page rap sheet showing only the offense for which he was sent to prison, along with a prison release date approximately four years later.

As Ben reviewed Racine's record, he tried to figure out what the connection between the two men was, other than the fact that at some point after they were released from prison Danny Villapando transferred title to the limousine to Jonathan Racine.

The rap sheets of the two men were completely different. But for the manslaughter conviction, appearing on Racine's criminal history, the man had led a clean life. Ben carefully looked at the information again, trying to find something that might connect the two men.

Both had been at Dannemora at the same time and both were paroled within the same month. Racine was a good five years younger than Villapando, though it was too much of a coincidence to believe that the two hadn't known each other in prison.

Ben shuffled through the papers until he found the final parole report on Jonathan Racine. The parole officer had typed a one-page report referring to Racine's conduct in prison and summarizing the criminal history dealing with the killing of Racine's father. It read much the same as that of Villapando, with the formal report containing no additional information as to the post-parole whereabouts of Jonathan Racine.

Ben thought that if Racine had been Villapando—if he'd had Villapando's criminal record—then LeGardy's information would have been more believable. With what he had received from Justice, it appeared to Ben that Jonathan Racine had led a law-abiding life but for what seemed an unfortunate and tragic act that was not entirely Racine's fault. Jonathan Racine had been a model prisoner, and had justifiably been paroled at an early date. He just didn't fit the picture of a hired gun.

Ben was about to file the information on the two men when he noticed a small piece of paper, a photostatic copy of a note, stuck to the back of the parole officer's final report. The photostat had some original handwriting on the top—from the agent at Justice, Ben figured—indicating that it was a copy of a note sent by Racine to his parole officer after his parole file had been closed. The parole officer had included it in Racine's package, which was what Justice had received and sent on to Ben.

Ben read the note. It was a request by Jonathan Racine that any communication received by the Department of Parole that related to his mother be forwarded to his new residence in California. He then listed the address, adding his thanks to the parole officer, and mentioning that he and Danny Villapando were sharing the rent and trying to make a go of it together.

Ben compared the Laurel Canyon address specified on the note with that listed in Racine's DMV printout. They were the same.

In Ben's mind, Darnell LeGardy was becoming increasingly more credible. The limousine, the personalized plate, and now the two ex-cons living together. Ben still would have liked it more if Racine was the one with the long arrest record, but even without it, his association with Villapando, and LeGardy's information, made Jonathan Racine someone that Ben would definitely have to check out.

He picked up the phone, dialed the Indian, and arranged for the two of them to pay a visit to Jonathan Racine.

CHAPTER 23 ━━━━━━━━

This was Ben's day for canyons. Pick up Joe Curzon at his place in Topanga Canyon, then head back to the Valley, hop on the Ventura Freeway, and take it to Laurel Canyon. Jonathan Racine's address, Ben figured, was somewhere midway between the freeway and West Hollywood, on one of the short winding roads that ran adjacent to Laurel Canyon Boulevard.

When Ben pulled up, the Indian was sitting out in front of his trailer on a toilet that somebody had discarded. He had his head down, and was reading a paperback. To Ben, and anyone else passing by, the Indian looked like he was relieving himself in his front yard. An outhouse without the house.

Curzon got up and walked toward the car as Ben pulled up in the dirt driveway.

"How you doin', Benny?"

Ben watched Curzon bend his way into the front seat, placing the paperback on his lap.

"Okay, Joe. How 'bout you?"

"Great. I like mornings like these. Clear, just a little overcast in spots, but not so as you think it's gonna rain. I like watching the fog moving in and out of the canyon. Kinda mysterious, ya know?"

Ben nodded his head, thinking that the Indian was full of surprises. "What're you reading?" he asked.

"Oh, this?" Curzon lifted the paperback off his lap.

"Elmore Leonard," he said. "Ya heard of him?"

"Yeah," said Ben. "Tough guys talking tough. Fast read, right?"

The Indian said, "Yeah. I like the way he does the cops. 'Specially the Latinos. No bullshit, ya know?"

Ben nodded, keeping his eyes on the road. They were coming back into the Valley on Topanga Canyon Boulevard, just the other side of Mulholland.

The last thing Ben felt like was a character in an Elmore Leonard book. It seemed like things were getting more and more complicated. And bullshit was definitely something that he could expect more of before the investigation was completed.

He had called Francis Powell's office and set up an appointment with the chief. Curzon had been right about having to make a decision. As it stood, Darnell LeGardy was dangling somewhere between being a suspect in a murder, and being the People's star witness in the Arnie Rosen case. Ben wasn't crazy about dealing with the gang-banger, but realized that they had little choice if they wanted to go after Romero, or Racine, or Villapando, or whoever it was that hit Arnie Rosen.

Ben was beginning to feel that going after Vincent Romero might not be worth what they were giving up. Dealing with LeGardy on the hunch that he might make Rosen's killer seemed like a long shot. Besides, Ben wanted LeGardy's hide for personal reasons.

Then there was the question of whether Romero even had anything to do with the killing at the mall. And if Vincent Romero wasn't involved in the Rosen murder, then who was? Racine? Was it worth cutting a deal with LeGardy to get Racine?

The shit, Ben mused, as he veered off the freeway at Laurel Canyon, was just about to hit the fan. He could just imagine Francis Powell, sitting behind that big desk of his, smiling, the wheels whirling, weighing the political benefits of each option.

Ben thought about his predicament. Yeah, just like an Elmore Leonard novel, he muttered to himself.

Curzon said, "You might be interested in something I found out the other night. Seems our boy has got something new in the works."

"Romero?"

"Yeah," said Curzon. "Followed him to a place, one of those adult motel places, ya know, that show porno on the TV. They also got a topless joint, I guess for when the guys get tired of beating off in their room. Place called the Honey Pot."

"You're shitting me."

"Nope. That's what they call it. Anyway, I'm sitting there watching Romero watching this broad shaking her tits, and in walks this greaseball muscle-builder in a T-shirt, sits down right next to Romero, and they both start watching the broad with the tits."

Curzon paused, lit a cigarette, then continued: "Then the broad, she comes over and joins them. I can't hear what they're saying. But what I see looks like Romero shaking Mr. Muscles down for cash. Can't be sure, though. They were arguing about something, at least the greaseball was looking pretty pissed."

"Did you see the money change hands?"

"Nah. It looked like Romero was playing it cool, like he enjoyed jerking the greaseball's chain. After a while, the girl left and so did Romero with the greaseball in the T-shirt."

"Together?"

"Yeah. Until they got outside. Then they split up, I guess."

"You guess?"

"Yeah, by the time I got out, Romero's car was gone." Curzon turned and smiled at Ben. "I caught a few minutes of the next show."

"I know," said Ben, grinning. "Great tits, right?"

"I got the name of the greaseball with the muscles," said Curzon. "Bartender says he hangs with the dancer. Goes by the name of Dirk Conrad."

"Nobody's named Dirk Conrad," said Ben.

"Yeah, that's what I figured," said Curzon. "So I ask around, find out his real name is Jesus Esquivel. He's one of these physical fitness trainers that come to your house and yell at you to exercise. Rich guys have 'em. I seen something like that on 'Lifestyles of the Rich and Famous.' You pay these guys a bundle and they come by in their Mercedes and watch you sweat for half an hour, then charge you a couple hundred bucks. It's real big with the rich-housewife set. Hubby goes off to work in the morning and wifey *gets off* with old Dirk in the afternoon."

Ben said, "This Esquivel got any record?"

"Funny you should ask," said Curzon. "Seems he did some state time a few years back. Grand theft. He's been clean since he got out, though."

"Until now, huh?"

Curzon didn't answer. He was looking out the window. The car was winding through Laurel Canyon. The fog had burned off and Ben could feel the heat of the sun through the side window. He switched on the air-conditioning.

Ben said, "You think our bodybuilder friend will be cooperative?"

Curzon answered, "No."

Ben said, "Maybe we can make it worth his while."

"That's what I figured," said Curzon.

Ben nodded his head, then slowed the car and pulled over to the curb. "That's it over there," he said, pointing to a small wooden frame house almost completely covered by eucalyptus branches.

The two men approached the house. Ben knocked on the front door, then waited.

"Check the side yard," he said to the Indian. He watched Curzon step off the porch and walk to the other side of the house. For a moment Curzon was out of Ben's sight, then he returned, pacing back toward the porch.

"Nothing," said Curzon. "No car. No sign of anyone."

Ben knocked on the door again and waited. "I guess we missed him," he said.

"Yeah," said Curzon, walking over to a front window and looking inside.

"Jeez, will you look at all them books!" he said, turning from the window and facing Ben. He turned back and looked inside, cupping his hands around his face. "The guy's gotta fucking library in there."

Ben walked over and took a look for himself. On the walls inside the small room, on shelves from the floor to the ceiling, were hundreds of books stacked closely together. On the floor around the oversized desk were stacks of books, along with cardboard boxes. The top of the desk was scattered with books and catalogs piled high.

Ben stepped back from the window and checked the address of the house. Joe Curzon turned from the window, put his hands in his pockets, and looked down at the ground, then at Ben.

"Interesting," he said. "A mob hit man that reads."

Ben clenched his jaw and thought, trying to make sense of the situation. Curzon was saying exactly what Ben had been thinking. Ben started to doubt Darnell LeGardy for about the hundredth time that week.

"Are you thinking what I think you're thinking?"

"Yeah," said Ben. "But we're both getting a little old for this kinda stuff."

"Speak for yourself, sonny." Curzon pulled out a thin metal pick from his wallet and inserted the pick in the front door lock. He looked to his left, then right. With a slight flick of the wrist he eased the lock open, holding the door closed with his other hand. He looked up, smiling at Ben.

"After you, old man," said Curzon, pushing open the door.

The two entered, Ben first. A small entryway with a wood floor led directly into the living room. A tall, narrow, mirrored armoire stood in the entryway against walls that had been covered in decorator paper of hand-painted flowers and vines. Off to the left was the kitchen. To the right was a hallway. Ben followed the hallway past a bedroom containing a twin bed, a small nightstand underneath a cut-crystal lamp, and a four-drawer dresser—another antique—to the book-filled room they had seen from outside.

The room smelled of must and eucalyptus. Ben noticed some leaves on the inside ledge of the window from the trees outside.

The room appeared much the same as the view they had seen from the front porch. A large desk was the only piece of furniture in the room other than the chair behind it. The desk dominated the center of the room, but even it was overwhelmed by the books. Lining the walls, everywhere, there were books.

On the desk was a picture of two young men. Ben recognized the faces as being slightly older, more relaxed versions of the booking photos that had accompanied the prison records of Jonathan Racine and Danny Villapando. Both men were smiling, bare-chested in swimming trunks, with their arms around one another.

Ben wondered what had become of Danny Villapando. The house showed sleeping arrangements for only one. Ben thought that that would be consistent with Villapando selling the limo to Racine. Maybe Villapando split. Maybe the two had gone their separate ways, but had remained friends.

"Find anything?" he said, absentmindedly, to Curzon.

"Just a whole lot of books," said the Indian. "Looks like Racine sells the things. There's lists of people from all over, with addresses and prices next to each name.''

''Hmm. Doesn't fit,'' said Ben. ''Does it?''

''Nope,'' said Curzon. ''We've both been doing this long enough to know that it takes all kinds. But I just can't picture this guy doing what was done to Rosen. He ain't the type.''

''Yeah,'' said Ben, lifting the picture of the two smiling men.

''We better make ourselves scarce,'' said Curzon. ''Racine's likely to come back any minute. There don't appear to be nothin' here that's gonna help us.''

Ben still had the picture in his hand. He was rubbing his thumb along the surface of the photo, thinking about Darnell LeGardy's story and trying to picture Jonathan Racine killing Arnie Rosen. It didn't work.

As he was about to put the picture back on the desk, Ben noticed that he had accidentally lifted one corner of the photo from inside the frame. He started to push the bottom of the photograph back into the slot when he spotted a folded piece of paper stuck between the photograph and the back of the frame. Ben removed the paper, which initially looked to be some sort of receipt that had been folded over. Once removed, it turned out to be two separate pieces, folded together. He opened the paper and separated the two pieces.

''What ya got?'' asked Curzon, coming over to get a better look. ''What are they?'' The Indian looked from Ben to the pieces of paper and back at Ben.

Ben's mind was racing, trying to condense all he knew about Racine and Villapando with all he knew about LeGardy, Vincent Romero, and the Arnie Rosen murder. It was too much. Nothing was clicking. Ben couldn't quite get a handle on exactly what the pieces of paper meant, but he knew they were important. One of the missing pieces of the puzzle, or puzzles, he thought.

Ben said, "They're blood test results."

The Indian said nothing, waiting for his partner to elaborate.

"This one here," said Ben, holding out one of the small pieces of paper, "is for Danny Villapando. It's dated over a year ago."

Ben flicked the corner of the other piece of paper with his fingernail. "This one," he said, "is for Jonathan Racine." He handed the blood test results to Curzon.

"Jesus," exclaimed Curzon. "These are for AIDS! These things are fucking test results." The Indian stared down at the pieces of paper, then quickly threw them on top of the desk, as if fearful that he would contract the disease by holding the paper test results.

Ben crossed his arms for a moment, thinking, then said, "Come on, Joe, let's get outta here." He took the two test results and refolded them, placing them behind the picture as he had found them.

Driving away from Racine's, Ben reviewed in his mind what he had seen. He now knew that Danny Villapando and Jonathan Racine had been more than just good friends, which he figured had something to do with the reason Danny Villapando was no longer around. He also knew that despite his lover having tested positive for AIDS, Jonathan Racine, at least as of a year ago, was not carrying the AIDS virus. But, Ben thought, given Jonathan Racine's sexual preference, a lot could happen in a year.

"Whadya think?" asked Curzon, once they were back on Laurel Canyon headed home.

Ben thought a moment, then said, "I don't know for sure." He thought about Rosen, the way he was killed. He thought about the stories he'd seen on TV about people dying of AIDS, the agony, and the expense involved. Desperate people, he thought. Then he thought of Jonathan Racine and his books.

Ben murmured to himself, "Desperate times . . . desperate measures."

"You say something?" asked Curzon.

"Nothing," said Ben. "Nothing."

CHAPTER 24 ━━━━━━━━━━

"For chrissake!"

Jesus Esquivel looked down at the speedometer. "Sixty-two fuckin' miles per hour," he said, looking in his rearview mirror and then pulling over onto the shoulder.

It was the convertible, he told himself, reaching in the rear pocket of his pants for his wallet. Cops see a Mexican tooling down the freeway in a Mercedes convertible, they get suspicious. It was the fourth time he'd been stopped in the two months since he'd leased the car.

Jesus said, "What seems to be the problem, Officer?" Be nice, he told himself. We both know what the *problem* is, but it won't do any good to piss the cop off, at least not yet.

The cop said, "Can I see your license, sir?"

Jesus said, Sure, and handed the license to the cop. "I was goin' the limit, Officer. Flow of traffic. You know." Jesus thought, just his luck, stopped by a motors cop, black storm-trooper boots nearly up to the knees, dark visor hiding the eyes. Be nice. These guys don't take to fucking around.

"Gee-sus Es-kee-vell," said the cop, looking at the license.

"That's '*Hay*-sus,' " corrected Esquivel. " '*Hay*-sus.' Not like the guy on the cross." He laughed. The storm trooper didn't.

"Please step from the car, Mr. Es-kee-vell," said the cop.

"What the hell!" exclaimed Jesus. "Shit! Just give me the fuckin' ticket and let me get outta here."

The storm trooper put his hand on the butt of his gun and took two steps back from the Mercedes. "Please," he said, leaving no doubt as to his intentions regarding the gun, "step from the vehicle, sir!"

"No problem," said Jesus, feigning a smile. "Listen, we can work this out, can't we?"

The storm trooper directed Jesus to the back of the convertible. It was then that Jesus noticed the other car, brown, without trim, parked behind the storm trooper's motorcycle. The driver of the brown car was still seated behind the wheel, his face obscured by the glare off the windshield glass.

The storm trooper said: "I'm going to ask you to perform some field sobriety tests, Mr. Es-kee-vell."

"Wha . . ." Jesus couldn't believe this was happening. With his back to the convertible he began walking an imaginary line, heel to toe, as the storm trooper had demonstrated.

"See," Jesus said, "I ain't drunk. Haven't had a drop." He looked up from watching his feet to catch a quick glance of the driver of the brown car leaning against the driver's door, watching him.

"Who's he?" said Jesus.

"Never mind," said the storm trooper. "You just keep doing what I say. Now, stand like this," he said, "with your feet together. Lift your right leg into the air, about a foot off the ground. That's it, just like I'm doing. Now, with the finger of your right hand I want you to touch the tip of your nose, like this." The cop demonstrated, then said, "See how I'm doing it? Then do it with your left. Back and forth. Okay, you try it."

"For chrissake, Officer," said Jesus, one foot in the air. "I got this old war injury. 'Nam, ya know. Have trouble doin' stuff like this even when I'm sober. Not that I'm not sober now, don't get me wrong."

Jesus did what the storm trooper had asked.

"How's that," he said, lowering his leg.

The storm trooper said, "One more test, Mr. Es-kee-vell. This one's easy. Put your left palm out, palm up, like this. Take your right hand and pat your left palm, alternating between the palm and back of your right hand. Like this."

Jesus watched the storm trooper clapping his hands.

"That's easy," said Jesus. He tried it.

"Very good, Mr. Es-kee-vell."

"That's Es-*qui*-vell," said Jesus, feeling cocky. He looked around. The driver of the brown car was nowhere to be seen.

"I got it," said Jesus. "You're a rookie, and that guy is puttin' you through your paces. Makin' sure you do it right. Well, I guess I did okay, huh? Or do you have to check it out with the other guy first?"

The storm trooper walked over to Jesus' convertible, glanced inside, then reached over the driver's door, bent down, and came up with a clear plastic Baggie containing white powder.

"What have we got here, Mr. Es-kee-vell?"

"What the shit! Oh, no . . . You ain't gonna get away with that shit, man. That ain't mine. I tell ya, that shit ain't mine!"

The storm trooper came back to the side of the road, holding the plastic bag. He said, "Turn around and put the palms of your hands on the hood."

"Shit, man! What's goin' on here? I never seen that stuff before. Truth, man. For chrissake, you gotta believe me, man. I don't do no cocaine."

"You recognize the stuff, huh," said the storm trooper.

"No, man, it's just . . . shit, you ain't gonna listen anyway. Fuck it, just fuck it."

"I'll take over from here, Officer." It was a new voice. Jesus was facing the hood of his Mercedes. "Yes, sir," he heard the storm trooper say.

"What's goin' on here?" said Jesus. He heard the

heavy clunk of the storm trooper's boots, then the rev of his motorcycle as he drove away.

"Who the hell are you?" asked Jesus.

"Just stay where you are," said the voice. Jesus could feel hands running up and down the outside of his legs, then the inside, patting him down. Then his arms were grabbed from behind and he felt the pinch of handcuffs.

"What about my rights," yelled Jesus. "Don't you guys read my fuckin' rights anymore?" He felt the firm pressure of a large hand pushing him toward the brown car.

"Have a seat, Mr. Esquivel," said the voice, directing him through the open passenger door. Jesus still had not seen the face that came with the voice.

Then he did. The biggest cop Jesus had ever seen. And he didn't look like any cop he had ever seen before, either. More like a Mexican wrestler in turquoise jewelry.

"Who the hell are you?" he asked.

"Just be quiet," said Joe Curzon. "I'm a cop. We're gonna go for a little ride. Then we'll talk."

"But . . ."

"I said *quiet,* Mr. Esquivel."

The Indian watched the greaseball out of the corner of his eye. He saw the sweat glistening on the greaseball's upper lip and chin, and the gray rings on his T-shirt getting darker around his armpits.

They drove on the 405 freeway to Sylmar, then headed east on the 210, getting off at Osborne Street. Curzon followed Osborne Street to the entrance to Hansen Dam. He entered the recreational facility, then took a quick turn into one of the many inlets and small coves that surrounded the reservoir. They were alone now, invisible. Just the way Curzon wanted it.

"Oh, no," muttered Esquivel, looking at the giant cop smiling down at him. "Listen, there's gotta be some mistake, man. That stuff back there ain't mine. And I don't know what you're doin' takin' me all the way out here, man. But I ain't the guy you think I am. Shit, man, I ain't nobody.''

''I know that,'' said the Indian.

''You what?''

Curzon looked straight at Jesus Esquivel. ''I want you to listen very carefully to what I'm going to say, Jesus. Don't interrupt, don't say a word. You understand?''

Jesus nodded.

''Good. Now I ain't interested in you. As far as I'm concerned, you're just another greasy sleazeball. The world's full of assholes like you and always will be. There ain't enough cops to arrest all you guys and not enough prisons to hold ya.

''What I *am* interested in,'' said the Indian, ''is someone you know. A cop with silver hair, goes by the name of Romero. Ring any bells?''

Jesus hesitated, then answered, ''Never heard of the guy.''

''Ah, I see,'' said the Indian, ''that I haven't made myself clear.'' He made a clucking sound with his tongue, then said: ''That's a pity, Jesus. A real pity. I guess you don't mind doing time for possession of cocaine for sale. Mighty stupid, if you ask me. With your record, you'll definitely go away for the max. Maybe even a little extra time for assaulting a police officer.''

''What!'' yelled Jesus. ''I never touched you, man!''

''Not yet, Mr. Esquivel. Not yet. But you see, I figure you're gonna get a little mad—when I start beating on your head, that is. And you're gonna fight back, naturally. And that's gonna cause you to incur—'incur,' that's the word I'll use in my report, it sounds so professional—like I said, you're gonna fight back and incur some serious bodily injury. And I'll write the whole thing up, nice and professional-like. I'll say that you resisted arrest and in an attempt to defend myself I was forced to use my departmentally issued baton on your head. It's unfortunate for you, but that's what everyone will read, including the judge that sends you away.''

Curzon continued, "Now, you're a big strong muscle-man, I can see that. But you'd have to be even more stupid than I know you are to believe that you're gonna be able to take me wearing those handcuffs. A man would have to be crazy to think that. You're not crazy, are you, Mr. Esquivel?"

"No," said Jesus, quietly. His entire face glistened with sweat now. Curzon could smell the man's fear.

"Good," he said. "Now, maybe you'd like to give my question a little more thought. Who knows? Something might just come to mind."

Jesus said, "I only met him once. At a bar. A friend told me about the guy."

"What'd he tell you?"

"Listen, man," said Jesus, "I don't wanna get no one else involved in this, okay? It was just a friend. He don't have anything to do with this."

"Okay, I'll go with that, for the moment," said Curzon. "Keep talking."

"Romero was supposed to do a job for us."

"Us?"

"Yeah, me and my girlfriend. I may as well tell you, you'll just find out about her anyway. She's got this old man, she's married to the guy. He's dyin' anyway. We just thought . . . well . . ."

"That you'd speed things up a little, huh," said Curzon.

"That's all there is, man," said Jesus. "Really. I'm not bullshittin' you. I ain't even paid the guy yet."

"When's it supposed to happen," said Curzon.

"Whenever I come up with the cash," said Jesus. "The guy made that real clear."

"Okay, Jesus," said Curzon, smiling. "I believe you. I think you're being real smart. Now I just have a few more things I want you to do for me."

Jesus sighed, shook his head, then looked at Curzon.

"Don't worry, Jesus," said Curzon, starting the car and backing out of the cove. "You're gonna be a fuckin' hero. Do the community a real service. Maybe even beat that cocaine rap you picked up today.''

"Cocaine? That's bullshit,'' said Jesus, but his previous anger had been replaced by resignation. "You planted that fuckin' stuff, man. You fuckin' set my ass up real good.''

"Yeah,'' said Curzon, chuckling to himself. "I gotta admit I'm good at what I do.''

"Fuckin' cops,'' muttered Jesus.

"Now is that any way to talk?'' said Curzon, laughing out loud.

CHAPTER 25 ━━━━━━━

Francis Powell sat reclined behind his desk, knees crossed, his fingertips together in a little tent, looking at the report Ben had submitted, which the chief had balanced on his lap. He was showing Ben his left profile, the one he used for the television cameras.

Ben was determined to go with the flow, knowing that Francis Powell would do what he decided was best for Francis Powell, and that any arguments to the contrary would be cordially received and then immediately discarded.

As Powell reviewed the lengthy report, Ben occupied himself by staring out the window at the Federal Building, still partially shrouded in morning gloom. Morrell and Osborne were in there somewhere, he thought.

Through the window, Ben could see wisps of smoke that spiraled high above the generators of the underground mall, like cloud-stilts supporting a gray sky. Ben knew the gray would later burn off, but for now it was the city's hat, rendering all it covered smoky, indistinct. Not much different than Francis Powell, he thought.

"A lot more complicated than when we set out, huh?" said Powell, looking up from the report.

Ben nodded.

"Whadya think?" said Powell.

"I think that we . . . I mean, that *you* have to make a decision pretty soon on the Romero bust."

"Yeah, I was afraid you were going to say that."

"You asked," said Ben.

Powell smiled, then looked out the window. The same view that Ben had been staring at.

"Run it by me again," said Powell. "Just so I'm sure I've got all the players right."

Ben said, "Okay. First, we've got Vincent Romero. We believe he's got something to do with the burglaries and insurance rip-offs at the Boulevard Mall, and elsewhere. We know he was having some sort of relationship with the woman who was shot up near Laurel Canyon. I wouldn't be at all surprised to find out that Romero was the shooter, and that he made it look like a rape/robbery to cover his tracks. But I can't prove that."

"The diamond," said Powell.

"That's right. Except, as we've already discussed, that case is weak without some concrete way to prove that the stone that he tried to hock was the same as the one the woman bought."

"Right," said Powell.

"Anyway," said Ben, "we now have new information that Romero is hiring himself out as a paid killer."

"I saw that in the report," said Powell. "The topless dancer and her boyfriend. I don't like the sound of that."

Ben nodded. "All he's waiting for on that one is for the boyfriend to come across with the cash. Curzon talked to the boyfriend. He's willing to cooperate with us."

Francis Powell smiled. "I'd like to have been a fly on the wall during that conversation."

"We'll wire the boyfriend and get Romero locked in on tape. But that case has also got its problems, what with having to use the boyfriend and the topless dancer as wits. First, they're both sleazeballs, and the boyfriend's got a record. Second, we'd have to wire one or both of them when the money changed hands, and Romero might be too smart for that.

"Then there's the Rosen case," Ben went on. "Arnold Rosen's found murdered in his office at the Boulevard Mall. Whoever did it was trying to send a message. His genitals were cut off and stuffed in his mouth. The only lead we have on that case is from a kid by the name of Darnell LeGardy who says he saw some guy running from the scene and getting into a limo."

"LeGardy's under arrest himself," said Powell.

"That's right, but I'll get to that in a minute. Besides LeGardy's story, we have Vincent Romero's name and address showing up in Rosen's wallet at the time his body was discovered. Now that might not mean anything since Romero was moonlighting at the mall as security, but given Romero's other activities, I don't think we can take anything for granted.

"Now back to Mr. LeGardy," said Ben. "Darnell Shapiro LeGardy is your basic sociopathic gang-banger. The guy, as far as I can see, has absolutely no sense of morality. He's a street kid who's out for himself and himself only.

"In addition to what I've already told you about LeGardy and the Rosen investigation, it turns out that besides a few warrants, probation violations, and a GTA in Ventura County, LeGardy is also the prime suspect in a drive-by shooting. The Dayna Adams murder."

"The little girl that was going out for a quart of milk," said Powell.

"And here's where we run into some unbelievable bad luck," said Ben. "The unit first at the scene of the Dayna Adams killing just happens to be Romero's car. The little girl makes a dying declaration that ties LeGardy into the case as the shooter. The only one that hears the little girl's statement is our boy Romero."

Francis Powell leaned back in his chair and closed his eyes for a few seconds. After a moment of silence, he opened his eyes, his head still resting against the chair, his face turned toward Ben.

Powell said: "So we can't convict LeGardy of the

Dayna Adams murder without the little girl's dying declaration, which is Vincent Romero's testimony. But if we arrest Romero, he's not going to testify against anybody, including Darnell LeGardy. And once LeGardy finds out that Romero has been arrested and isn't going to testify to the little girl's dying declaration, LeGardy's lawyer will know that we have no case against LeGardy, and there won't be any reason for LeGardy to cooperate and finger Arnold Rosen's killer. That just about sum it up?''

"You got it," said Ben.

"Did you check out LeGardy's story?"

"Yeah," said Ben. "He gave us a license plate, and we traced it to a guy by the name of Jonathan Racine. Lives over just off Laurel Canyon. A bookseller of some sort.''

"Bookseller?''

"Yeah," said Ben. "That's the funny part. Seems this Racine did some time in New York for manslaughter. Killed his father, and from the reports, it looks like he did the community and the rest of his family a public service. They dropped the murder to manslaughter, and with good time and work time he was out in three or four years.

"While he was in the joint," said Ben, "Racine met up with a guy named Danny Villapando—juvenile record in New York, your basic medium-grade punk. They hit it off. They spent some time in the New York area after they were paroled, then came out west.''

Ben went on: "Racine and Villapando set up shop in Laurel Canyon. From what I can gather, Villapando drove a limo and Racine ran his book business. No problems with the police.

"The Indian and I checked out Racine's place. Seems that Racine and Villapando were more than just good friends, if you catch my drift.''

Francis Powell nodded. As if quoting a commercial jingle, he said wryly, "I fell in love with your joint while in the joint.''

"That's about it. Anyway, the records show Villapando transferred title to the limo about a year ago, then Villapando just seems to have disappeared. I have reason to believe that he died of AIDS. I've got one of the guys checking hospital records to make sure."

"AIDS, huh? So what's Racine's motive?" asked Powell.

"I'm not sure," said Ben. "I suspect it might have something to do with Danny Villapando. Villapando had been active with the mob before he went to prison. It's possible that Rosen's murder was linked with Villapando in some way. It might explain that genitals-in-the-mouth business."

"Very interesting," said Powell. "That might also explain the presence of our FBI friends and their interest in Rosen's death."

Ben jerked to attention. He hadn't mentioned anything about Morrell and Osborne in his report.

"Yes," said Powell. "I've received a couple of calls from Mr. Morrell. 'Matter of national security,' " he said, mimicking the FBI agent, and laughed. "Bit of an arrogant asshole, wouldn't you say?"

"I wouldn't argue with you there," said Ben. He stared at a spot on the wall behind Francis Powell, while Powell looked down at the sheaf of papers on his lap.

Powell said, "Looks to me like we gotta make a choice, Benny."

Ben didn't answer. This one was all Francis Powell. Ben braced himself for the bullshit.

"The way I look at it," said Powell, "we gotta give someone up in order to salvage anything in these investigations."

Ben nodded silently.

"LeGardy, Romero, Racine . . . One of them is going to get a deal, maybe a complete walk, so that we can make the others. The question is, who?"

"Funtime, eh, Francis?" said Ben.

Francis Powell looked over his desk at Ben. "It's not an easy one to make," he said. "You see, Benny, the prosecution of each of these cases has its own individual set of benefits and drawbacks. I have to weigh those benefits and drawbacks, then decide.

"Take for instance the Dayna Adams case. Tragic. Undeniably sad for the community and, of course, for the family." Francis Powell paused momentarily, then went on. "But when was the last time you saw anything in the press about it? A few weeks have passed and it's already old news. Twenty other ghetto kids have been shot or shot at since the Adams girl was killed."

Powell continued, "Now I feel for that mother and her family—believe me, I do. And it's a tough decision. One that I don't mind telling you I'll likely lose some sleep over."

Ben doubted the veracity of Powell's last statement, but let it pass.

"However," said Powell, "I have to look at the other cases. From what I see, the Adams girl's dying declaration is weak. The only way this LeGardy is really made is via the statements of some other gang-bangers, who we both know aren't going to be around at the time of trial. We could try this case and lose it. Then where would we be?

"On the other hand," said Powell, "the papers out in the Valley are still running articles about the Rosen killing. You know how things go out there. Somebody gets killed, there's the slightest whiff of gang activity or organized crime, and everybody and their brother are writing their city councilman demanding more police protection."

"The squeaky wheel gets the grease, huh?" said Ben.

"You know what I mean," said Powell. "It's just a fact of life. Besides, the feds are real interested in resolving that one. We could take care of two birds, so to speak, if we successfully wrapped up the Rosen case.

"And there ain't no way," Powell added emphatically, throwing the report on his desk, "that I'm going to let Vincent Romero skate on anything. That cop's going down for the count and I'm going to be right there to count him out.''

''Your decision,'' said Ben, figuring he had nothing to lose since Powell had already made up his mind, and wanting to see the chief twist in the wind for rolling over on the little girl's murder, ''wouldn't have anything to do with your political ambitions, would it, Francis?''

Powell acted surprised. Ben was pleased to see the initial flash of anger in his friend's eyes; at least the old emotion was still there. Then, just as fast as his composure broke, he was back to the unflappable politician, face composed, reclined in his chair, hands clasped behind his head.

''I'm gonna make believe I didn't hear that,'' said Powell.

''No, you aren't,'' answered Ben. The image of the little girl lying in a puddle of her own blood was stuck in his mind. The coroner's photos made everything look so clinical, so impersonal. Except to him. He'd changed the face on those pictures. For him, the Dayna Adams murder was anything but impersonal.

''You're right,'' said Powell.

The two men stared at each other in silence for at least thirty seconds.

''If that's all you need,'' said Ben, getting up, ''I'll be going.'' He turned and headed for the door.

''Benny,'' said Powell. ''Sit down for a minute. There's something I want to explain.''

Francis Powell waited until Ben had returned to his seat before beginning.

''You think I'm full of shit, don't you?''

No answer.

''Well,'' said Powell, turning and blankly gazing out the window, ''I wish I could convince you otherwise.'' He turned back to Ben, his eyes focused, intense. ''Each one of these cases has problems, Ben. I've only told you what you already know, what the D.A. would say.

You gotta give up one of these cases to make the others."

Francis Powell continued, "Now, you may take issue with my choice. You might think, 'Why not one of the other cases? Why the little girl?' Well, it's like I said, I've gotta be aware of what benefits the department. Taking a chance on convicting Darnell LeGardy, and giving up Racine or Romero in the process, is not in the department's best interest. Shit, Benny, they already caught the guys who were supposed to have been with LeGardy when he did it. You wrote that yourself in your report."

"On other beefs," said Ben. "Not on murder."

"What does it matter?" said Powell. "Those guys are going to be locked up for a while anyway. We'd never be able to prove that they were with him. So what does it matter?

"Meanwhile," said Powell, "we have a chance to solve the Rosen case and get the citizens and the city council off our backs. And we can do that without giving up a damn thing on Romero."

Powell paused. He was leaning over his desk, gesturing with his right hand. Ben saw no anger in his friend's eyes, only the sincere desire to have his beliefs confirmed. Powell waited, still poised over his desk, eyebrows raised above an uncertain smile.

Ben thought about his conversations with Beth Mellnor, and the promise he had made to himself and to Julie. He saw it all going down the drain, along with, perhaps, his own mental stability. He understood, but could do nothing to alter his feeling that his own emotional well-being was somehow in limbo awaiting the resolution of the Dayna Adams murder investigation. He saw himself hanging by a thread over a dark abyss, with only the punishment of the little girl's killer acting as a safety net, keeping him from falling in.

Ben said, "I don't suppose there's any way we could try and get LeGardy to testify against Racine, then get Romero to testify against LeGardy in the

Dayna Adams case, and *then* bust Romero?'' Ben knew the answer to his own question. He asked it more to confirm the impossibility of his suggestion than anything else.

Powell smiled a knowing smile. "That's it, isn't it, Benny?'' he said. "We just don't have the time to do it the way we want. It could take six months to a year to bring LeGardy to trial. That's six months to a year before Romero would have to testify. Can we afford to have him out there capering, running his scams, his murder-for-hire schemes for that long? Romero's just too dangerous. You said it, Benny: I've gotta make a decision, and now. Romero's getting too close to doing it again. We can't let that happen. Romero's got to be arrested immediately, even if we lose his testimony against LeGardy because of it.

"Sure," said Powell, more as an afterthought to his last comment, "it would be great if we could get LeGardy to finger Racine in court without having to offer him some sort of deal first. But Benny, we both know that LeGardy's not going to do us any favors for free. LeGardy won't come through against Racine unless we give him something on the Dayna Adams murder.

"I've made my decision, Ben. We'll use LeGardy's testimony to get Arnie Rosen's killer, and we'll bust Vincent Romero's ass before he has a chance to do any more damage. As for Dayna Adams, well . . .''

Both men looked away from each other, each dissatisfied with the limited options. In his gut Ben told himself that it wasn't going to happen that way, Powell's way. That he'd do something to bring the child-killer to justice. His mind, though, was sending other messages. Telling him that he'd lost again. Another wasted life.

"I read that you're a declared candidate," said Ben, intentionally changing the subject. "I wish you all the luck in the world, Francis. I really do. This wrap-up of Rosen and Romero shouldn't hurt you a bit.''

Powell was silent. He watched his friend get up and start for the door a second time.

"I'll make sure," said Ben, opening the office door, "that Curzon is up front when we bust Romero."

Francis Powell said, "Thanks, Benny." It was too late. Ben was already out the door.

When he got back to his desk there were three messages. The Indian had called, and wanted Ben to call back. There was a call from the homicide detective handling the Dayna Adams case. And there was a call from the watch commander at county jail. Ben called county jail first.

"Front desk, Deputy Walker," said the young military-sounding voice. Ben told the deputy who he was and asked to speak to the watch commander. He was put on hold while the call was transferred.

Ben waited, listening to the Muzak, thinking about his conversation with Francis Powell. Maybe he'd been a little hard on the chief. After all, Powell was right, the Adams case was weak, there was no getting around that. They could put all their efforts into convicting Darnell LeGardy for the Adams murder and still fail. The evidence, even with Romero testifying to the girl's dying declaration, was inconclusive. And then, without LeGardy's testimony, they'd be giving up the case against Arnie Rosen's killer.

The chief was right. It went against Ben's grain to admit that, but he could see no logical way to refute Powell's thinking. With LeGardy's testimony, they would have a better than decent chance to convict Jonathan Racine of killing Arnie Rosen. Maybe they'd get lucky, Ben thought, and get Racine to cop out. In any event, under Francis Powell's plan, they could pop Vincent Romero immediately and not have to worry about Romero and LeGardy, through their attorneys, each playing games with the D.A., trying to get a better deal for their testimony.

Ben's first inclination was to discount the Rosen

murder. The way it looked, Rosen was involved in some way with the mob. Ben figured the feds wouldn't be as interested in a local homicide if the mob didn't have their hand in the pie somewhere. What's the big deal, he thought, one mobster hitting another. Either way, everybody was better off: one less gangster in the world.

Yet Ben couldn't fault Francis Powell's reasoning in not wanting to pass up the Rosen conviction. The residents of the Valley had mounted an organized campaign to put forth their views and exert pressure on their elected officials. They weren't about to tolerate such vicious acts in their own backyard. Even if it were commonplace downtown.

And Francis Powell, future mayor of the city of Los Angeles, was not stupid. He needed the support of those Valley voters in the upcoming election. Scoring some points with the feds in the process was just icing on his cake.

"Sergeant Flannigan," grumbled the gravelly voice into the telephone.

"This is Ben Green returning your call."

"Yeah," said the watch commander. "You got a fish down here by the name of LeGardy. Darnell LeGardy."

"That's right," said Ben.

"Just wanted to let you know that we're transferring him to another module. Gotta keep him in a keep-away unit. Seems like he's on the most-wanted list of almost every gang-banger down here. Word is that there's a price on his head."

"Keep him healthy, Sergeant. At least for now. We need him as a witness on a homicide."

"No sweat. Just thought I'd let you know since your name showed up on the computer. This guy's big-time, huh?"

"Yeah, you might say that." Ben hung up the phone. He smiled to himself, thinking about his directions to the watch commander to keep Darnell LeGardy healthy. Sure, he wanted LeGardy's testimony in the Rosen case, but he also wanted LeGardy around so that he could see him tried, convicted, and sentenced to death for killing Dayna Adams. Francis Powell be damned. He was going to see Darnell LeGardy fry.

CHAPTER 26 ━━━━━━━━

They put LeGardy on tape—Ben and Joe Curzon and LeGardy's lawyer, Harold Stein—in the same interview room at county jail in which Ben and the Indian had had their first conversation with him. The four of them had gone over his story a couple times off the tape, before recording. The recorded testimony was a short, concise statement of exactly what Darnell LeGardy saw the night Arnie Rosen was murdered. The tape would ensure that at the time of trial, LeGardy would be locked into his story about Racine, the limousine, and seeing Racine running from the scene of the Rosen murder.

Ben and Joe could now go out and arrest Vincent Romero. With LeGardy's story memorialized on tape, Darnell would still have to be called as a witness, but he'd be unable to change his story later, even if he discovered that Romero had been arrested and was thus unavailable to testify against him as to Dayna Adams' dying declaration.

On the morning following Darnell LeGardy's taped statement, Ben and the Indian drove out to Romero's place to make the arrest. They'd arranged for two backup units, just in case, but Romero proved cooperative. Dressed in a pair of Nike jogging shorts, running shoes, a silky red tank top, and a baseball cap with the letters L.A.P.D. monogrammed on the front, Vincent Romero had merely nodded his head when advised of the reasons for his arrest, and turned to his girlfriend, still groggy in her pink nightie, telling her to make sure the alarm on his BMW was activated while he was gone. He then smiled calmly in Ben's direction and headed for the front door.

That was the last thing Ben had heard Romero say, except for his request, once they reached the station, that he be allowed to make a phone call to his lawyer.

Ben now sat behind his desk in the detective room. From where he was, he could keep an eye on Romero and his lawyer sitting in the glass-enclosed interview room. Ben put his feet on top of the desk, pushed his chair back a little, then crossed his legs.

Romero still seemed in control, sitting upright behind the small metal desk in the interview room, speaking calmly, as if he and his lawyer were discussing a business venture. He was not looking at Ben through the glass.

He knows I'm watching him, Ben thought. He's been through this whole thing a thousand times, and he knows all the little mind games.

Ben looked at his watch, then flicked on the portable nine-inch television that he kept on his desk. He paid only half-attention to the blonde Barbie-type newscaster. He adjusted the antenna, trying to get a clearer picture while he waited for the story of Romero's arrest and Francis Powell's subsequent press conference.

The Indian had told him about it. Said it would be carried on the local stations. Curzon had said that Powell had directed that he, Curzon, stand directly behind him and to the right once the press conference began. Powell had done all the talking, referring to Ben on one occasion, and to Curzon repeatedly. He had, according to the Indian, even put his arm around the Indian's shoulders at one point, giving him credit for cracking the case.

Ben watched the tape of the press conference on the small screen, with Francis Powell going through his act, just like the Indian had said. Powell was in his glory, surrounded by eager reporters, cameras whirring, lights flashing. He gave them what they wanted: a show. Displaying his good side for the cameras, the one Ben had seen in his office the day the chief had decided to make political hay out of the Romero investigation. The day Francis Powell had decided to do a tank-job on the Dayna Adams case.

Ben wondered what Romero would think if he could see Francis Powell on TV. Romero was now quiet, patiently listening to his lawyer. And why shouldn't he? Romero was no fool. He had used his one phone call wisely. He had called Saul David Miller. Miller was an ex-prosecutor who had left the D.A.'s office after a few years, only to spend the next fifteen years racking up an impressive list of trial victories over that same D.A.'s office that had given him his start. In the process, Miller had garnered all the trappings of a successful law practice: suits and cars from Italy, vacation homes in Aspen and Cannes, and standing reservations at the week's trendiest restaurant.

It was reputed that Miller was well-connected, and that the numerous dope dealers he represented in state and federal court were mob clients. Nobody had ever been able to pin anything on him, though, and Ben figured that those kinds of stories always seemed to come to the surface when a lawyer won more than his share of cases, especially against the feds.

The phone rang, startling Ben from his thoughts of Vincent Romero and his lawyer.

"Green!" he barked, instead of saying hello.

"Green, you won't believe this."

"Flannigan, is that you?" Ben had immediately recognized the gravelly indifference of the watch commander's voice.

"Listen to me, Green," said Flannigan. "They just called me from the jail ward at County USC Hospital. Your future star witness, Darnell LeGardy, was stabbed this morning. The doctors at the hospital pronounced him dead on arrival.''

With a flick of his perfectly manicured finger, Saul David Miller sent a piece of errant lint flying into the air. He quickly brushed his silk jacket, smoothing the cool material with his fingertips. He had just bought the suit at his usual shop in Beverly Hills, and he liked the feel of the rich tailored fabric, custom-made for him, against his skin. He could almost taste the champagne, Taittinger, he was informed by the owner, in the fluted glass served to him by the gorgeous young saleslady—perhaps a model?—who Miller suspected did nothing more than pour champagne and serve spoonfuls of caviar on miniature crackers. She had done a convincing sales job on him. He made a mental note to return to the shop and order two more suits.

It wasn't the first call he'd received from a client in jail. Not even the first call from a cop in trouble. He sat patiently, legs crossed, letting the client tell his story. He nodded periodically to keep the client going and to make the client feel as if he were listening attentively. It was a habit he had acquired, and like all of his professional habits, it was consciously designed to generate income for Saul David Miller.

"So that's about it," said Romero. "Whadya think?"

Miller ran a finger across his lips, savoring the look of eager anticipation on the client's face. He knew the client hadn't told him everything. They rarely did. Especially the smart ones, or the ones that thought they were being smart. The smart ones always thought they could put one over on their attorney. That they could pick and choose the facts to feed to their lawyer, and by doing that, indirectly control the outcome of their case.

Miller thought that this cop definitely fit into that category. A smart one. Arrogant. Well, he thought, it didn't really matter. All that was really important was the money. If the cop had the money, than Saul David

Miller would be his. If not, then it was "Nice to make your acquaintance and I'm sure you'll be happy with the public defender."

"Mr. Romero," said Miller. "Perhaps we should get the matter of finances out of the way first."

"No problem," said Vincent, all business. "I can have my girlfriend deliver the cash to your office whenever you like."

Saul David Miller smiled. "You are aware of my standard retainer in such cases?" he asked.

Vincent paused, looked the attorney in the eye, then smiled a partial smile. He said, "Would a hundred thousand cover it?"

"That will do nicely," said Miller, evenly, without emotion. "Now let's set a few ground rules. I'll do all the talking. And by that I mean *all* the talking. Do we agree on that?"

Vincent nodded.

"Good. I find," said Miller, "that with my police officer clients there are normally few problems between attorney and client. Coming from your professional background, you can appreciate the value of what I do. But, by the same token, police officers are by virtue of their professional training, and by nature I think, quite authoritarian. They want to take control. They feel uncomfortable if they are not in control of their case, in a position of authority. I trust that you and I will not have such a problem, Mr. Romero?"

"You're the boss," said Vincent.

"Perfect," said Miller. "Now, tell me again what the police know about you, and what you know about them. And leave out the bullshit this time."

Ben suddenly realized that he'd been gone, he didn't know for how long, daydreaming. Thinking about what Flannigan had said.

"Green!" He heard Flannigan's voice, yelling, but sounding small, like he was actually inside the telephone receiver calling out to him. He saw that he had placed the receiver on his desk.

"Yes, I'm sorry," said Ben, grabbing the receiver and trying to gather his thoughts.

"Are you okay?"

"Yeah, yeah," he said. "Just a little surprised." He was watching Romero and Miller. They had stopped talking and were looking at him through the glass window.

"Rotten luck," said Flannigan.

"Yeah," said Ben, absentmindedly. He was thinking that he had to make some quick decisions about Romero. There was also, in the back of his mind, in a place that he couldn't quite reach, an uneasy sense of relief that washed over him. Uneasy in that he was surprisingly embarrassed to experience it. And uneasy in that the relief was colored with personal uncertainty over what effect Darnell LeGardy's death would have on his own mental stability.

"Listen," Ben said. "I'll call you back later." He hung up the phone. Saul David Miller was beckoning to him from inside the interview room.

"Can we talk for a moment," said Miller. "In private." Ben was standing at the open door to the interview room. He motioned Miller to a similar room down the hall, closing and locking the door to the room in which Romero was seated.

The two men sat in identical wooden chairs on the opposite sides of a square Formica-topped table. Ben could smell the spicy-sweet odor of Miller's cologne as the attorney attempted to find a comfortable position on the hard wooden chair.

Miller craned his neck and adjusted the knot in his tie, as if in front of an imaginary mirror, then crossed his legs, careful not to upset the still-crisp pleat of his pants.

"When is the arraignment?" asked Miller.

"Tomorrow."

"And bail?"

"It's a no-bail case, Counselor. Murder, conspiracy to commit murder, insurance fraud, you name it." As Ben watched Miller pursing his lips in thought, he was wrestling with his own thoughts. The entire investigation seemed to be unraveling, and here he was, doing battle with one of the sharpest lawyers in the city, trying to salvage his one remaining suspect.

His suspect? That was a real joke. Ben's investigation of Romero had spilled over into the investigations of LeGardy and Racine. By direction of Francis Powell, Ben had been given carte blanche, complete access to all information and reports. All case developments on any of the investigations were to be immediately reported to Ben. Ben was in control of each individual investigation, city-wide, on a day-to-day basis. The result was that the detectives assigned to each investigation, who would normally take charge in each case, deferred to Ben, making the ultimate responsibility for the outcome of each investigation his and his alone.

"I know it's a little early in the game to start talking deal . . ." said Miller. "And my client certainly continues to deny any wrongdoing, and will enter a plea of not guilty at his arraignment . . ."

Ben shrugged, pretending indifference.

"Yet," said Miller, "one has to face the realities of these situations. Mr. Romero has informed me he would consider trading information for favorable treatment. A deal, in other words."

"That's not up to me," said Ben.

"Come now, Detective Green. My sources tell me that you're the man to speak with on this case."

"Your sources?" said Ben.

"You'd be surprised how much one can find out by making a few well-placed phone calls."

"You've been misinformed, Counsel," said Ben. He was trying to figure out what information Romero might have that would be important enough for an experienced attorney like Miller to bring up so early in the game.

Ben said, "And even if we were open to some sort of *deal*, as you say, I doubt whether your client has anything that we would be interested enough in to cut him any slack on these charges."

Miller said, "Let's just say that I have reason to believe, from what my client has related to me, that he could possibly finger the killer in the Arnold Rosen murder."

Ben strained to remain emotionless. No smile, no raised eyebrows. Keep the breathing even and steady, he told himself. Don't blink too much, and maintain eye contact.

What in hell could Romero know about that?

"That case is in the can," said Ben. "We already have a witness to the crime. I'm afraid your client's information, even if it is true, is too little, too late." The words were coming out automatically, without thinking—Ben's built-in defense mechanism when dealing with the enemy. His mind raced, trying to keep up with the situation.

With LeGardy gone, there's no case against Racine. Unless . . . But if Romero finds out we need him to convict Racine, he'll use it to cut a deal for himself. But Powell wouldn't allow that, would he? What if the feds find out that Romero is their only means of getting Racine? Would they overrule Powell?

"Just keep it in mind," said Miller. The dapper attorney stood, straightening his tie once more, then shrugged his shoulders and buttoned the lower button of his jacket. "If you don't mind," he said, heading for the door, "I'd like a few more minutes with my client."

Ben unlocked the door to Romero's interview room and returned to his desk. Romero and Miller resumed their conversation, with Ben watching but unable to hear. Ben opened the metal file cabinet below his desk and pulled out the Arnold Rosen murder file. He'd had a duplicate made of the entire homicide file, including the coroner's photos. Ben found the small manila en-

velope containing the photographs, opened the clasp,
and poured the packet of color pictures onto his desk.

He then put the pictures in a sort of order, eliminat-
ing the coroner's meat-market shots of Rosen's torso
ripped open and turned inside out for examination. He
made a small pile of those and set it aside.

The remaining dozen or so pictures he placed side
by side in three rows on his desk. These were the photos of Rosen's office and of Arnold Rosen as he was
found by the first officers at the scene. Ben then separated the three rows of photographs, keeping only those
that showed the body of Arnold Rosen slumped in the
back room of his office.

He paid particular attention to the close-ups of Rosen's face, bloated and discolored, covered in blood,
the penis and partial genitals inside Rosen's mouth displayed by the coroner by use of a small stick placed
between Rosen's upper and lower jaw, holding the
mouth open.

Ben looked over to Vincent Romero, calmly conversing with his lawyer, and wondered what his involvement was in Rosen's death. He now thought it
unlikely that he'd ever find out. Francis Powell was not
about to make any deals with Vincent Romero. Not for
Jonathan Racine or anybody else. The feds were the
only ones who could put enough pressure on Powell to
make a deal for Vincent Romero's information. And if
Ben knew his friend Francis Powell, the feds would
never find out about it.

Vincent Romero sat alone in the interview room
waiting for his lawyer to return. He went over the last
few hours in his mind, like a newsreel, short clips of
faces and action, one right after the next.

The bit about Rosen was a gamble. Vincent knew
the baby-faced guy in the garage had nothing to do with
the Rosen hit. But a guy like Rosen had probably pissed
off a lot of people. The D.A. just might buy that. Yeah,
that's what he'd tell them. That one of them just lost

it—some crazy who'd lost all his money in one of the little Jew's rip-offs.

Vincent figured they'd have trouble pinning anything on him that would stick. Too many witnesses who were involved themselves. As long as everybody stayed cool, didn't get scared, he'd come out okay.

But that was the problem, relying on others. Like he always told himself: Leave loose ends and you pay for it. Now he wasn't around to make sure nobody talked. The muscle-man and the girl with the tits . . . Lots of loose ends. The kind of problems that could mean a bus ticket for him to Chino.

He'd have to scramble. Maybe use a little leverage, make a trade. The Rosen thing was still big in the Valley. They had no real suspect. As long as he got immunity before he opened his mouth, the D.A. couldn't use what he said. Even if they got the surprise of their lives by what he said. Even if they found out too late that they'd given the killer a free ride. It was his best bet. He couldn't tell them what really happened, at least not and expect to live afterward. This way he might find out what kind of hand the cops were holding against him.

"How sure are you that this guy you saw is the killer?" asked Miller. He'd entered the interview room, leaving Ben Green outside, and had resumed his seat opposite Romero at the desk.

"I'm sure," said Vincent, trying to maintain his air of confidence.

"Mmm." Miller ran his finger across his lower lip as before, looking down and away from Vincent. He finally looked up, saying, "This thing cuts both ways, you know that? Even assuming that you have information that the cops want, there'll be a lot of questions. Like how you got the information and what your relationship was with Arnold Rosen. And that assumes that the cops need you to testify. Green tells me that the case is already a lock. They have an eyewitness."

"Then why haven't they made an arrest?" asked Vincent.

"I don't know," answered Miller. "I didn't want to push the cop into a corner. It's still early. No use forcing anyone into taking positions that their egos won't let them escape from later. If they've got enough to make the Rosen case, we'll soon find out. If not, then I would expect to hear something in the form of an offer. We'll just let them think about it for now."

Miller said, "You've got two major problems in this case, the way I see it. Let's assume that they need your information. First, you're a cop. A cop who's abused his power and position in the community. There is nobody that a jury would rather convict than a cop who has abused his sacred trust. Anybody who's ever gotten a ticket or been stopped for drunk driving by some surly police officer, who didn't say enough 'Please, sirs,' and 'Thank you, sirs,' is going to vent all that pent-up anger against you. You'll get hammered.

"The second problem is that we have to be very careful in telling the D.A. about your relationship with Mr. Rosen. I mean, what do you think their attitude is going to be when you tell them you have information about Rosen's killer, and that you *got* that information because Rosen had heard of your reputation and wanted to hire you to lay some muscle on the guy! That's the last thing I want coming out."

Vincent nodded his agreement. Inside he smiled at what the lawyer didn't know. "What do we do?" he asked. He'd have to take it slow with the lawyer, make him think that he was in charge.

Miller got up and headed for the door. "I'll make some more calls," he said. "See what I can find out about their case. Meantime, I'll see you in court tomorrow."

"What about bail?"

"I'll see what I can do," said Miller.

Vincent saw Ben Green walking toward the interview room.

"And start thinking," said Miller, his voice lowered, "about a story that has you knowing Rosen without being his hit man, okay?"

Vincent nodded, holding back a smile at the lawyer's unintentional pun.

CHAPTER 27 ▬▬▬▬▬

It was one of those uncommonly warm summer evenings when with eyes closed it seemed like mid-afternoon, the heat was so intense. The night air seemed to hang, suffocating, unmoving—like the inside of a child's small glass jar in which a spider has been placed for observation, the lid fastened tightly and without holes. In the distance, the rhythmic alternating hiss of lawn sprinklers rasped their slow, lazy cadence in the darkness, counterpoint to the soft modulating hum of the insects.

Ben and Bryan sat at a round glass table in the apartment courtyard, bathing in the uncertain glow of the underwater light from the swimming pool. Overhead, a string of small plastic Chinese lanterns that some former tenant had attached to the side of the building cast a faint, but more steady, illumination. Both men sat with legs crossed, relaxed, gazing into the pool and sipping their beers.

These weekly sessions around the pool had become a sort of therapy for the both of them. Over the weeks, Ben had taken Bryan more into his confidence, unfolding the entire story about himself and Julie, even his sessions with Beth Mellnor. Ben felt the need to unload, to tell somebody. And Bryan was a good listener, never offering advice, but instead asking questions when he felt there was something Ben should consider more closely.

They'd also talked about the Romero investigation, since the news of Vincent Romero's arrest and subsequent courtroom maneuvering was plastered all over the local papers. Ben mentioned his concern over the Dayna Adams killing and his promise to himself that her killer would be brought to justice.

"All right," said Bryan. "Since I'm taking the place of your Dr. Mellnor, I want to know all the facts. I have a vague idea about how all these people relate to one another, but I want to make sure I've got it right. Before I sit down to write our Emmy-winning screenplay, that is."

"First of all," said Ben, "you could never take the place of Beth Mellnor, your legs aren't near good enough. Besides, I'm going back to her eventually, as soon as I wrap up this investigation."

"So you're just using me, huh?" Both men laughed.

"And second," said Ben, "this Romero case, and probably all the other suspects along with him, are going to be around for quite a while. By the time these cases wind their ways through the courts, it could be years. There's no way you can be doing a Movie of the Week while these guys are still on trial."

"Okay, okay," Bryan agreed, holding up a restraining hand. "I'll wait. Or we'll change the names. Just let me ask a few more questions."

"Feel free," said Ben.

"What's happening with Vincent Romero?"

"He's still pending trial," said Ben. "Held to answer at his preliminary hearing. The bail was set at a million dollars. He's still in custody."

Bryan said, "And this kid, LeGardy, was the only witness, other than Vincent Romero, to the guy who supposedly killed Arnold Rosen, right?"

"Darnell LeGardy," said Ben. "The late, unlamented Darnell LeGardy, I might add. In a way, you could say that everything has worked out for the best. Darnell LeGardy deserved to die. The world's a much better place without him. Saves the taxpayers all that

money in having him arrested a few more times, all the
court expense of putting him on trial. And that's not
even considering all those tax dollars wasted in trying
to rehabilitate the little asshole while he's pounding out
license plates up at Folsom for the rest of his life.''

Ben continued, ''It also seems that the FBI is more
than just casually interested in the death of Mr. Arnold
Rosen. They've contacted Francis Powell and me about
keeping track of the murder investigation. And they've
been very close to the vest about the whole thing. I
wouldn't be at all surprised to learn that Arnold Rosen
is not who we think he is, and that the land swindles
over at the Vacation Villas are just the tip of the ice-
berg.''

''Geez, this is really getting good,'' said Bryan.
''The hell with Jake Stone. There might be a whole
series in this!''

''Finally,'' said Ben, ''we come back full circle to
Vincent Romero. We know he's involved in at least one
murder, maybe more. He's been actively involved in
setting up insurance rip-offs for some of the merchants
at the Boulevard Mall and elsewhere. God only knows
how many other officers he's got working for him.

''Romero now says he's got information on the Rosen
killing.'' Ben paused momentarily, enjoying the look
of excitement on Bryan's face. He had to admit that
even he was getting a little excited about this one. But
it sounded almost too unbelievable, even for TV.

''Well,'' Ben went on, ''Darnell LeGardy has already fingered a suspect by the name of Jonathan Racine as Rosen's killer. But without LeGardy's in-court
testimony, there's no convicting Racine. It would be
inadmissible hearsay.''

''Unless you use Romero,'' said Bryan.

''Which,'' answered Ben, ''is not going to happen.
Not as long as Francis Powell gets his way.''

''But what about the feds?'' said Bryan. ''You mentioned they were anxious to find out who killed Arnold
Rosen.''

"Oh, they're anxious, all right," said Ben. "They already know about Darnell LeGardy. What they don't know is that LeGardy is no longer with us. They still think that LeGardy's going to lead us to a conviction of Rosen's killer."

"You haven't told them he's dead?" asked Bryan, incredulous.

"Nope. And neither has Powell. We will, eventually. We need to buy a little more time. If the feds find out that LeGardy is out of the picture, and that Romero might be able to take his place, then they'll want us to deal with Romero."

"And Francis Powell will lose his political pawn," exclaimed Bryan, shaking his head in disbelief. "And you said being a cop was boring!"

Ben snickered.

"It seems," said Bryan, "that under your plan, you still don't get Rosen's killer."

"You're right," said Ben. "Not unless we turn something up on Jonathan Racine, assuming he *is* the killer, which is a big assumption since it rests totally on the uncorroborated statement of Darnell LeGardy."

Bryan said, "Why don't you just go out to Racine's place and confront him? That's what Jake Stone would do. Go right out to where the guy lives and put it to him.

"I can see it now," said Bryan, pushing his chair away from the table a few inches and raising his hands in the air as he sketched the scene. "You go out to this bookseller's place. There's a confrontation. You know he's the killer, and he knows that you know. There's some small talk, both of you sparring with each other, trying to feel each other out. Then you tell him about LeGardy, and that you know he's the one that snuffed out Rosen. You move toward him. He reaches into his desk and pulls out a gun. He's pointing the gun at you. With a sly little grin on his face, he says, 'You know too much, Detective Green, and therefore I must kill you.' "

" 'Therefore I must kill you'?" said Ben, eyebrows raised in mild disbelief.

"Well . . ." said Bryan, racking his brain. "He says something like that, okay? After all, he is a bookseller, right? The guy's gotta be more literate than your run-of-the-mill murderer.

"Anyway," said Bryan, continuing his scenario, "with the gun still pointed at your chest, Racine admits that he killed Arnold Rosen, but he says that you'll never live to tell the story. He moves closer to you. You leap at him over the desk. There's a struggle over the gun. You both fall to the ground. A shot's fired. We don't know whether anybody's been hit. Then dramatic music and the picture fades to commercial." Bryan sat back in his chair, smiling, slightly out of breath, hands clasped behind his head, perfectly pleased with himself.

"Let me guess," said Ben. "We return from the commercial to find our hero telling the story to his sexy secretary. And the bad guy—who is still alive so that he can stand trial over the next three or four episodes and receive the full force of the law, just like we all want to see—is being lifted into the back of an ambulance, cursing and threatening to get even."

"That's a great ending, Ben!" exclaimed Bryan. "I knew you had the knack for this stuff." He grinned. "Maybe even an end-of-the-season cliff-hanger."

Ben sighed. "You know what I think?" he said. "I think that the both of us have been watching too much TV."

CHAPTER 28 ■■■■■■■

Up and down the court, there was the echoing thud of rubber on hardwood in the small gym at the downtown Eastlake Juvenile Facility, where on most afternoons Ben could find a pick-up game of some sort. Lawyers, probation officers, cops, and juvenile hall staff, mostly middle-aged men, grunting and wheezing their way back and forth across the court, trying to stay in shape, and trying to remember what it was like when it was all so much easier.

It had been nearly two months since the Romero arrest. Ben had returned to the old routine of playing basketball two or three days a week down at Eastlake, biding his time until the trial. Most of his normal caseload had already been shifted to other people in the department to allow him to concentrate on the Vincent Romero investigation, so that by the time Romero was actually busted, Ben found himself with a lot of time on his hands. A sort of well-earned vacation, he figured.

Romero's trial was scheduled three weeks hence. Francis Powell was still holding firm to his no-deal position. For Ben, the only thing remaining was to work with the D.A. on the trial preparation. His job was to be around if the phone rang, and to occasionally run a piece of evidence or a police report over to the Criminal Courts Building if requested. It was waiting time. The interim period before a big trial was usually one big long wait. Once both sides had already discovered most of what the opponent's trial strategy was, there wasn't much left to do but fine-tune your case and wait some more.

For Ben, standing under the steaming locker room shower, waiting for his muscles to send their signal that it was safe for him to try and walk again, the time since Vincent Romero's arrest had been filled with a mild uneasiness, a feeling that something was wrong, or about to go wrong. He couldn't exactly pinpoint the reason, though he had thought about it off and on over the last several weeks. He tried to reassure himself that it was nothing. Just overcautiousness: the desire to be as well-prepared as possible after a lengthy investigation leading to a big arrest. Still, the uncertainty persisted.

The feds had been uncharacteristically quiet about the whole affair. Not a word from Morrell or Osborne about LeGardy or the status of the Romero case. That was one of the things that bothered Ben. It was just too easy. Nobody, he figured, not even some East Coast prep school rich boy like Randall Morrell *The Third* could be that stupid.

And then there was Jonathan Racine. Another piece that didn't fit into the puzzle. The feds had been told of Racine. They'd been given Darnell LeGardy's statement, along with the supplemental reports tracing LeGardy's description of the limo to Danny Villapando and Jonathan Racine. Yet they'd done nothing about it. Weeks had passed, and it was as if Morrell and his group had gone on permanent leave, disappeared. They seemed content to just sit by and wait for the D.A. to get around to going after Jonathan Racine.

There was something missing. Some fact or piece of evidence that Ben was unaware of. Like a wheel that will roll along, wobbling with an untrue spoke, Ben knew he was getting to the heart of the case, but he still felt an unsteadiness, an uncertainty.

Randall Morrell and his boys already knew about

Jonathan Racine. No matter how Ben tried to stretch the facts, it just didn't make sense, in light of their initial interest in the case, that the feds hadn't stepped into the investigation, thrown their weight around, and demanded that Racine's case be given priority.

Ben toweled himself off in front of his locker, his every movement slow and deliberate. He was determined not to pick up the half-used tube of Ben-Gay that stared at him from the metal shelf, an unwanted but necessary reminder of his own mortality. His mind wandered to Beth Mellnor, and to his poolside talks with Bryan. The scenes were going through Ben's mind in no exact order as he dressed. Tying his tie in front of the small rectangle of glass attached to the inside of his locker, Ben's thoughts flashed back to what Bryan had said about Jonathan Racine.

It wasn't the first time since that summer's evening that Ben had thought about squaring off with Racine. He wouldn't admit as much to Bryan, but he had given the idea serious consideration. He thought that if he could just confront the man, then maybe something would happen. Maybe he'd find that missing element, whatever it was, that was making him feel unsettled.

But each time his mind went through the scenario, logic and experience set in. Ben knew that he had no case against Jonathan Racine. It would likely turn out badly for him to confront Racine on the off chance that he might get lucky. It was a bush-league move. Powell wouldn't like it, and neither, Ben thought, would the feds.

He finished dressing, closed his locker, and headed for his car. He couldn't stop thinking about Racine. The rest of the afternoon is free, he thought. No appointments and no paperwork to catch up on. The other guys would cover for him if anything came up.

Ben eased his car into the bumper-to-bumper mid-afternoon traffic, heading in the general direction of his apartment. He was on automatic pilot, only half-paying attention to the road. His mind was still presenting him with the same unorganized, disordered slide show. The same images that had been playing over and over until he was, by this time, almost used to the feeling of the fist in his stomach, pulling on him from the inside out. It started, as it always did, with Julie, the trial, and Sara looking at him from across the grave with that moribund expression of defeat and accusation. But now the face of Vincent Romero was added, smiling at him from inside the custody interview room. And there were the meat-market photographs of Arnold Rosen slumped in the back of his office with his genitals dangling over his lower lip. The images faded with the sweet, inno-cent face of Dayna Adams, her dead, questioning eyes gazing up at him from the sidewalk.

He wasn't certain exactly where it happened, but somewhere between the Ben-Gay and the Santa Monica Freeway, Ben decided it was about time he had his talk with Jonathan Racine.

CHAPTER 29 ━━━━━━━━━━

Ben was reaching into his coat pocket when the door opened halfway, Jonathan Racine's slender, well-muscled body taking up the space between door and frame.

"Yes?" That's all he said, looking like he wanted to get back to what he'd been doing before Ben interrupted him.

Racine was dressed in white canvas pants and a loose-fitting poncho-type shirt made of a thin woven material. The shirt was worn on the outside of his pants and was brightly colored. It looked like the handmade clothing Ben had seen in Mexico. Racine wore leather sandals—also handmade, probably Mexican, Ben figured—without socks. His hair was freshly combed and looked wet, like he had just come from the shower.

"Ben Green," said Ben, flapping open the black leather wallet containing his Investigator's shield and identification card. He held it open long enough to let Racine read the name and check the picture.

"I'd like to ask you a few questions, Mr. Racine," said Ben.

Racine smiled, then said, "That sounds like a line from about a dozen movies." The smile then quickly disappeared and he was all business. "Questions about what?" he asked. He had opened the door a little further, but was still wedged in the space between door and frame, his hand at the ready on the doorknob.

"We've received information," said Ben, "that you might know something about a murder that occurred at the Boulevard Mall a while back. You may have read about it. The victim's name was Arnold Rosen. He had an office over at the mall. That's where they found him."

Racine looked away for a split second, then back at Ben, who registered the other man's momentary loss of composure.

Racine said, "Ah, I'm afraid that I don't know anything about that, Investigator. You must have the wrong person." He smiled a nervous smile. Ben could see his hand, the one holding the doorknob, start to move, tightening the grip. Racine looked away from Ben into the house, then leaned against the door slightly, blocking off the doorway.

"If I could have just a few minutes of your time?" said Ben, telling as much as asking. He set his jaw and looked Racine directly in the eyes. He stood straighter, not as relaxed. The informal approach wasn't going to work with this guy.

Racine looked around for a moment, feigning nonchalance at Ben's authority. "Sure," he said, "Come on in. This won't take too long, will it?" He opened the door and stepped back.

"Just a few minutes," said Ben, entering the house. He quickly looked around, remembering the layout of the house from the last time. He wanted the conversation to take place in the study. Maybe it was the picture of Racine and Villapando, he wasn't sure, but he felt there was something about that room that would explain what Jonathan Racine was all about.

"How about in here," said Ben, pointing toward the open study door and taking a step in that direction.

Racine didn't answer initially. His eyes caught Ben's, then quickly glanced away, and, as if finally deciding that the study was as good a place as any, he followed Ben into the room, saying, "You'll have to excuse the mess. I'm getting ready to move."

"Oh, really?" said Ben, his back to Racine. "Goodness," he said, stepping into the study. "I don't think I've ever seen this many books, except in a library."

"I sell them," said Racine. He motioned for Ben to have a seat on one of the dozen or so large wooden crates that were scattered and stacked on the floor. The crates were filled with books of all sizes and shapes. Ben noticed that the shelves which had been overflowing with volumes when he and the Indian had been in the house were now almost empty.

"Where you moving to?" asked Ben, pulling out a pen and a small spiral notebook and removing the cap from the pen. He wasn't looking at Racine, as if he were uninterested in the answer to his question.

Racine didn't reply immediately. He took a seat on one of the wooden crates a few feet from Ben. The large desk that had occupied a good part of the room was gone. Ben quickly glanced about the room but couldn't find the picture of Racine and Danny Villapando.

"Relatives," is all Racine said. He brought one knee to his chest and held it there, his heel balanced on the edge of the crate.

"You said something about a murder, Investigator?"

Ben was trying to picture Jonathan Racine killing Arnold Rosen and then stuffing his genitals in his mouth. It didn't work. Not unless Racine had somebody else with him doing all the dirty work. Racine was big enough to do the job, that wasn't the problem. It was that beautiful face of his: handsome, but too pretty to do anything like the job that had been done on Arnold Rosen. Racine was like those guys with the chiseled masculine features in the after-shave ads. Ben could easily picture Jonathan Racine stepping from the shower, a towel wrapped around his waist, smoothing some after-shave or cologne on his face, some half-dressed gorgeous blonde at his side looking at him longingly.

But that wasn't real either. Ben knew that. He knew enough about Jonathan Racine and Danny Villapando to know that Racine's life did not include half-dressed gorgeous blondes. At least not of the female variety.

"Yes, well, it's like this, Mr. Racine." Ben flipped through his notebook as if looking for a particular item. He was thinking. Trying to figure out just how much to tell Racine.

"Ah ha," said Ben, after sifting past the first few pages. "Here it is." He paused a moment, then continued. "Mr. Racine, it seems that in the course of our normal investigation of Mr. Rosen's death, we came upon a witness who said he was in the area of the mall on the evening of the murder. He said he saw a tall, dark-haired man running from the area of Arnold Rosen's office. That the man got into a limousine and sped off. We traced the license number of the limo to a Mr. Danny Villapando." Ben glanced at Racine for any sign of recognition. There was none. Just the same cool stare.

Ben continued, "The DMV records show that Villapando transferred title to the limousine to you."

Racine said, "Listen, Investigator—Green, is it?"

Ben nodded.

"Let's level with each other. You must have seen the limo parked out on the side of the house, so you know that I still have it. I also do a lot of shopping at the Boulevard Mall. So it is quite conceivable that I could have been at the mall on or about the time that this Rosen person was murdered. I may have even been running, as your witness said. That's not unusual, is it? Certainly it's no crime to run through a shopping mall these days?"

"Oh, nobody's pointing the finger at anybody," said Ben. "I just wanted to let you know why I'm here. Nobody's saying that *you* killed Arnold Rosen, Mr. Racine." Ben watched the other man shift positions on the wooden crate. "I mean," he added, "that would be ridiculous, wouldn't it?" Both men stared at each other.

"I don't know what to tell you," said Racine. "It is

possible that I was where your witness said, but I have no recollection of the evening, and I certainly don't know anything about any murder.''

"Uh huh," murmured Ben, writing in his notebook. He looked up, then gazed around the room. "Much of a market for books these days?" he asked.

Racine looked at Ben and smiled. "I do all right," he answered.

"Nothing personal," said Ben. "It's just that I wouldn't figure a small operation could compete with the big bookstores."

"If you really want to know," said Racine, still choosing his words cautiously, but clearly feeling more confident on his own turf, "the big stores can't compete with me. At least not with the service that I provide. We don't sell the same items. I sell to the collector. Rare or special editions. The hard-to-get volume. If you want the latest Danielle Steel, you go down to the drugstore and buy it. If you want a signed limited edition of a book that is no longer in print, of let's say Robert Frost's *A Way Out,* then you come to me.''

"I see," said Ben. "A book like that must carry a pretty hefty price, huh? I remember reading Frost in school. Something about the road not taken . . . ? Something like that.''

Jonathan Racine put his cupped hand to his mouth and coughed, a bit too politely. He asked, "Do you see yourself, investigator, as a traveler wondering about the road not taken?''

"Sometimes," said Ben. "We're not all automatons, you know. I have my moments.''

"I'm impressed," said Racine. He looked at his wrist, but there was no watch. "Investigator Green," he said abruptly, "I'm sure you're not here to discuss the book business. Now, if you've got the information you came for, I have some business to take care of myself.'' He got up as if to leave. Ben remained seated.

"Just one more question," said Ben. He motioned for Racine to sit down. "This won't take long." Ben again flipped through the pages of his notebook before speaking, then asked his question without lifting his eyes from the notebook.

"What's your relationship with Danny Villapando?"

Racine stared at Ben for a full ten seconds before replying.

"You must already know the answer to that question," he said, "otherwise you wouldn't be asking."

Ben didn't answer.

"But," said Racine, "that's all right. I have nothing to hide. Danny and I were lovers. We met in prison, but you probably already know that, too. He'd dead. Anything else?"

"He was from New York, wasn't he?" said Ben. "Lots of bad guys in the Big Apple, so I hear. Well-connected bad guys. You know, wiseguys."

Racine—still cool, still emotionless—glared at Ben only momentarily. He remembered how all the trouble started with Danny telling his bosses about how he had this roommate who was just like them, one of the family. And how easily everyone, from the East Coast bosses to the investigator who stood before him, adhered to the view that ex-cons were incapable of changing their stripes.

Jonathan stood up. "I wouldn't know," he said, barely moving his lips, his jaw rigid. He headed for the door, saying, with strained good manners: "Now, if you'll excuse me, Investigator Green, I've got things to do."

Ben quickly stood up and followed him out of the study.

Racine was already holding the front door open when Ben reached the small foyer. Ben said, "There's another of Frost's poems that sticks in my mind. How does it go . . . let's see . . . 'The heart can think of no devotion greater than being shore to the ocean . . .' " Ben paused, his eyebrows furrowed, then added, "I can't seem to remember the rest."

Racine stood motionless by the door, looking wistfully at a spot somewhere behind Ben, alone with his thoughts.

"West-Running Brook," said Racine, monotone, still looking through Ben. "It's from a poem called 'Devotion' by Robert Frost. The collection is *West-Running Brook."*

"Yeah," said Ben. "That sounds familiar. I wish I had the knack to remember those things. I'm not a big one on poetry, ya know. I never could remember the whole poem. Only parts. I guess that's better than nothing, huh?" He headed out the door, saying, "Thank you for your cooperation, Mr. Racine. If we find out anything more, rest assured, we'll be in touch."

Racine didn't respond.

Ben had already stepped off the front porch when he turned around. "Oh, by the way," he asked, "where did you say you were moving?"

"I didn't," said Racine, closing and locking the door.

CHAPTER 30 ━━━━━━━━━

The morning after his conversation with Jonathan Racine, Ben lay in bed, about to get up, savoring the few minutes of peace and quiet before the day began. Soon his alarm would sound and he'd go through the morning rituals precedent to fighting the fender-bending traffic to the office. Once there, yet another series of rituals would begin.

It was during this peaceful morning-in-bed period, as Ben rolled over, dreaming of another ten minutes of half-sleep and running bits and pieces of the previous day's conversation with Jonathan Racine through his mind, that Francis Powell called.

It was unusual for Francis Powell to make any of his own telephone calls, let alone for him to call Ben at home. After the perfunctory "I hope I didn't wake you," Powell told Ben that he wanted Ben to meet him at Morrell's office in the Federal Building first thing. He wouldn't elaborate, saying only that it was important.

When he arrived, Morrell's secretary led Ben into her boss' office. Francis Powell was already there, seated next to Randall Morrell, both men occupying the leather couch near the window. Two cups of coffee, partially full, sat upon the small glass coffee table in front of the couch.

Francis Powell wore a dark blue suit, white shirt, and yellow paisley tie. He sat with his legs crossed, looking surprisingly at home and relaxed, conversing with Randall Morrell.

"Ah, Ben," said Powell, uncrossing his legs and standing up. He approached Ben, extending his hand.

"Sorry about the last-minute call," he said. "I think you already know Randall Morrell here."

"Yes," said Ben, cautiously moving from Powell to Morrell, who remained seated on the couch. Morrell reached out over the coffee table to shake Ben's hand. Morrell's slight smile as they shook hands gave Ben the impression that Morrell and Powell had been discussing him prior to his arrival. Just a guess, but Ben would have laid money on it.

Morrell got up off the couch and walked behind his desk where he remained standing. He seemed more relaxed than the last time they had met. He wore a tan summer suit of a light material, crisply pressed. No vest, only burgundy suspenders contrasting against a starched white shirt with French cuffs. His tie was a burgundy stripe, knotted tightly at the neck and highlighted by a gold tie bar through the collar. He removed his jacket and hung it on a coat rack in the corner behind his desk. Ben could see that Morrell's cuff links were also gold, and had his initials on them, as did the pocket of his shirt. He motioned for Francis Powell and Ben to be seated on the couch, and plopped down atop his desk, balancing himself with one wing-tipped shoe on the floor.

"This is going to come as a bit of a surprise to you, Mr. Green," said Morrell. He looked slightly uncomfortable, as if he wasn't quite sure how to tell Ben what he intended to tell him.

Morrell said: "I hear you paid a little visit yesterday to Jonathan Racine." Ben looked at Francis Powell, who was having a difficult time trying to remain expressionless. Then back at Morrell.

"All right," said Ben, after the five-second pause. "I'll ask the stupid question: how did you find that out?"

Morrell looked Ben straight in the eyes, unblinking. "Jonathan Racine told us," he said.

"Racine?"

"That's right, Mr. Green," said Morrell, getting up off the desk and walking toward the window. He peered out the window for a few moments, putting his hands on his hips. The office was quiet. Still facing the window, Morrell said: "Jonathan Racine works for us. He has for quite some time now."

"But . . ."

"He's an informant," said Morrell, turning away from the window and facing Ben. "Chief Powell knew about our relationship with Mr. Racine, but was under strict orders not to disclose it to anybody, including you."

"Sorry about that, Benny," said Powell.

Morrell said, "You see, Mr. Green, as you already know, Mr. Racine had a friend, a lover, by the name of Danny Villapando. Villapando was providing muscle to the mob. We're still uncertain exactly how much of that Racine knew about, but that's not important now.

"Villapando," said Morrell, "contracted AIDS a little over a year ago. Racine tried to take care of him, but it was a losing battle. Villapando eventually died, but not before racking up some hefty medical expenses. Racine had been dipping into the mob coffers via some loan sharks, to help pay Villapando's bills. An admirable gesture, but unfortunately doomed to failure. Once Villapando died, it was time to pay up. But Racine had no money. At least not the kind of money, or the kind of interest, that the wiseguys charge."

Morrell continued, "So Mr. Racine found himself in a spot of trouble, you might say. And it only gets worse. It seems that one of the old-time East Coast big shots, by the name of Anthony Ruggerio—otherwise known as Big Tony—had a vendetta against a small-time hustler by the name of Leonard Fine. Fine had turned State's evidence against the mobster and some of his cronies back in the fifties. The mobster ended up doing some time behind that, while Fine disappeared.

"At least," said Morrell, pointing a finger into the air, "the mob could never find Leonard Fine. Until recently, that is."

Ben looked over at Francis Powell, who had barely uttered a word since Morrell had begun speaking.

"Arnold Rosen," said Powell, turning toward Ben. "Arnold Rosen was Leonard Fine."

Morrell continued, "We put Mr. Fine into the Witness Protection Program. By 'we,' I mean the bureau. Changed his name and identity, plastic surgery, the whole bit. Made him into an entirely new person. It was part of the deal that the agents made with him at the time in order to get him to testify."

"And the Rosen murder," said Ben, "was the payback."

Morrell paused a few seconds before answering.

"That's what we thought, at first," he said. "It had all the trappings of the typical mob hit."

"But what does all this have to do with Racine?" asked Ben.

"Racine," said Morrell, "was the guy the mob contacted to kill Rosen. They had Racine by the balls. They gave him an ultimatum: either pay up on Villapando's debt, or do them this little favor and hit Rosen.

"That's when Racine came to us. He decided to take a chance. He knew he couldn't pay back the debt, and he didn't have it in him to kill Arnold Rosen.

"I have to admit," said Morrell, smiling, "for a while there we weren't too sure about that last part. After we got news of the Rosen murder, I don't mind telling you that we were more than a little suspicious about Mr. Racine's involvement.

"But, as it turns out," said Morrell, "Racine had nothing to do with Rosen's death. We're convinced of that. You see, Mr. Green, we wanted Jonathan Racine to string along the mob guys for as long as possible, make them think that he was actually planning on killing Arnie Rosen. We had wiretaps installed on both coasts, and we were collecting all kinds of incriminating evidence. The longer Racine was able to delay the actual hit, the more stuff we got.

"After Rosen was hit, we called Racine in for questioning. It was risky, but we had no choice. After talking with him, we were convinced, the other agents and myself, that he had nothing to do with the murder."

Powell said, "Benny, they suspect that Vincent Romero is Arnie Rosen's killer. That Rosen got spooked when Racine began tailing him and went to Romero for protection. Romero, always in the market to the highest bidder, went to Ruggerio himself and offered to kill Rosen, for the right price, that is."

"And you knew about this all the time?" asked Ben.

"Most of it," said Powell. "I was told to handle the matter just like any other case, not to do or say anything that might send the wrong signal."

"You see," said Morrell, "up until Rosen's death, we had to be careful not to tip off the mob that Racine was working for us. Once Rosen was hit, we had the initial worry that Racine might blow it. You know, say something to the wrong person so that the bad guys would get suspicious. It was still important to us that the mob believe that Racine was Rosen's killer."

"And what about Romero?" asked Ben. "Why bother with two hit men? And how do you explain Romero trying to cut a deal to testify against Racine if he, in fact, was Rosen's killer?"

"Ruggerio wanted Rosen dead," said Morrell. "He didn't much care who did it. Our best guess, and it is only a guess at this point, is that Romero found out about Racine from Ruggerio's people. We checked Romero's phone records, and there are three calls to Miami about the time that we think he contacted Big Tony. We've got some of our agents working on trying to actually place him in Miami.

"After he was arrested, Romero figured he'd try and save himself by trading what he said he knew about

Racine being Rosen's killer for years off his sentence
on the other cases. The guy's got balls, you gotta give
him that. It's like the F. Lee Bailey gambit in the Boston Strangler case. After his arrest, Romero figured his
lawyer would have no problem getting him complete
immunity for his statements on the Rosen murder, since
nobody suspected he was the killer. His lawyer would
tie the deal to a decreased sentence on his other cases.
Then he'd tell his tale about Racine, and if it backfired,
he'd still be completely immunized. There'd be no way
he could be charged with killing Rosen.

"And to complicate this whole thing even further,"
said Morrell, "we were not only out to get the mob
guys who were setting up the Rosen hit, but also the
person who had given them their information in the first
place."

"That wouldn't have anything to do with Mr. Osborne, would it?" asked Ben.

Morrell smiled. "You've got your Vincent Romero," he said, "we've got D. David Osborne. It
seems Osborne had been feeding the mob inside information—more specifically in this case, the identity and
whereabouts of one Leonard Fine. From what we've
gathered, it appears that Osborne's motive was solely
financial. He'd supply the information for cash. The
funny thing about it is that the mob apparently never
totally trusted him. They used their own people every
inch of the way to confirm his information. They must
have feared that he might be putting out bad information as part of some sort of sting operation."

Ben said: "I don't know why they'd figure that. Every
time you pick up the paper you guys are posing as some
kind of sheik or Saudi oil magnate, putting some poor
slob on videotape in his hotel room."

Morrell laughed, saying, "Yes, well, the East Coast
wiseguys must have shared your opinion. They had Osborne double-checked. One of their local operators set
Rosen up with a hooker, just to make sure that Osborne's information was on the up-and-up."

"No honor among thieves, eh?" said Ben.

"Apparently not," said Morrell. "Anyway, Osborne's been indicted. The federal marshals have got him in custody downstairs. He's already agreed to cooperate against the wiseguys that were involved in setting up the hit. There's going to be a press conference sometime next week, after all the indictments are handed down. Jonathan Racine's to be the government's star witness. An interesting turn of events, don't you think?"

Ben said, "And all that arrogant crap from you in the beginning was just part of the show, huh?"

Morrell laughed. "We had to walk a tightrope with you," he said. "We wanted you to go through the motions with Racine, make it look real, but not to do anything that might screw up our investigation. We didn't want anyone to get suspicious about why we, and you, weren't interested in getting at Racine. At the same time, arresting Jonathan Racine was the last thing we wanted."

"And LeGardy's statement?" said Ben.

"That was my decision," said Francis Powell. "I talked it over with Mr. Morrell here but the decision was mine, ultimately. We didn't have a case against LeGardy on the murder. Just some declaration by a dying victim that the guy had a shiny smile. Not enough to go to court. All we had against Racine was Darnell LeGardy's statement that he saw Racine running from the mall on the evening of Rosen's murder, which in itself was also insufficient to get a conviction, had we wanted one. The main thing I wanted to do was buy some time on LeGardy's case and keep you away from arresting Jonathan Racine." Francis Powell smiled, first at Morrell, then at Ben. "I never intended to give up LeGardy like I said, and I don't mind telling you, Benny, that I'm still pissed off that you thought I would."

"You see," said Powell, "I authorized a deal for LeGardy based on his testifying against Racine. I knew *that* would never happen. We never asked LeGardy anything about his own case, the Dayna Adams murder, so there were no self-incrimination problems. I figured once the lid had blown off on Jonathan Racine, we'd still have LeGardy in custody. I'd tell his attorney that the deal was off and that we no longer needed his testimony against Racine. Everything would go back to square one, and hopefully, by then, we might have had enough evidence to convict LeGardy on the Dayna Adams murder.

"Then LeGardy was killed in jail," said Powell. "It couldn't have worked out better. No embarrassment down the road at having to pull his deal, LeGardy got what he deserved, Jonathan Racine's cover was still intact, and . . ."

"And you got Vincent Romero tied up nice and neat," said Ben.

"Exactly," said Powell. "We already have Romero on tape agreeing to kill the topless dancer's husband, Jed Rickert. Plus, the lab boys are doing a recheck on the semen and pubic hair samples taken from the victim over on Laurel Canyon. Randy says he'll see about getting us some help from the FBI's DNA-typing facility. It's still pretty experimental stuff, but every little bit helps. We'll tie Romero into that one, one way or the other, you can bet on it."

"And who knows," offered Morrell. "Once we get Tony Ruggerio convicted he might decide that it's in his best interest to tell us about his arrangement with Vincent Romero. As you put it, Mr. Green, there's no honor among thieves."

Ben got up and walked over to the window. He could see his fifteenth-floor office in Parker Center high above the blare of horns and squealing of tires on Temple Street. For a moment, Ben felt like he always did when looking down from his office at the confusion of the street: insulated, protected—not a part of the chaos.

Then he thought of what Randall Morrell and Francis Powell had said to him over the last twenty minutes, and his feeling of insulation, of safety, disappeared. Instead, there was part anger, part confusion, but mostly a sense of disappointment.

"What's going to happen to Racine," Ben asked, still staring out the window. He thought about the picture of the two smiling young men that he'd seen on Racine's desk.

"Oh, he'll be all right," said Randall Morrell. "We'll find a place for him in the program. Change his identity, maybe a little plastic surgery, who knows."

"And he wants to do that?" asked Ben, incredulously.

"He doesn't have much choice, does he?" said Morrell. "We're the only game in town. If he stays out there on the street, they'll kill him sooner or later. He knows that."

"We saw how effective you were with Rosen," said Ben, then regretted that he had said it. Morrell was just doing his job.

"Well," said Morrell, clearing his throat. "Let's hope for Mr. Racine's sake that there are no more D. David Osbornes in the bureau. In any event, it's Racine's choice. It's the way he wanted it. My job is to keep him safe until the time of trial. After he's testified, the bureau will do its best to make him disappear. There are no sure things in this business. There's no guarantee that they won't find him. But it's the best anybody can do."

Morrell paused, smiled, then pursed his lips, signaling a change of subject.

"Apparently," he said, "Mr. Racine was quite taken with you, Mr. Green."

"Taken?" asked Ben.

"The poetry bit. Quoting Robert Frost."

Ben shrugged.

"Well," said Morrell, "it seems that whatever you said got to him."

Ben thought of Jonathan Racine standing in the foyer, daydreaming, blankly staring at the wall. In Racine's face Ben had not only seen the photograph of the two young men, but had seen himself, drifting, inexorably drawn toward that bottomless black hole where too-painful memories of loved ones never remained buried for very long. For the first time since it all began Ben felt like an intruder, and that feeling surprised him.

"I didn't get to him," he said. "The memories did."

Christmas that year was filled with the usual last-minute running around, only busier. Bryan had managed to get a mountain cabin for a few days from one of the other writers on the series. He and Ben were to spend the week between Christmas and New Year's in the snow at Mammoth.

Ben was so busy getting things taken care of at the office and at home that he almost missed the article in the Metro section of the *Times*. In fact, it was Bryan who pointed it out to him the evening before they were about to leave.

"Isn't this the same guy you were after?" asked Bryan, lifting the newspaper off the kitchen table. They had their gear strewn about Ben's living room floor in semi-organized piles.

Bryan handed Ben the newspaper, on which he had already circled the headline with a felt-tipped pen.

ORGANIZED CRIME PROSECUTION IN JEOPARDY

The prosecution of organized crime kingpin Anthony Ruggerio and other crime figures may have been placed in jeopardy, prosecutors announced, with the loss of the prosecution's star witness, Jonathan Racine.

Randall Morrell III, of the Federal Bureau of Investigation's Organized Crime Task Force, announced yesterday that Racine was to testify next

March in the upcoming racketeering and extortion trial of Ruggerio and four other organized crime figures.

Reporters learned that Racine recently checked into St. John's Hospital with what doctors diagnosed as an advanced case of pneumonia. His identity was kept secret by federal authorities. It was learned that Racine was subsequently transferred to the U.C.L.A. Medical Center where he died yesterday of pneumonia complicated by the AIDS virus.

Racine was part of the FBI's Federal Witness Protection Program and had been working with federal agents in gathering evidence against Ruggerio and others. It is rumored that Racine contracted the deadly virus from his ex-roommate, who himself died of AIDS last year.

Federal authorities had no comment on whether they will be able to proceed with the prosecutions now that Racine's testimony has been lost.

Ben tossed the paper on the table.

"Tough luck, huh?" said Bryan. "You guys go to all that trouble to keep him away from the mob and the guy dies of AIDS. It's hard to figure."

"It doesn't make sense," Ben whispered to himself, thinking of the picture of Villapando and Racine, and the hidden test results. "It just doesn't make sense."

"What doesn't?" said Bryan. He was busy stuffing sweaters into his suitcase.

"He looked healthy three months ago," said Ben.

Bryan got up from the floor and looked at the newspaper article for a moment. "This AIDS stuff is crazy," he said. "People are dying all over the place. Some seem to hang on for years before they eventually go under. Others, I've heard, carry the disease themselves but remain in other respects unaffected. Racine might have contracted it years ago. Who knows. Maybe it just finally caught up with him.''

"Yeah," said Ben, still thinking about Racine. "Maybe you're right."

"That doesn't mean that the feds are blown out of the water, does it? I mean, can't they use his deposition or something?"

"No such luck," said Ben. "It's a criminal case. They need to have a live body in court testifying and subject to cross-examination. Take a look at the Sixth Amendment."

Bryan asked, "So without Racine they've got no case against those mobsters?"

"Looks that way," said Ben.

CHAPTER 31 ━━━━━━━━

In March, Bryan talked Ben into going on location with him to Santa Barbara for a few days. The writers, director, producers, and actors were put up at the Four Seasons Hotel overlooking the beach. It was just the diversion that everyone sorely needed, Ben included. A short respite from the lung-searing smog of the city and the daily battle with the rush-hour throngs for a parking space. A vacation from the numbing morning hours spent listening to tedious traffic reports on the radio while staring, transfixed, at the rear bumper of the car in front of you.

If this was what TV writing was like, Ben told Bryan once they were there, then he was all for it. Hell, he'd even make up stories if that's what they wanted. Bryan was quick to inform Ben that this pampering was the exception rather than the rule. That usually they stayed in the Motel 6, or worse, but since the show was doing so well in the ratings, and the season's shooting was coming to an end, the producers and studio had decided to treat everybody to a few days of cool ocean breezes, panoramic sea views, excellent food, and the quiet luxury that the Four Seasons was famous for.

Ben spent his days hanging around the set, kibbitzing with the crew, and going on late-afternoon strolls with Bryan along the beach, where the two of them buried their fists into the pockets of windbreakers pulled tightly against winter ocean flurries and sketched out what they jokingly referred to as their Big Blockbuster Screenplay. For Ben, it was a time for relaxation. A time for self-evaluation and changing perspectives. Within him, he rediscovered the flicker of recognition, transitory as it was, that things could get better; that hope, like a buoy held captive at the ocean's bottom by some monstrous wave, could once again bob to the surface.

When the filming was over, he hated to leave. He spent most of the drive home reconciling the familiar images of Los Angeles with his newfound sense of acceptance, and daydreaming of their proposed screenplay.

As Bryan pulled the car into the lot parking behind their apartment, one of the images that came to mind was Jonathan Racine. Ben remembered that the Tony Ruggerio trial was scheduled to begin in two days. Ben had called Randall Morrell shortly after reading the newspaper article about Jonathan Racine's death to confirm the details. When they spoke, Morrell had expressed serious doubt whether the prosecution would get past an opening statement without Racine's testimony.

Ben's job was done. Vincent Romero had been tried and convicted of solicitation of murder in the Jed Rickert case. He was currently sitting in the Chino Men's Colony working on his appeal. Francis Powell, true to his word, had the boys working overtime and had come up with a witness, a housewife driving a station wagon, who said that she recognized Romero from his picture in the paper as having illegally passed her on Mulholland Drive. According to the housewife, she was so angry at Romero for recklessly endangering the lives of her children that she followed him to an address off Laurel Canyon Boulevard, where, she said, she spotted his BMW parked in the driveway, and saw Romero entering a house with a woman who was wearing a fur coat. The D.A.'s office was in the process of pinning down the exact time and date before filing additional murder charges.

It was ironic, and more than a little disappointing, Ben thought, that Jonathan Racine's testimony against Tony Ruggerio was the only part of the original puzzle that apparently was never going to come together.

Ben walked over to the kitchen table where Bryan had dumped the mail that had collected while they'd been gone. There was a note on his bulletin board reminding him of his next appointment with Beth Mellnor. This time he didn't dread it, though. In fact, he felt stronger than ever, and figured he was ready for another try. He was even optimistic about what might happen once she saw this new, stronger Ben Green. Over the last several months, he had come to the realization that he'd never be in total control of his memories. But that was okay with him. He had accepted the fact that he'd always have the dreams about Julie, the uncertain, awkward moments that broke into his everyday life.

But, for the time being, the fist that was inside his stomach now rested silently. He knew it was still there, but that it was under control. He wasn't at all sure how long this new feeling would last—but he was determined to enjoy it while he could, one day at a time.

To the side of the pile of envelopes and junk mail was a small package, wrapped in brown paper, taped on the ends, and addressed to "Investigator Ben Green," with no return address.

"What's this?" asked Ben.

Bryan was busy moving the suitcases.

"It was with the magazines," he said. "I just threw it on the table with the rest of the stuff. You expecting a gift or something?"

"Not that I know of," said Ben. He opened one end of the wrapper, then tilted the package, allowing the contents to slide into his hand. It was a book.

"What is it?" yelled Bryan from the other room.

Ben didn't answer. He held the book, with its slightly worn cover, in both hands, reading the title: *West-Running Brook*, by Robert Frost. He opened the book to a page that had been marked with a small folded piece of paper, on which there was an unsigned hand-written note:

> *Investigator Green:*
> *The reports of my death have been greatly exag-gerated. (I've always wanted to be able to say that.) You've probably figured out by now that the bad guys were starting to get a little too close for comfort. The obituary number was our friendly G-man's idea. You might say that I've been forced underground until the trial. (No pun intended!)*
> *Anyway, this might look like just an old book to you, but believe me, it's worth something, so don't get rid of it.*
> *This is the last you'll hear from old J.R. And after next week, the last anyone will hear for that matter.*
> *See you in my next life.*

Ben folded the paper and put it back inside the book. He noticed that the note marked a place in the book where the poem "Devotion" appeared.

"Hey, Ben," Bryan said, walking into the kitchen. "I almost forgot to tell you. The director and producers were very impressed with you. They mentioned that they'd like to see some of your ideas for next season. I happened to let it slip at lunch that you worked in In-ternal Affairs for L.A.P.D. and their chins just about dropped into their angel-hair pasta. Whadya think about that?"

Ben was laughing silently to himself. Bryan would never believe this one.

"So listen, Ben," said Bryan, "whadya say? All they want is to pick your brain a little. Maybe come up with some new twists on the cops-and-robbers story line."

"Well, Bryan," Ben replied, trying to keep a straight face, "you know what I've always said. Actual police work is pretty boring stuff. Nothing very interesting ever happens. Not like the cops on TV."

"I know," said Bryan. "It's mostly just pushing paper."

"That's right." Ben smiled. "But don't worry," he added, gripping the volume of poetry with both hands. "I'm sure we'll come up with something."